PENGUIN BOOKS

THE AUTUMN OF THE PATRIARCH

'Delights with its quirky humanity and black humour and impresses by its total originality' *Vogue*

'It asks to be read more than twice, and the rewards are dazzling' *Observer*

'Captures perfectly the moral squalor and political paralysis that enshrouds a society awaiting the death of a long-term dictator' *Guardian*

'Márquez writes in this lyrical, magical language that no one else can do' Salman Rushdie

'Majestic, mystic, surrealistic – a stunning portrait of a monstrous tyrant' *The New York Times*

'Mesmeric, ornate, horrifying . . . a magnificat to harsh Latin American reality' *Sunday Times*

'In every respect an amazing piece of writing, in which cruelty and comedy are placed in perfect balance' *Washington Post*

'One of this century's most evocative writers' Anne Tyler

'The most important writer of fiction in any language' Bill Clinton

'Márquez has insights and sympathies which he can project with the intensity of a reflecting mirror in a bright sun. He dazzles us with powerful effect' *New Statesman*

'The vigour and coherence of Márquez's vision, the brilliance and beauty of his imagery, the narrative tension . . . coursing through his pages . . . makes it difficult to put down' *Daily Telegraph*

'Sentence for sentence, there is hardly another writer in the world so generous with incidental pleasures' *Independent*

'Márquez is the master weaver of the real and the conjectured. His descriptive power astounds' *New Statesman*

'Underlying the marvellous wit, the inimitable humour and the superbly paced dialogue, there is the author's own anger, always controlled' *The Times*

'Every word and incident counts, everything hangs together, the work is a neatly perfect organism' *Financial Times*

ABOUT THE AUTHOR

Gabriel García Márquez was born in Aracataca, Colombia, in 1927. He studied at the National University of Colombia at Bogotá and later worked as a reporter for the Colombian newspaper *El Espectador* and as a foreign correspondent in Rome, Paris, Barcelona, Caracas and New York. He is the author of several novels and collections of stories, including *Eyes of a Blue Dog* (1947), *Leaf Storm* (1955), *No One Writes to the Colonel* (1958), *In Evil Hour* (1962), *Big Mama's Funeral* (1962), *One Hundred Years of Solitude* (1967), *Innocent Erendira and Other Stories* (1972), *The Autumn of the Patriarch* (1975), *Chronicle of a Death Foretold* (1981), *Love in the Time of Cholera* (1985), *The General in His Labyrinth* (1989), *Strange Pilgrims* (1992), *Of Love and Other Demons* (1994) and *Memories of My Melancholy Whores* (2005). Many of his books are published by Penguin. He was awarded the Nobel Prize for Literature in 1982. Gabriel García Márquez died in 2014.

GABRIEL GARCÍA MÁRQUEZ

THE AUTUMN OF
THE PATRIARCH

TRANSLATED FROM THE SPANISH
BY GREGORY RABASSA

PENGUIN BOOKS

PENGUIN BOOKS

Published by the Penguin Group
Penguin Books Ltd, 80 Strand, London WC2R ORL, England
Penguin Group (USA) Inc., 375 Hudson Street, New York, New York 10014, USA
Penguin Group (Canada), 90 Eglinton Avenue East, Suite 700, Toronto, Ontario, Canada M4P 2Y3
(a division of Pearson Penguin Canada Inc.)
Penguin Ireland, 25 St Stephen's Green, Dublin 2, Ireland (a division of Penguin Books Ltd)
Penguin Group (Australia), 707 Collins Street, Melbourne, Victoria 3008, Australia
(a division of Pearson Australia Group Pty Ltd)
Penguin Books India Pvt Ltd, 11 Community Centre, Panchsheel Park, New Delhi – 110 017, India
Penguin Group (NZ), 67 Apollo Drive, Rosedale, Auckland 0632, New Zealand
(a division of Pearson New Zealand Ltd)
Penguin Books (South Africa) (Pty) Ltd, Block D, Rosebank Office Park,
181 Jan Smuts Avenue, Parktown North, Gauteng 2193, South Africa

Penguin Books Ltd, Registered Offices: 80 Strand, London WC2R ORL, England

www.penguin.com

First published in Spanish as *El Otoño del Patriarca* 1975
This English translation first published in the United States of America
by Harper & Row, Publishers, Inc. 1976
First published in Great Britain by Jonathan Cape 1977
Published in Penguin Books 1996
This edition published 2014
001

Copyright © Gabriel García Márquez, 1975
English translation copyright © Harper & Row, Publishers, Inc., 1976
All rights reserved

Portions of this work originally appeared in the *New Yorker*

The moral right of the author and translator has been asserted

Printed in England by Clays Ltd, St Ives plc

Except in the United States of America, this book is sold subject
to the condition that it shall not, by way of trade or otherwise, be lent,
re-sold, hired out, or otherwise circulated without the publisher's
prior consent in any form of binding or cover other than that in
which it is published and without a similar condition including this
condition being imposed on the subsequent purchaser

ISBN: 978-0-241-98042-2

www.greenpenguin.co.uk

MIX
Paper from
responsible sources
FSC
www.fsc.org
FSC™ C018179

Penguin Books is committed to a sustainable
future for our business, our readers and our planet.
This book is made from Forest Stewardship
Council™ certified paper.

THE AUTUMN
OF THE
PATRIARCH

OVER THE WEEKEND the vultures got into the presidential palace by pecking through the screens on the balcony windows and the flapping of their wings stirred up the stagnant time inside, and at dawn on Monday the city awoke out of its lethargy of centuries with the warm, soft breeze of a great man dead and rotting grandeur. Only then did we dare go in without attacking the crumbling walls of reinforced stone, as the more resolute had wished, and without using oxbows to knock the main door off its hinges, as others had proposed, because all that was needed was for someone to give a push and the great armored doors that had resisted the lombards of William Dampier during the building's heroic days gave way. It was like entering the atmosphere of another age, because the air was thinner in the rubble pits of the vast lair of power, and the silence was more ancient, and things were hard to see in the decrepit light. All across the first courtyard, where the paving stones had given way to the underground thrust of weeds, we saw the disorder of the post of the guard who had fled, the weapons abandoned in their racks, the big, long rough-planked tables with plates containing the leftovers of the Sunday lunch that had been interrupted by panic, in shadows we saw the annex where government house had been, colored fungi and pale irises among the unresolved briefs whose normal course had been slower than the pace of the dryest of lives, in the center of the courtyard we saw the baptismal font where more than five generations had been christened with martial sacraments, in the rear we saw the ancient viceregal stable which had been transformed into a coach house, and among the camellias and butterflies we saw the berlin from stirring days, the wagon from the time of the plague, the coach from the year of the comet, the hearse from progress in order, the sleep-walking limousine of the first century of peace, all in good shape under the dusty cobwebs and all painted with the colors of the flag. In the next courtyard, behind an iron grille, were the lunar-dust-covered rosebushes under which the lepers had slept during the great days of the house, and they had proliferated to such a degree in their abandonment that there was scarcely an odorless chink in that atmosphere of roses which mingled with the stench that came to us from the rear of the garden and the stink of the henhouse and the smell of dung and urine ferment of cows and soldiers from the colonial basilica that had been converted into a milking barn. Opening a way through the asphyxiating growth we saw the arches of the gallery with potted carnations and sprigs of astromelias and pansies where the concubines' quarters had been, and from the variety of domestic leftovers and the quantity of sewing machines we thought it possible that more than a thousand women had lived there with their crews of seven-month runts, we saw the battlefield disorder of the kitchens, clothes rotting in the sun by the wash basins, the open slit trench shared by concubines and soldiers, and in back we saw the Babylonian willows that had been carried alive from Asia Minor in great seagoing hothouses, with their own soil, their sap, and their drizzle, and behind the willows we saw government house, immense and sad, where the vultures were still entering through the chipped blinds. We did not have to knock down the door, as we had thought, for the main door seemed to open by itself with just the push of a voice, so we went up to the main floor along a bare stone stairway where the opera-house carpeting had been torn by the hoofs of the cows, and from the first vestibule on down to the private bedrooms we saw the ruined offices and protocol salons through which the brazen cows wandered, eating the velvet curtains and nibbling at the trim on the chairs, we saw heroic portraits of saints and soldiers thrown to the floor among broken furniture and fresh cow flops, we saw a dining room that had been eaten up by the cows, the music room profaned by the cows' breakage, the domino tables destroyed and the felt on the billiard tables cropped by the cows, abandoned in a corner we saw the wind machine, the one which counterfeited any phenomenon from the four points of the compass so that the people in the house could bear up under their nostalgia for the sea that had gone away, we saw birdcages hanging everywhere, still covered with the sleeping cloths put on some night the week before, and through the numerous windows we saw the broad and sleeping animal that was the city, still innocent of the historic Monday that was beginning to come to life, and beyond the city, up to the horizon, we saw the dead craters of harsh moon ash on the endless plain where the sea had been. In that forbidden corner which only a few people of privilege had ever come to know, we smelled the vultures' carnage for the first time, we caught their age-old asthma, their premonitory instinct, and guiding ourselves by the putrefaction of their wing flaps in the reception room we found the wormy shells of the cows, their female animal hindquarters repeated many times in the full-length mirrors, and then we pushed open a side door that connected with an office hidden in the wall, and there we saw him, in his denim uniform without insignia, boots, the gold spur on his left heel, older than all old men and all old animals on land or sea, and he was stretched out on the floor, face down, his right arm bent under his head as a pillow, as he had slept night after night

3

every night of his ever so long life of a solitary despot. Only when we turned him over to look at his face did we realize that it was impossible to recognize him, even though his face had not been pecked away by vultures, because none of us had ever seen him, and even though his profile was on both sides of all coins, on postage stamps, on condom labels, on trusses and scapulars, and even though his engraved picture with the flag across his chest and the dragon of the fatherland was displayed at all times in all places, we knew that they were copies of copies of portraits that had already been considered unfaithful during the time of the comet, when our own parents knew who he was because they had heard tell from theirs, as they had from theirs before them, and from childhood on we grew accustomed to believe that he was alive in the house of power because someone had seen him light the Chinese lanterns at some festival, someone had told about seeing his sad eyes, his pale lips, his pensive hand waving through the liturgical decorations of the presidential coach, because one Sunday many years ago they had brought him the blind man on the street who for five cents would recite the verses of the forgotten poet Rubén Darío and he had come away happy with the nice wad they had paid him for a recital that had been only for him, even though he had not seen him, of course, not because he was blind, but because no mortal had ever seen him since the days of the black vomit and yet we knew that he was there, we knew it because the world went on, life went on, the mail was delivered, the municipal band played its retreat of silly waltzes on Saturday under the dusty palm trees and the dim street lights of the main square, and other old musicians took the places of the dead musicians in the band. In recent years when human sounds or the singing of birds were no longer heard inside and the armored doors were closed forever, we knew that there was someone in government house because at night lights that looked like a ship's beacons could be seen through the windows of the side that faced the sea, and those who dared go closer could hear a disaster of hoofs and animal sighs from behind the fortified walls, and one January afternoon we had seen a cow contemplating the sunset from the presidential balcony, just imagine, a cow on the balcony of the nation, what an awful thing, what a shitty country, and all sorts of conjectures were made about how it was possible for a cow to get onto a balcony since everybody knew that cows can't climb stairs, and even less carpeted ones, so in the end we never knew if we had really seen it or whether we had been spending an afternoon on the main square and as we strolled along had dreamed that we had seen a cow on the presidential balcony where nothing had been seen or would ever be seen again for many years until dawn last Friday when the first vultures began to arrive, rising up from where they had always dozed on the cornices of the charity hospital, they came from farther inland, they came in successive waves, out of the horizon of the sea of dust where the sea had been, for a whole day they flew in slow circles over the house of power until a king with bridal feathers and a crimson ruff gave a silent order and that breaking of glass began, that breeze of a great man dead, that in and out of vultures through the windows imaginable only in a house which lacked authority, so we dared go in too and in the deserted sanctuary we found the rubble of grandeur, the body that had been pecked at, the smooth maiden hands with the ring of power on the bone of the third finger, and his whole body was sprouting tiny lichens and parasitic animals from the depths of the sea, especially in the armpits and the groin, and he had the canvas truss on his herniated testicle, which was the only thing that had escaped the vultures in spite of its being the size of an ox kidney, but even then we did not dare believe in his death because it was the second time he had been found in that office, alone and dressed and dead seemingly of natural causes during his sleep, as had been announced a long time ago in the prophetic waters of soothsayers' basins. The first time they found him had been at the beginning of his autumn, the nation was still lively enough for him to feel menaced by death even in the solitude of his bedroom, and still he governed as if he knew he was predestined never to die, for at that time it did not look like a presidential palace

5

but rather a marketplace where a person had to make his way through barefoot orderlies unloading vegetables and chicken cages from donkeys in the corridors, stepping over beggar women with famished godchildren who were sleeping in a huddle on the stairs awaiting the miracle of official charity, it was necessary to elude the flow of dirty water from the foul-mouthed concubines who were putting fresh flowers in the vases in the place of nocturnal flowers and swabbing the floor and singing songs of illusory loves to the rhythm of the dry branches that beat rugs on the balconies and all of it in the midst of the uproar of tenured civil servants who found hens laying eggs in desk drawers, and the traffic of whores and soldiers in the toilets, and a tumult of birds, and the fighting of street dogs in the midst of audiences because no one knew who was who or by whom in that palace with open doors in the grand disorder of which it was impossible to locate the government. The man of the house not only participated in that marketplace disaster but he had set it up himself and ruled over it, for as soon as the lights in his bedroom went on, before the cocks began to crow, the reveille of the presidential guard gave the notice of the new day to the nearby Conde barracks, and from there it was repeated for the San Jerónimo base, and from there to the harbor fort, and there it would be repeated in the six successive reveilles that would first awaken the city and then the whole country, while he meditated in the portable latrine trying to stifle with his hands the buzzing in his ears, which was beginning to show itself at that time, and watching the passage of the lights of ships along the fickle topaz sea which in those days of glory was still beneath his window. Every day, ever since he had taken possession of the house, he had supervised the milking in the cow barns to measure with his own hand the quantity of milk that the three presidential wagons would carry to the barracks in the city, in the kitchen he would have a mug of black coffee and some cassava without knowing too well the direction in which the whimsical winds of the new day would blow him, always attent on the gabbling of the servants, who were the people in the house who spoke the same

6

language as he, whose serious blandishments he respected most, and whose hearts he best deciphered, and a short time before nine o'clock he would take a slow bath in water with boiled leaves in the granite cistern built in the shadow of the almond trees of his private courtyard, and only after eleven o'clock would he manage to overcome the drowsiness of dawn and confront the hazards of reality. Previously, during the occupation by the marines, he would shut himself up in his office to decide the destiny of the nation with the commandant of the forces of the landing and sign all manner of laws and decrees with his thumbprint, for in those days he did not know how to read or write, but when they left him alone with his nation and his power again he did not poison his blood again with the sluggishness of written law, but governed orally and physically, present at every moment and everywhere with a flinty parsimony but also with a diligence inconceivable at his age, besieged by mobs of lepers, blind people and cripples who begged for the salt of health from his hands, and lettered politicians and dauntless adulators who proclaimed him the corrector of earthquakes, eclipses, leap years and other errors of God, dragging his great feet of an elephant walking in the snow all through the house as he resolved problems of state and household matters with the same simplicity with which he gave the order take that door away from here and put it over there for me, they took it away, put it back again for me, they put it back, the clock in the tower should not strike twelve at twelve o'clock but two times so that life would seem longer, the order was carried out, without an instant of hesitation, without a pause, except for the mortal hour of siesta time when he would take refuge in the shade of the concubines, he would choose one by assault, without undressing her or getting undressed himself, without closing the door, and all through the house one could hear his heartless panting of an urgent spouse, the craving tinkle of his gold spur, his dog whimper, the surprise of the woman who wasted her time at love in trying to get rid of the squalid stares of the seven-month runts, her shouts of get out of here, go play in the courtyard, this isn't for children

7

to see, and it was as if an angel had flown across the skies of the nation, voices were muffled, life came to a halt, everybody remained stone-still with a finger to his lips, not breathing, silence, the general is screwing, but those who knew him best had no faith even in the respite of that sacred moment, for it always seemed that he was in two places at once, they would see him playing dominoes at seven o'clock at night and at the same time he had been seen lighting cow chips to drive the mosquitoes out of the reception room, nor did anyone harbor any illusions until the lights in the last of the windows went out and they heard the noise of the three crossbars, the three locks, the three bolts on the door of the presidential bedroom, and they heard the thump of the body as it collapsed from fatigue onto the stone floor, and the breathing of a decrepit child that grew deeper as the tide rose, until the nocturnal harp of the wind silenced the cicadas and their fiddling and a broad big sea wave swept through the streets of the ancient city of viceroys and buccaneers and poured into government house through all the windows like a tremendous August Saturday that caused barnacles to grow on the mirrors and left the reception room at the mercy of the sharks and it rose higher than the highest levels of prehistoric oceans and overflowed the face of the land and space and time, and only he remained floating face down on the lunar water of his dreams of a solitary drowned man, in his denim private soldier's uniform, his boots, his gold spur, and his right arm folded under his head to serve as a pillow. That simultaneous presence everywhere during the flinty years that preceded his first death, that going up as he went down, that going into ecstasy in the sea while in agony in unsuccessful loves, were not a privilege of his nature, as his adulators proclaimed, or a mass hallucination, as his critics said, but his luck in counting on the complete service and doglike loyalty of Patricio Aragonés, his perfect double, who had been found without anyone's searching for him when they came to him with the news general sir a false presidential coach was driving around to Indian villages doing a prosperous business of impostoring, they had seen

8

the taciturn eyes in the morguelike shadows, they had seen the pale lips, the hand of a sensitive bride with a velvet glove that went along throwing handfuls of salt to sick people kneeling in the street, and behind the coach followed two bogus cavalry officers collecting hard cash for the favor of health, just imagine general sir, what a sacrilege, and he gave no order against the impostor, but asked instead that they bring him secretly to the presidential palace with his head stuck in a burlap bag so that people would not get them mixed up, and then he suffered the humiliation of seeing himself in such a state of equality, God damn it, this man is me, he said, because it really was as if he were, except for the authority of the voice, which the other one never managed to imitate, and for the clearness of the lines on the hand where the life line went along without obstacles all around the base of the thumb, and if he did not have him shot immediately it was not because he was interested in keeping him as his official impostor, that occurred to him later, but because the illusion that the cipher of his own fate should be written on the hand of an impostor bothered him. When he became convinced of the vanity of that dream Patricio Aragonés had already impassively survived six assassination attempts, had acquired the habit of dragging his feet which had been flattened out with a mallet, his ears buzzed, and his hernia ached at dawn in the winter, and he had learned to take off and put on the golden spur as if the straps were tangled up simply to gain time at audiences muttering God damn it these buckles Flemish blacksmiths make aren't even good for this, and from the jokester and gabbler that he had been when he was a glass-blower in his father's carquaise he became thoughtful and somber and paid no attention to what people were saying to him but scrutinized the shadows of their eyes to guess what they were not saying to him, and he never answered a question without first asking in turn what do you think and from the slothful wastrel he had been in his business as a vendor of miracles, he became diligent to the point of torture and an implacable walker, he became tight-fisted and rapacious, he resigned himself to sleeping on the floor,

9

his clothes on, face down and with no pillow, and he renounced his precocious presumption of an identity of his own and all hereditary vocation for the golden flightiness of simply blowing and making bottles, and he confronted the most terrible risks of power laying cornerstones where the second stone was never to be laid, cutting ribbons in enemy territory and bearing up under so many soft-boiled dreams and so many repressed sighs of impossible illusions as he crowned and did not so much as touch all those ephemeral and unattainable beauty queens, for he had become resigned forever to live a destiny that was not his, even though he did not do it out of greed or conviction but because he had exchanged his life for his in the lifetime job of official impostor with a nominal salary of fifty pesos a month and the advantage of living like a king without the calamity of being one, what more could you ask? That mix-up of identities reached its high point one night when the wind was long and he found Patricio Aragonés sighing out toward the sea amidst the fragrant vapor of the jasmines and he asked him with legitimate alarm if they had put wolfbane in the food because he was drifting off as if pierced by evil air, and Patricio Aragonés answered him no general, it's worse than that, on Saturday he had crowned a carnival queen and had danced the first waltz with her and now he couldn't find any exit out of that memory, because she was the most beautiful woman on earth, the kind you never get for yourself general, if you could only see her, but he answered with a sigh of relief and what the hell, this is the kind of trouble a man gets into when he gets all tied up with women, he proposed abducting her as he had done with so many good-looking women who had become his concubines, I'll have her held down by force on the bed with four troopers at her arms and legs while you take care of her with your soup ladle, God damn it, you can take her while she's bulldogged, he told him, even the tightest of them roll around with rage at first and then they beg you don't leave me like this general like a sad rose apple whose seed has fallen off, but Patricio Aragonés didn't want as much as that he wanted more, he wanted them to love him, because this girl is one of those who know where the tune comes from general, you'll see when you get a look at her, so as a formula for relief he pointed out the nocturnal pathways to the rooms of his concubines to him and authorized him to make use of them as if it were he himself, by assault and quickly and with his clothes on, and Patricio Aragonés in good faith sank into that morass of loves even believing that he could put a gag on his urges through them, but such was his anxiety that sometimes he forgot the conditions of the loan, he would unbutton his fly absentmindedly, linger over details, carelessly stumble across the hidden jewels of the basest of women, draw out their deepest sighs, and even make them laugh with surprise in the shadows, you old devil general, they would tell him, you're growing greedy on us in your old age, and from then on neither of them or any of the women either ever knew whose child was whose or by whom, because Patricio Aragonés's children were seven-monthers just like his. So it came to pass that Patricio Aragonés became the man most essential to the seat of power, the most beloved and also perhaps the most feared, and he had more time available to take care of the armed forces, not because the armed forces were what sustained his power, as we all thought, quite the contrary, because they were his most feared natural enemy, so he made some officers believe that they were being watched by others, he shuffled their assignments to prevent their plotting, every army post received a ration of eight blank cartridges for every ten live rounds and he sent them gunpowder mixed with beach sand while he kept the good ammunition within reach in an arsenal in the presidential palace the keys to which hung on a ring with other keys that had no duplicates and opened other doors that no one else could open, protected by the tranquil shadow of my lifelong comrade General Rodrigo de Aguilar, an artilleryman and academy graduate who was also his minister of defense and at the same time commander of the presidential guard, director of the state security services, and one of the very few mortals authorized to beat him in a game of dominoes, because he had lost his right arm trying to defuse a dynamite charge minutes before the presidential berlin was to pass by the site of the assassination attempt. He felt so safe under the protection of General Rodrigo de Aguilar and with the presence of Patricio Aragonés that he began to relax his concern with self-preservation and was becoming more and more visible, he dared take a ride through the city with only one aide in a covered wagon bearing insignia looking through the peepholes at the arrogant gilt stone cathedral which he had declared by decree the most beautiful in the world, he peeped at the ancient stone mansions with entranceways from times when all was drowsy and the sunflowers turned seaward, the cobbled streets with the smell of snuff in the viceregal quarter, the pale young ladies making bobbin lace with ineluctable decency among the pots of carnations and the bunches of pansies in the light of balconies, the checkerboard convent of the Biscayan sisters with the same harpsichord exercise at three in the afternoon with which they had celebrated the first passage of the comet, he went through the Babelic labyrinth of the commercial district, its lethal music, the labara of lottery tickets, the pushcarts with cane juice, the strings of iguana eggs, the Turks and their sunlight-faded bargains, the fearsome tapestry of the woman who had been changed into a scorpion for having disobeyed her parents, the alley of misery of women without men who would emerge naked at dusk to buy blue corbinas and red snappers and exchange mother-directed curses with the women selling vegetables while their clothes were drying on the carved wooden balconies, he smelled the rotten shellfish wind, the everyday light of the pelicans around the corner, the disorder of colors of the Negro shacks on the promontories of the bay, and suddenly there it was, the waterfront, alas, the waterfront, the dock and its spongy planks, the old battleship of the marines longer and gloomier than truth, the black dockworker woman who was too late in getting out of the way of the fearsome little wagon and felt touched by death with the sight of the sunset old man who was contemplating the waterfront with the saddest look in the world, it's him, she exclaimed with surprise, hurray for the stud, she shouted, hurray, shouted the men, the women, the children who came running out of the Chinese bars and lunchrooms, hurray, shouted the ones who held the horses' legs and blocked the coach's way so they could shake the hand of the power that was, a maneuver so swift and unforeseen that he barely had time to push aside the armed hand of his aide scolding him in a tense voice, don't be a damned fool, lieutenant, let them love me, so overwhelmed by that out-pouring of love and by similar ones during the days that followed that it was hard for General Rodrigo de Aguilar to make him get out of his head the idea of riding about in an open carriage so that the patriots of the nation could see me full length, what the hell, because he didn't even sus-pect that the assault at the waterfront may have been spon-taneous but that the ones that followed had been organized by his own security services in order to please him but without any risks, so honeyed by the breezes of love on the eve of his autumn that he dared go out of the city after many years, he started up the old train painted with the colors of the flag again and went creeping and crawling about the cornices of his vast mournful realm, opening a path through orchid sprigs and Amazonian balsam apples, rousing up monkeys, birds of paradise, jaguars sleeping on the tracks, even the glacial and deserted villages of his native barren uplands where they waited for him at the station with mournful-music bands, tolling death bells, dis-playing signs of welcome for the nameless patriot who sits at the right hand of the Holy Trinity, they recruited rustics from the back reaches who came down to meet the hidden power in the funereal shadows of the presidential coach, and those who managed to get close enough only saw the quivering lips, the palm of a hand with no origins which waved from the limbo of glory, while a member of the escort tried to get him away from the window, be careful, general, the nation needs you, but he would reply sleepily don't worry, colonel, these people love me, as it was on the train in the barren lands so it was the same on the wooden paddle-wheeler that went along leaving a wake of player-piano waltzes in the midst of the sweet fragrance of gardenias and rotting salamanders of the equatorial tributaries, eluding prehistoric dragons in their leather gun cases, providential isles where sirens lay down to give birth, sunsets which were the disasters of immense disappeared cities, even the burning and desolate shantytowns where the inhabitants appeared on the riverbank to see the wooden boat painted with the national colors and they could just make out an anonymous hand with a velvet glove which waved from a window of the presidential stateroom, but he saw the groups on shore who were waving malanga leaves for lack of flags, he saw those who jumped into the water with a live tapir, a gigantic yam that was as big as an elephant's foot, a cage of partridges for the presidential stewpot, and he sighed with emotion in the ecclesiastical penumbra of the stateroom, see how they come, captain, see how they love me. In December, when the Caribbean world turned to glass, he would take the closed carriage on a climb along the cornices of crags until he came to the house perched on top of the reefs and he would spend the afternoon playing dominoes with the former dictators of other nations of the continent, the dethroned fathers of other countries to whom he had granted asylum over the course of many years and who were now growing old in the shadow of his mercy dreaming in chairs on the terrace about the chimerical vessel of their second chance, talking to themselves, dying dead in the rest home he had built for them on the balcony of the sea after having received all of them as if each were the only one, for they all appeared at dawn in the dress uniform they had put on inside out over their pajamas, with a chest of money they had pilfered from the public treasury and a suitcase with a box of decorations, newspaper clippings pasted into old ledgers, and a photograph album they would show him at the first audience, as if they were credentials, saying look general, that's me when I was a lieutenant, this was the day I was inaugurated, this was the sixteenth anniversary of my taking power, here, look general, but he would give them asylum without paying any more attention to them or inspecting credentials because the only document of identity for an overthrown president should be his death certificate, he would say, and with the same disdain he would listen to the illusory little speech of I accept for this short time your noble hospitality while the justice of the people brings the usurper to account, the eternal formula of puerile solemnity which a while later he would hear from the usurper, and then from the usurper's usurper as if the God-damned fools didn't know that in this business of men if you fall, you fall, and he put all of them up for a few months in the presidential palace, made them play dominoes until he had fleeced them down to their last cent, and then he took me by the arm over to the window looking out onto the sea, he helped me grieve over this meat-beating life that only goes in one direction, he consoled me with the illusion that I go over there, look, over there to that big house that looked like an ocean liner aground on the top of the reefs where I have some lodgings with good light and good food, and plenty of time to forget along with other companions of misfortune, and with a terrace overlooking the sea where he liked to sit on December afternoons not so much for the pleasure of playing dominoes with that bunch of boobs but to enjoy the base good fortune of not being one of them, to look at himself in the instructive mirror of their misery while he wallowed in the great slough of felicity, dreaming alone, tiptoing like an evil thought in pursuit of the tame mulatto girls who swept government house in the dimness of dawn, he sniffed out their public dormitory and drugstore hairgrease trail, he would lie in wait for the chance to catch one alone and make rooster love to her behind office doors while they would burst with laughter in the shadows, what a devil you are general, such a great man and still so horny, but he would be sad after making love and would start singing to console himself where no one could hear him, bright January moon, he would sing, see how sad I am standing on the gallows by your window, he would sing, so sure of his people's love on those Octobers with no evil omens that he would put up a hammock in the courtyard of the suburban mansion where his mother Bendición Al-

varado lived and slept his siesta in the shade of the tamarind trees, without an escort, dreaming about the errant
fish who swam in the colored waters of the bedrooms, a
nation is the best thing that was ever invented, mother, he
would sigh, but he never waited for the answer from the
only person in the world who dared scold him for the
rancid onion smell of his armpits, but he returned to the
presidential palace through the main door in exaltation
with that miraculous season of the Caribbean in January,
that reconciliation with the world at the end of old age,
those mellow soft afternoons after he had made peace with
the papal nuncio and the latter would visit him without an
appointment to attempt to convert him to the faith of
Christ while they had chocolate and cookies, and bursting
with laughter he would allege that if God is the man you say
he is tell him to rid me of this beetle that's buzzing in my
ear, he would tell him, he would unbutton the nine buttons
of his fly and show him his huge tool, tell him to deflate this
creature, he would tell him, but the nuncio went along with
his shepherd's work with patient stoicism, tried to convince
him that everything that is truth, no matter who says it,
comes from the Holy Spirit, and he would see him to the
door when the first lights went on, dying with laughter as
had rarely been seen, don't waste your gunpowder on buzzards, father, he told him, why should you want to convert
me since everything I'm doing is just what you people want,
what the hell. That floating calmness shattered its hull suddenly at a cockpit on a faraway plain when a bloodthirsty
cock tore the head off his adversary and ate it, pecking at
it before an audience that was maddened by blood and a
drunken brass band that celebrated the horror with festive
music, and he was the only one who spotted the evil omen,
and he sensed that it was so clear and so imminent that he
secretly ordered his escort to arrest one of the musicians,
that one, the one playing the tuba, and, indeed, they found
a sawed-off shotgun on him and under torture he confessed
that he had planned to shoot him during the confusion as
the people left, it was quite obvious, of course, he explained, because I was looking at everybody and everybody

was looking back at me, but the only one who didn't dare look at me one single time was that son of a bitch with the tuba, poor devil, and still he knew that that wasn't the ultimate reason for his anxiety, because he kept on feeling it at night in government house even after his security service had shown that there was no reason for worry general sir, everything was in order, but he had clung to Patricio Aragonés as if he were himself after he had received the omen at the cockpit, he gave him his own food to eat, he gave him his own honey to drink with the same spoon so that he would at least die with the consolation that they had both died together in case the things had been poisoned, and they went like fugitives through forgotten rooms, walking on the rugs so that no one would hear their great furtive Siamese elephant steps, navigating together in the intermittent light from the beacon as it came in through the windows and flooded the rooms of the house every thirty seconds with green amidst the vapor from cow flops and the mournful greetings of nocturnal ships on the sleeping seas, they would spend whole afternoons watching it rain, counting swallows on languid September afternoons like two aged lovers, so far removed from the world that he himself did not realize that his fierce struggle to exist twice was feeding the contrary suspicion that he was existing less and less, that he was lying in a lethargy, that the guard had been doubled and no one was allowed in or out of the presidential quarters, that someone had still managed to get through that strict filter and had seen the birds silent in their cages, the cows drinking at the baptismal font, the lepers and cripples sleeping in the rose beds, and everybody at midday seemed to be waiting for dawn to come since he had died as had been announced in the prophetic basins of natural causes during his sleep but the high command was delaying the notice while they tried to settle in bloody secret meetings their postponed quarrels. Although he did not know of those rumors he was aware that something was about to occur in his life, he would interrupt the slow domino games to ask General Rodrigo de Aguilar how the mess was going, friend, everything under control sir, the nation was calm, he watched for signs of premonition in the funeral pyres of cow chips that burned on the court-yard corridors and in the wells with their ancient waters but he could find no answer for his anxiety, he visited his mother Bendición Alvarado in the suburban mansion when the heat died down, they would sit and take in the cool afternoon breezes under the tamarinds, she in her maternal rocking chair, decrepit but with her soul intact, tossing handfuls of grain to the hens and the peacocks who pecked about the courtyard, and he in the large wicker chair, fan-ning himself with his hat, following with his look of old hunger the big mulatto women who brought him colored fruit juices to quench his hot thirst, general, thinking oh Bendición Alvarado, my mother, if you only knew that I can't stand the world any more, that I'd like to go away I don't know where, mother, far away from so much injus-tice, but not even his mother was shown the inside of his sighs but he would return to the presidential palace with the first lights of evening, go in through the service en-trance hearing the clicking of sentries' heels as he went along the corridors and they saluted him all's well general sir, everything in order, but he knew that it wasn't true, that they were dissembling from habit, that they lied to him out of fear, that nothing was true in that crisis of uncertainty which was rendering his glory bitter and had been taking away his old desire to command ever since that fateful night at the cockpit, until very late he would stay stretched out face down on the floor without sleeping, through the open window facing the sea he could hear the distant drums and sad bagpipes that were celebrating some wedding among the poor with the same uproar with which they would have celebrated his death, he could hear the farewell of a vaga-bond steamer that was weighing anchor at two o'clock in the morning without permission from the port captain, he could hear the paper sound of the roses as they opened at dawn, without one moment of rest, sensing with a woods-man's instinct the imminence of the afternoon when he would be on his way back from the suburban mansion and be surprised by a mob in the street, an opening and closing

18

of windows and a panic of swallows in the diaphanous December sky and he peeped through the curtain of the carriage to see what was going on and he said to himself this is it, mother, this is it, he said to himself, with a terrible feeling of relief, seeing the colored balloons in the sky, the red and green balloons, the yellow balloons like great blue oranges, the innumerable wandering balloons that took flight in the midst of swallows' fright and floated for an instant in the crystal light of four o'clock and suddenly broke with a silent and unanimous explosion releasing thousands and thousands of bits of paper over the city, a blizzard of broadsides which the coachman took advantage of in order to slip through the tumult of the public market without anyone's recognizing the coach of power, because everybody was busy in the scramble for the papers from the balloons general sir, they were shouting out the words on them from the balconies, from memory they repeated down with oppression, they shouted death to the tyrant, and even the sentries along the corridors of the presidential palace were reading aloud about the union of all without distinction of class against the despotism of centuries, patriotic reconciliation against the corruption and the arrogance of the military, no more blood, they shouted, no more pillaging, the whole country was awakening from its age-old sleep at the moment he was going through the coach house door and he ran into the terrible news general sir that Patricio Aragonés had been fatally wounded by a poisoned dart. Years before one night of bad moods he had proposed to Patricio Aragonés that they gamble their lives on heads or tails, heads you die, tails I die, but Patricio Aragonés made him see that they would both meet death in a tie because all coins had both their faces on both sides, he then proposed that they gamble their lives at the domino table, the best out of twenty games, and Patricio Aragonés accepted with great honor general sir, with the proviso that you grant me the privilege of being allowed to beat you, and he accepted, agreed, so they played one game, they played two, they played twenty, and Patricio Aragonés always won because he only used to win because it was for-

19

bidden to beat him, a long and bloody battle was joined and they reached the last game without his having won a single match, and Patricio Aragonés dried the sweat of his brow with his shirt sleeve sighing I'm deeply sorry general but I don't want to die, and then he went about picking up the pieces, placed them in order in the little wooden box while he said like a schoolmaster chanting a rote lesson that he had no need to die at the domino table either but in his own time and his own place from natural causes in his sleep as had been predicted ever since the beginning of his days by the sibylline basins, and not even that way, when you come to think of it, because Bendición Alvarado didn't bring me into the world to pay any heed to basins but to command, and after all I am what I am, and not you, so give thanks to God that this was only a game, he told him laughing, not having imagined then or ever that the terrible joke was to come true the night he went into Patricio Aragonés's room and found him facing the demands of death, hopeless, with no chance of surviving the poison, and he greeted him from the door with his hand outstretched, God save you, stud, it's a great honor to die for your country. He stayed with him during his slow agony, the two of them alone in the room, giving him the spoonfuls of anodyne with his own hand, and Patricio Aragonés took them without gratitude telling him between spoonfuls I will leave you here for a while my general with your world of shit because my heart tells me that quite soon we shall meet again in the depths of hell, I all twisted up worse than a mullet because of this poison and you with your head in your hand looking for a place to put it, let it be said without the least bit of respect general sir, that I can tell you now that I never loved you as you think but that ever since the days of the filibusters when I had the evil misfortune to chance into your domains I've been praying that you would be killed, in a good way even, so that you would pay me back for this life of an orphan you gave me, first by flattening my feet with tamping hands so that they would be those of a sleepwalker like yours, then by piercing my nuts with a shoemaker's awl so I would develop a rupture, then by making me drink turpentine so

I would forget how to read and write after all the work it took my mother to teach me, and always obliging me to go through the public ceremonies you didn't dare face, and not because the nation needs you alive as you say but because even the toughest man can feel his ass freeze up when he crowns a beauty whore and doesn't know from what direction death will explode in on him, let it be said without the least respect general, but he wasn't bothered by the insolence but rather by the ingratitude of Patricio Aragonés who I set up in life like a king in a palace and I gave you what no one has ever given anybody in this world even lending you my own women, although we'd best not talk about that general because it's better to be gelded by a mace than to go about laying mothers on the ground as if it were a matter of branding calves, just because those poor heartless bitch waifs don't even feel the brand or kick or twist or complain like calves, and they don't smoke from the haunches or smell of singed flesh which is the least one asks of good women, but they lay down their dead-cow bodies so a person can do his duty while they go on peeling potatoes and shouting to the other women please keep an eye on the kitchen for me while I take a breather here so my rice doesn't burn, only you would think that stuff like that is love general, because it's the only kind you know, without the least respect of course, and then he began to roar shut up, God damn it, shut up or you'll pay for it, but Patricio Aragonés kept on saying without the slightest intention of a joke why should I shut up when all you can do is kill me and you're already killing me, it would be better now to take advantage and look truth in the face general, so you can know that no one has ever told you what he really thinks but that everyone tells you what he knows you want to hear while he bows to your face and thumbs his nose at you from behind, you might even thank fate that I'm the man who most pities you in this world because I'm the only one who looks like you, the only one honorable enough to sing out to you what everyone says that you're president of nobody and that you're not on the throne because of your big guns but because the English sat you there and the gringos kept you there with the pair of balls on their battleship, because I saw you scurrying like a cockroach this way and that, back and forth when the gringos shouted to you we're leaving you here with your nigger whorehouse so let's see if you can put it all together without us, and if you never got out of your chair since that time or have never gotten out it's probably not because you don't want to but because you can't, recognize it, because you know that the moment they see you on the street dressed as a mortal they're going to fall on you like a pack of dogs to collect from you in one case for the killings at Santa María del Altar, in another for the prisoners thrown into the moat of the harbor fort to be eaten by crocodiles, in another for the people you skin alive and send their hides to their families as a lesson, he said, dipping into the bottomless well of his long-postponed rancor and drawing out the string of atrocities of his regime of infamy, until he could no longer tell him any more because a fiery rake tore his guts apart, his heart softened again and he ended with no intent of offense but almost one of supplication I'm serious general, take advantage of the fact that I'm dying now and die with me, no one has more right than I to tell you this because I never had any intention of looking like anyone much less a national hero but only a sad little glassblower making bottles like my father, take a chance, general, it doesn't hurt as much as it seems, and he said it with an air of such serene truth that the rage to answer did not overcome him but rather he tried to hold him up in his chair when he saw that he was starting to twist about and hold his belly in his hands and was sobbing with tears of pain and shame I'm so sorry general but I'm shitting in my pants and he thought he meant it in a figurative sense that he was dying of fear, but Patricio Aragonés answered him no, I mean real shit shitting general and he managed to beseech him hold on Patricio Aragonés, hold on, we generals of the fatherland have to die like men even if we pay for it with our lives, but he said it too late because Patricio Aragonés fell face down and on top of him kicking with fear and soaked in shit and tears. In the office next to the hearing room he had to scrub the body with a dishrag and soap to get rid of the bad smell, he dressed it in the clothes he was wearing, he put the canvas truss on, the boots, the gold spur on the left heel, feeling as he did it that he was changing into the most solitary man on earth, and last of all he erased all traces of the farce and reproduced the perfection down to the tiniest details that he had seen with his own eyes in the premonitory waters of the basins so that at dawn on the next day the cleaning women would find the body as they did find it stretched out face down on the floor of the office, dead for the first time of natural causes in his sleep with his denim uniform with no insignia, boots, the gold spur, and his right arm folded under his head as a pillow. They did not spread the news immediately that time either, contrary to what he expected, but many prudent hours passed with clandestine investigations, secret agreements among the heirs of the regime who were trying to gain time by denying the rumor of death with all manner of contrary versions, they brought his mother Bendición Alvarado out into the commercial district to show that she was not wearing a mourning face, they dressed me in a flowered dress like a chippy, sir, they made me buy a macaw-feather hat so that everybody would see me happy, they made me buy every piece of junk to be found in the stores in spite of my telling them no, sir, it wasn't a time for buying but for crying because even I believed that it was really my son who had died, and they forced me to smile when people took full-length pictures of me because the military men said it had to be done for the good of the country while he wondered confused in his hiding place what's happening out in the world since nothing had changed with the trick of his death, how was it that the sun had risen and had risen again without stumbling, why that Sunday look, mother, why the same heat without me, he was wondering in surprise when a sudden cannon shot sounded from the fortress on the harbor and the main bells of the cathedral began to toll and all the way up to government house came the surge of the crowds that were rising up out of the age-old morass with the greatest piece of news in the world, and then he half-opened the bedroom door and peeped into the audience room and saw himself laid out more dead and more decorated than all the dead popes of Christendom, wounded by the horror and the shame of his own body of a military stud lying among the flowers, his face pale with powder, his lips painted, the hard hands of a dauntless young lady crossed over the chest armored with military decorations, the showy dress uniform with the ten pips of general of the universe, a rank someone had invented for him after death, the king-of-spades saber he never used, the patent leather boots with two gold spurs, the vast paraphernalia of power and the lugubrious martial glories reduced to his human size of a fagot lying in state, God damn it, that can't be me, he said to himself in a fury it's not right, God damn it, he said to himself, contemplating the procession that was parading around his corpse, and for an instant he forgot the murky reasons for the farce and felt raped and diminished by the inclemency of death toward the majesty of power, he saw life without him, he saw with a certain compassion how men were bereft of his authority, he saw with a hidden uneasiness those who had only come to decipher the enigma of whether it really was or was not he, he saw a very old man who gave the masonic salute from the days of the federalist war, he saw a man in mourning who kissed his ring, he saw a schoolgirl who laid a flower on him, he saw a fishwife who could not resist the truth of his death and strewed her basket of fresh fish all over the floor and embraced the perfumed corpse sobbing aloud that it was him, my God, what's going to become of us without him, she wept, so it was him, they shouted, it was him, shouted the throng suffocated by the sun in the main square and then the bells of the cathedral stopped tolling their knell and those of all the churches announced a Wednesday of jubilation, Easter rockets exploded, Roman candles, drums of liberation, and he watched the assault groups that came in through the windows in the face of the silent complacency of the guard, he watched the ferocious leaders who dispersed the procession with clubs and knocked down the inconsolable fishwife, he watched the ones who attacked the corpse, the eight men who took it out of its immemorial state and its chimerical time of agapanthus lilies and sunflowers and dragged it down the stairs, those who gutted the insides of that paradise of opulence and misfortune thinking they were destroying the lair of power forever, knocking over the papier-mâché Doric capitals, velvet curtains and Babylonic columns crowned with alabaster palm trees, throwing birdcages out the window, the throne of the viceroys, the grand piano, breaking the funeral urns with the ashes of unknown patriots and Gobelin tapestries of maidens asleep in gondolas of disillusion and enormous oil paintings of bishops and archaic military men and inconceivable naval battles, annihilating that world so that in the memory of future generations not the slightest memory of the cursed line of men of arms would remain, and then he peeped into the street through the slats in the blinds to see what degree the ravages of defenestration had reached and with just one glance he saw more infamy and more ingratitude than had ever been seen and wept over by my eyes since the day I was born, mother, he saw his merry widows leaving the building through the service entrance leading the cows from my stables by the halter, carrying off government furniture, the jars of honey from your hives, mother, he saw his seven-month runts making music of jubilation with kitchen pots and treasures from the crystal set and the table service for pontifical banquets singing with street-urchin shouts my papa is dead, hurray for freedom, he saw the bonfire that had been lighted on the main square to burn the official portraits and the almanac lithographs that had been in all places and at all times ever since the beginning of his regime, and he saw his own body dragged by as it left behind along the street a trail of medals and epaulets, dolman buttons, strands of brocade and frog embroidery and tassels from playing-card sabers and the ten sad pips of the king of the universe, mother, look what they've done to me, he said, feeling in his own flesh the ignominy of the spitting and the sickbed pans that were thrown on him from the balconies as he went by, horrified with the idea of being quartered and devoured by dogs and vultures amidst the delirious howls and the roar of fireworks celebrating the carnival of my death. When the cataclysm had passed he still heard the distant music of the windless afternoon, he went on killing mosquitoes and with the same slaps trying to kill the katydids in his ears which hindered him in his thinking, he still saw the light of the fires on the horizon, the lighthouse that tinted him with green every thirty seconds through the slits in the blinds, the natural breathing of daily life which was getting to be the same again while his death was changing into a different death more like so many others in the past, the incessant torrent of reality which was carrying him off toward the no man's land of compassion and oblivion, God damn it, fuck death, he exclaimed, and then he left his hiding place exalted by the certainty that his grandest hour had struck, he went through the sacked salons dragging his thick phantom feet in the midst of the ruins of his former life in the shadows that smelled of dying flowers and burial candlewicks, he pushed open the door of the cabinet room, heard through the smoky air the thin voices around the long walnut table, and saw through the smoke that all the ones he wanted to be there were there, the liberals who had sold the federalist war, the conservatives who had bought it, the generals of the high command, three of his cabinet ministers, the archbishop primate and Ambassador Schontner, all together in one single plot calling for the unity of all against the despotism of centuries so that they could divide up among themselves the booty of his death, so absorbed in the depths of greed that no one noticed the appearance of the unburied president who gave a single blow with the palm of his hand on the table, and shouted aha! and that was all he had to do, for when he lifted his hand from the table the stampede of panic was over and all that was left in the room were the overflowing ashtrays, the coffee mugs, the chairs flung on the floor, and my comrade of a lifetime General Rodrigo de Aguilar in battle dress, minute, impassive, wafting away the smoke with his one hand and indicating to him to drop to the floor general sir because now the fun is going to begin, and they both dropped to the floor at the instant the machine guns' death jubilation started up by the front of the building, the butcher feast of the presidential guard who with great pleasure and great honor general sir carried out his fierce orders that no one should escape alive from the meeting where treason was being hatched, any who tried to escape through the main door were mowed down with machine-gun bursts, the ones who were hanging out the windows were shot down like birds from a blind, the ones who were able to escape the encirclement and took refuge in nearby houses were degutted with phosphorus grenades, and they finished off the wounded in accordance with the presidential criterion that any survivor is a dangerous enemy as long as he lives, while he remained lying face down on the floor two feet away from General Rodrigo de Aguilar tolerating the hail of glass and plaster that came through the windows with every explosion, murmuring without pause as if he were praying, that's it, old friend, that's it, the trouble's over, from now on I'm going to rule alone with no dogs to bark at me, tomorrow we'll have to see what good has come out of this mother fucking mess and what hasn't and if we don't have anything to sit on in the meantime we'll get six leather stools of the cheapest sort, some straw mats and put them here and there to cover up the holes, we'll buy a few more odds and ends, and that's it, no plàtes, no spoons, no nothing, I'll bring it all from the barracks, because I'm not going to have any military men or officers around, God damn it, all they're good for is to waste more milk and when there's trouble, as we've seen, they spit on the hand that feeds them, I'll only keep the presidential guard who are straight shooters and brave fellows and I'm not going to name any cabinet, God damn it, just a good minister of health which is the only thing anyone really needs in life, and maybe another one with a good hand for what has to be put in writing, and that way we can rent out the ministries and barracks and save the money for help, because what's needed here isn't people but money, we'll get two good maids, one for cleaning and cooking and the other to wash and iron, and I'll take care of the cows and the birds myself when we get some, and no more of jumping whores in the toilets or lepers in the rosebushes or doctors of philosophy who know everything or wise politicians who see everything, because after all this is a presidential palace and not a nigger whorehouse as Patricio Aragonés said the gringos said, and I'm more than enough all alone to keep on ruling until the comet comes by again, and not just once but ten times, because the way I am I don't intend to die again, God damn it, let other people die, he said, talking without any pauses to think, as if he were reciting by heart, because he had known ever since the war that thinking aloud was driving off the fear of the dynamite charges that were shaking the building, making plans for tomorrow in the morning and for the coming century at dusk until the last coup de grace rang out in the street and General Rodrigo de Aguilar crawled over to the window and gave the order to get the garbage wagons and take away the dead bodies and he left the room saying have a good night general, the same for you old friend, he answered, thank you very much, lying face down on the funereal marble of the cabinet room, and then he folded his right arm to serve as a pillow and fell asleep at once, more alone than ever, lulled by the sound of the trail of yellow leaves of his autumn of pain which had begun forever that night with the smoking bodies and the puddles of red moons of the massacre. He did not have to take any of the predicted measures because the army broke up on its own, the troops scattered, the few officers who resisted until the last moments in the garrisons in the city and in another six in the countryside were wiped out by the presidential guards with the help of civilian volunteers, the surviving ministers fled into exile at dawn and only the two most faithful remained, one who was also his private physician and the other who had the best handwriting in the country, and he did not have to kowtow to any foreign power because the government coffers were overflowing with wedding rings held as surety by instant partisans, nor did he have to buy any mats or leather stools of the cheapest sort to repair the ravages of defenestration, because even be-

fore the pacification of the country was over the audience
room was restored and more sumptuous than ever, and
there were birdcages everywhere, chattering macaws, royal
lory parrots who sang in the cornices for Spain and not for
Portugal, discreet and serviceable women who kept the
building as neat and clean as a battleship, and in through
the windows came the music of glory, the same Roman
candles of excitement, the same bells of jubilation that had
begun celebrating his death and went on celebrating his
immortality, and there was a great permanent rally on the
main square with shouts of eternal support and large signs
saying God Save the Magnificent who arose from the dead
on the third day, an endless celebration that he did not have
to prolong with any secret maneuvers as he had done at
other times, because affairs of state took care of themselves
without any help, the nation went along, he alone was the
government, and no one bothered the aims of his will
whether by word or deed, because he was so alone in his
glory that he no longer had any enemies left, and he was
so thankful for his comrade of a lifetime Rodrigo de Aguilar
that he did not get nervous again over the expense of the
milk but ordered the private soldiers who had distinguished themselves by their ferocity and sense of duty to
form in the courtyard, and pointing to them according to
the impulses of his inspiration he promoted them to the
highest ranks knowing that he was restoring the armed
forces who were going to spit in the hand that fed them, you
to captain, you to major, you to colonel, what am I saying,
to general, and all the rest to lieutenant, what the hell old
friend, here's your army, and he was so moved by those
who had been grieved by his death that he had them fetch
the old man with the masonic salute and the gentleman in
mourning who had kissed his ring and he decorated them
with the medal of peace, he had them bring in the fishwife
and he gave her what she said she needed most which was
a house with a lot of rooms where she could live with her
fourteen children, he had them bring in the schoolgirl who
had laid a flower on the corpse and granted her what I most
want in this world which was to get married to a man of the

sea, but in spite of those acts of relief his confused heart did
not have a moment of rest until in the courtyard of the San
Jerónimo barracks he saw bound and spat upon the assault
groups who had sacked the presidential palace, he recognized them one by one with the remorseless memory of
rancor and he went about separating them into different
groups according to the intensity of the offense, you here,
the one who led the assault, you over there, the ones who
had thrown the inconsolable fishwife to the floor, you here,
the ones who had taken the corpse out of the coffin and
dragged it down the stairs and through the mire, and all the
rest on this side, you bastards, although he was really not
interested in the punishment but in proving to himself that
the profanation of the body and the attack on the building
had not been a spontaneous and popular act but an infamous mercenary deal, so he took charge of the interroga-
tion of the prisoners physically present and doing the talking himself to get them to tell him willingly the illusory
truth that his heart needed, but he could not manage it, he
had them hung from a horizontal beam like parrots tied
hand and foot with their heads down for hours on end, but
he could not manage it, he had one thrown into the moat
of the courtyard and the others saw him quartered and
devoured by the crocodiles, but he could not manage it, he
chose one out of the main group and had him skinned alive
in the presence of all and they saw his flesh tender and
yellow like a newborn placenta and they felt the soaking of
the warm blood broth of the body that had been laid bare
as it went through its throes thrashing about on the courtyard stones, and then they confessed what he wanted that
they had been paid four hundred gold pesos to drag the
corpse to the dung heap in the marketplace, that they didn't
want to do it for love nor money because they had nothing
against him, all the less so since he was dead, but that at a
secret meeting where they even saw two generals from the
high command they had all been frightened with every
manner of threat and that was why we did it general sir,
word of honor, and then he exhaled a great mouthful of
relief, ordered them to be fed, that they be allowed to rest

that night and in the morning they would be thrown to the crocodiles, poor deceived boys, he sighed and went back to the presidential palace with his heart free of the hair shirt of doubt, murmuring you all saw it, God damn it, you all saw it, these people love me. Resolved to dissipate even the dregs of the uneasiness that Patricio Aragonés had sown in his heart, he decided that those acts of torture would be the last of his regime, the crocodiles were killed, the torture chambers where it was possible to crumble every bone in the body one by one without killing were dismantled, he proclaimed a general amnesty, he looked to the future with the magical idea that came to him that the trouble with this country is that the people have too much time to think on their hands, and looking for a way to keep them busy he restored the March poetry festival and the annual contest for the election of a beauty queen, he built the largest baseball stadium in the Caribbean and imparted to our team the motto of victory or death, and he ordered a free school established in each province to teach sweeping where the pupils fanaticized by the presidential stimulus went on to sweep the streets after having swept their houses and then the nearby highways and roads so that piles of trash were carried back and forth from one province to another without anyone's knowing what to do with it in official processions with the national flag and large banners saying God Save the All Pure who watches over the cleanliness of the nation, while he dragged his slow feet of a meditative beast about in search of new formulas to keep the civilian population busy, opening a way among the lepers and blind men and cripples who begged the salt of health from his hands, baptizing with his name at the font in the courtyard the children of his godchildren among persistent adulators who proclaimed him the one and only because now he could not count on the resources of any look-alike and he had to make himself double in a market-place of a palace where every day cages and more cages of rare birds arrived ever since the secret was let out that his mother Bendición Alvarado followed the trade of bird-woman, and even though some sent them out of adulation

and others sent them as a joke after a short time there was
no room to hang any more cages, and he tried to attend to
so many public matters at the same time that among the
crowds in the courtyards and the offices it was impossible
to tell who were the servants and who were the ones served,
and they knocked down so many walls to make more room
and opened so many windows for a view of the sea that the
simple act of going from one room to another was like
crossing the deck of a sailboat adrift in a crosswind autumn.
They were the March trade winds which had always come
in through the windows of the building, but now they said
they were the winds of peace general sir, it was the same
buzzing in the eardrums that he had had for many years,
but even his physician told him that it was the buzz of peace
general sir, because ever since they had found him dead the
first time all things on heaven and earth had changed into
things of peace general sir, and he believed it, and he believed it so much that in December he went back to going
up to the house on the reef to seek solace in the misfortune
of the brotherhood of nostalgic former dictators who
would interrupt the game of dominoes to tell him that he
was for example the double six and let's say that the doc-
trinaire conservatives were double three, only I wasn't
aware of the clandestine alliance between Masons and
priests, who in hell would have thought of it, without worrying about the soup that was jelling in the plate while one
of them explained that for example this sugar bowl was the
presidential palace, here, and the only cannon the enemy
had left had a range of four hundred yards with the wind
in its favor, here, so if you people see me in this state it's
only because of nineteen inches of bad luck, that is to say,
and even those most encrusted by the barnacles of exile
wasted their hopes scanning the horizon and spotting ships
from their homelands, they could recognize them from the
color of their smoke, from the rust on their foghorns, they
would go down to the harbor in the drizzle of early dawn
in search of the newspapers the crewmen had used to wrap
up the lunch they took ashore, they found them in the
garbage cans and read them up and down and left to right

down to the last lines to predict the future of their countries from the news of who had died, who had got married, who had invited whom and whom they had not invited to a birthday party, deciphering their destiny according to the direction of a providential storm cloud that was going to roar down on their country in an apocalyptic tempest that would overflow the rivers which would burst the dams that would devastate the fields and spread misery and plague in the cities, and they will come here to beg me to save them from disaster and anarchy, you'll see, but while they waited for the great hour they had to call aside the youngest exile and ask him to do them the favor of threading their needles to patch these pants that I don't want to throw away for sentimental reasons, they washed their clothes in secret, they honed the razor blades that the new arrivals had used, they would shut themselves up in their rooms to eat so that the others would not see that they were living off leftovers, so that they would not see the shame of pants stained by senile incontinence, and on some unexpected Thursday we would use pins to fasten medals on the last shirt of one of them, wrap his body in his flag, sing his national anthem, and send him off to govern the forgotten people at the base of the sea cliffs with no other ballast than that of his own eroded heart and without leaving any more gap in the world than an easy chair on the terrace without horizons where we would sit down to cast lots for the dead man's possessions, if there were any left general, just imagine this life as civilians after so much glory. On another distant December when the house was inaugurated, he had seen from that terrace the line of the hallucinated isles of the Antilles which someone pointed out to him in the showcase of the sea, he had seen the perfumed volcano of Martinique, over there general, he had seen the tuberculosis hospital, the gigantic black man with a lace blouse selling bouquets of gardenias to governors' wives on the church steps, he had seen the infernal market of Paramaribo, there general, the crabs that came out of the sea and up through the toilets, climbing up onto the tables of ice cream parlors, the diamonds embedded in the teeth of black grandmothers who sold heads of Indians and ginger roots sitting on their safe buttocks under the drenching rain, he had see the solid gold cows on Tanaguarena beach general, the blind visionary of La Guayra who charged two reals to scare off the blandishments of death with a one-string violin, he had seen Trinidad's burning August, automobiles going the wrong way, the green Hindus who shat in the middle of the street in front of their shops with genuine silkworm shirts and mandarins carved from the whole tusk of an elephant, he had seen Haiti's nightmare, its blue dogs, the oxcart that collected the dead off the streets at dawn, he had seen the rebirth of Dutch tulips in the gasoline drums of Curaçao, the windmill houses with roofs built for snow, the mysterious ocean liner that passed through the center of the city among the hotel kitchens, he had seen the stone enclosure of Cartagena de Indias, its bay closed off by a chain, the light lingering on the balconies, the filthy horses of the hacks who still yawned for the viceroys' fodder, its smell of shit general sir, how marvelous, tell me, isn't the world large, and it was, really, and not just large but insidious, because if he went up to the house on the reefs in December it was not to pass the time with those refugees whom he detested as much as his own image in the mirror of misfortune but to be there at the moment of miracles when the December light came out, mother—true and he could see once more the whole universe of the Antilles from Barbados to Veracruz, and then he would forget who had the double-three piece and go to the overlook to contemplate the line of islands as lunatic as sleeping crocodiles in the cistern of the sea, and contemplating the islands he evoked again and relived that historic October Friday when he left his room at dawn and discovered that everybody in the presidential palace was wearing a red biretta, that the new concubines were sweeping the parlors and changing the water in the cages wearing red birettas, that the milkers in the stables, the sentries in their boxes, the cripples on the stairs and the lepers in the rose beds were going about with the red birettas of a carnival Sunday, so he began to look into what had happened to the world while he was sleeping for the people in his house and the inhabitants of the city to be going around wearing red birettas and dragging a string of jingle bells everywhere, and finally he found someone to tell him the truth general sir, that some strangers had arrived who gabbled in funny old talk because they made the word for sea feminine and not masculine, they called macaws poll parrots, canoes rafts, harpoons javelins, and when they saw us going out to greet them and swim around their ships they climbed up onto the yardarms and shouted to each other look there how well-formed, of beauteous body and fine face, and thick-haired and almost like horsehair silk, and when they saw that we were painted so as not to get sunburned they got all excited like wet little parrots and shouted look there how they daub themselves gray, and they are the hue of canary birds, not white nor yet black, and what there be of them, and we didn't understand why the hell they were making so much fun of us general sir since we were just as normal as the day our mothers bore us and on the other hand they were decked out like the jack of clubs in all that heat, which they made feminine the way Dutch smugglers do, and they wore their hair like women even though they were all men and they shouted that they didn't understand us in Christian tongue when they were the ones who couldn't understand what we were shouting, and then they came toward us in their canoes which they called rafts, as we said before, and they were amazed that our harpoons had a shad bone for a tip which they called a fishy tooth, and we traded everything we had for these red birettas and these strings of glass beads that we hung around our necks to please them, and also for these brass bells that can't be worth more than a penny and for chamber pots and eyeglasses and other goods from Flanders, of the cheapest sort general sir, and since we saw that they were good people and men of good will we went on leading them to the beach without their realizing it, but the trouble was that among the I'll swap you this for that and that for the other a wild motherfucking trade grew up and after a while everybody was swapping his parrots, his tobacco, his wads of chocolate, his iguana eggs, everything God ever created, because they took and gave everything willingly, and they even wanted to trade a velvet doublet for one of us to show off in Europeland, just imagine general, what a wild affair, but he was so confused that he could not decide whether that lunatic business came within the incumbency of his government, so he went back to his bedroom, opened the window that looked out onto the sea so that perhaps he might discover some new light to shed on the mix-up they had told him about, and he saw the usual battleship that the marines had left behind at the dock, and beyond the battleship, anchored in the shadowy sea, he saw the three caravels.

THE SECOND TIME he was found, chewed away by vultures in the same office, wearing the same clothes and in the same position, none of us was old enough to remember what had happened the first time, but we knew that no evidence of his death was final, because there was always another truth behind the truth. Not even the least prudent among us would accept appearances because so many times it had been a given fact that he was prostrate with epilepsy and would fall off his throne during the course of audiences twisting with convulsions as gall froth foamed out of his mouth, that he had lost his speech from so much talking and had ventriloquists stationed behind the curtains to make it appear that he was speaking, that shad scales were breaking out all over his body as punishment for his perversions, that in the coolness of December the rupture sang sea chanties to him and he could only walk with the aid of a small orthopedic cart which bore his herniated testicle, that a military van had brought in a coffin with gold echini and purple ribbons and that someone had seen Leticia Nazareno bleeding to death from weeping in the rain garden, but the more certain the rumors of his death seemed, he would appear even more alive and authoritarian at the least expected moment to impose other unforeseen directions to our destiny. It would have been easier for a person to let himself be convinced by the immediate indications of the ring with the presidential seal or the supernatural size of his feet of an implacable walker or the strange evidence of the herniated testicle which the vultures had not dared peck, but there was always someone who had memories of other similar indications in the case of other less important dead men in the past. Nor did the meticulous scrutiny of the house bring forth any valid element to establish his identity. In the bedroom of Bendición Alvarado, about whom we only remembered the tale of her canonization by decree, we found broken-down birdcages with little bird bones changed to stone by the years, we saw a wicker easy chair nibbled by the cows, we saw watercolor sets and glasses with paintbrushes of the kind used by birdwomen of the plains so they could sell faded birds by passing them off as orioles, we saw a tub with a balm bush that had kept on growing in neglect and its branches had climbed up the wall and peeped out through the eyes of the portraits and had gone out through the window and ended up getting all entangled with the wild bushes in the rear courtyards, but we couldn't find the most insignificant trace of his ever having been in that room. In the bridal bedroom of Leticia Nazareno, of whom we had a clearer image, not just because she had reigned in a more recent period but also because of the éclat of her public acts, we saw a bed good for the outrages of love with the embroidered canopy converted into a nesting place for hens, in the closets we saw what the moths had left of blue-fox stoles, the wire framework of hoopskirts, the glacial powder of the petticoats, the Brussels lace bodices, the men's high-cut shoes that she wore in the house and the velvet high-heeled pumps with straps that she wore at receptions, the full-length shroud with felt violets and taffeta ribbons from her gala funeral as first lady and the homespun novice's habit

like the hide of a gray sheep in which she had been kid-
napped from Jamaica inside a crate of party crystal to be
placed upon her throne as wife of a hidden president, but
we didn't find any vestige in that room either, nothing
which would allow us to establish at least whether that
kidnapping by corsairs had been inspired by love. In the
presidential bedroom, which was the part of the house
where he spent the greater part of his last years, we found
only an unused barracks bed, a portable latrine of the kind
that antiquarians removed from the mansions abandoned
by the marines, an iron coffer with his ninety-two medals,
and a denim suit just like the one the corpse had on, per-
forated by six large-caliber bullets that had left singe damage as they entered through the back and came out through
the chest, which made us think there was truth to the legend going around that a bullet shot into his back would go
right through without harming him, and if shot from the
front it would rebound off his body back at the attacker, and
that he was only vulnerable to a coup de grace fired by
someone who loved him so much that he would die for him.
Both uniforms were too small for the corpse, but it was not
for that reason that we put aside the possibility that they
were his, because it had also been said at one time that he
had kept on growing until the age of one hundred and at
one hundred fifty he grew a third set of teeth, although in
truth the vulture-ravaged body was no larger than that of
any average man of our day and it had some healthy teeth,
small and stubby that looked like milk teeth, the skin was
the color of gall speckled with liver spots without a single
scar and empty pouches all over as if he had been quite fat
in some other day, there were only empty sockets for the
eyes that had been taciturn, and the only thing that seemed
out of proportion, except for the herniated testicle, was the
pair of enormous feet, square and flat with the calluses and
twisted talons of a hawk. Contrary to what his clothing
showed, the descriptions made by his historians made him
very big and official schoolboy texts referred to him as a
patriarch of huge size who never left his house because he
could not fit through the doors, who loved children and

swallows, who knew the language of certain animals, who had the virtue of being able to anticipate the designs of nature, who could guess a person's thoughts by one look in the eyes, and who had the secret of a salt with the virtue of curing lepers' sores and making cripples walk. Although all trace of his origins had disappeared from the texts, it was thought that he was a man of the upland plains because of his immense appetite for power, the nature of his government, his mournful bearing, the inconceivable evil of a heart which had sold the sea to a foreign power and condemned us to live facing this limitless plain of harsh lunar dust where the bottomless sunsets pain us in our souls. It was calculated that in the course of his life he must have sired five thousand children, all seven-monthers, by the countless number of loveless beloveds he had who succeeded each other in his seraglio until the moment he was ready to enjoy them, but none bore his name or surname, except for the one he had by Leticia Nazareno, who was appointed a major general with jurisdiction and command at the moment of his birth, for he considered no one the son of anyone except his mother, and only her. That certainty seemed valid even for him, as he knew that he was a man without a father like the most illustrious despots of history, that the only relative known to him and perhaps the only one he had was his mother of my heart Bendición Alvarado to whom the school texts attributed the miracle of having conceived him without recourse to any male and of having received in a dream the hermetical keys to his messianic destiny, and whom he proclaimed matriarch of the land by decree with the simple argument that there is no mother but one, mine, a strange woman of uncertain origins whose simpleness of soul had been the scandal of the fanatics of presidential dignity during the beginnings of the regime, because they could not admit that the mother of the chief of state would hang a pouch of camphor around her neck to ward off all contagion and tried to jab the caviar with her fork and staggered about in her patent leather pumps, nor could they accept the fact that she kept a bee-hive on the terrace of the music room, or bred turkeys and watercolor-painted birds in public offices or put the sheets out to dry on the balcony from which speeches were made, nor could they bear the fact that at a diplomatic party she had said I'm tired of begging God to overthrow my son, because all this business of living in the presidential palace is like having the lights on all the time, sir, and she had said it with the same naturalness with which on one national holiday she had made her way through the guard of honor with a basket of empty bottles and reached the presidential limousine that was leading the parade of celebration in an uproar of ovations and martial music and storms of flowers and she shoved the basket through the window and shouted to her son that since you'll be passing right by take advantage and return these bottles to the store on the corner, poor mother. That lack of a sense of history would have its night of splendor at the formal banquet with which we celebrate the landing of the marines under the command of Admiral Higgingson when Bendición Alvarado saw her son in dress uniform with his gold medals and velvet gloves which he continued to wear for the rest of his life and she could not repress her impulse of maternal pride and exclaimed aloud in front of the whole diplomatic corps that if I'd known my son was going to be president of the republic I'd have sent him to school, yes sir, how shameful it must have been after that when they exiled her to the suburban mansion, an eleven-room palace that he had won on a good night of dice when the leaders of the federalist war had used the gaming tables to divide up the splendid residential district of the fugitive conservatives, except that Bendición Alvarado disdained the imperial décor which makes me feel I'm the wife of the Pope himself and she preferred the servants' quarters next to the six barefoot maids who had been assigned to her, she set up her sewing machine and her cages of painted-up birds in a forgotten back room where the heat never reached and it was easier to drive off the six o'clock mosquitoes, she would sit down to sew across from the lazy light of the main courtyard and the medicinal breeze of the tamarinds while the hens wandered through the parlors and the soldiers of the guard lay in wait for the housemaids in the empty bedrooms, she would sit down to paint orioles and lament with the servants over the misfortunes of my poor son whom the marines had set up in the presidential palace so far from his mother, lord, without a loving wife who could take care of him if he woke up with an ache in the middle of the night, and all involved with that job of president of the republic for a measly salary of three hundred pesos a month, poor boy. She knew quite well what she was talking about because he visited her every day while the city sloshed in the mire of siesta time, he would bring her the candied fruit she liked so much and he took advantage of the occasion to unwind with her about his bitter position as the marines' pratboy, he told her how he had to sneak out the sugar oranges and syrup figs in napkins because the occupation authorities had accountants who in their books kept track even of lunch leftovers, he lamented that the other day the captain of the battleship came to the presidential palace with some kind of land astronomers who took measurements of everything and didn't even say hello but put their tape measure around my head while they made their calculations in English and shouted at me through the interpreter to get out of here and he got out, for him to get out of the light, and he got out, go somewhere where you won't be in the way, God damn it, and he didn't know where to go without getting in the way because there were measurers measuring everything down to the size of the light from the balconies, but that wasn't the worst, mother, they threw out the last two skinny concubines he had left because the admiral had said they weren't worthy of a president, and he was really in such want of women that on some afternoons he would pretend that he was leaving the suburban mansion but his mother heard him chasing after the maids in the shadows of the bedrooms, and her sorrow was such that she roused up the birds in their cages so that no one would find out about her son's troubles, she forced them to sing so that the neighbors would not hear the sounds of the attack, the shame of the struggle, the repressed threats of quiet down general or I'll tell your mama, and she would ruin the siesta of the troupials and make them burst with song so that no one would hear his heartless panting of an urgent mate, his misfortune of a lover with all his clothes on, his doggish whine, his solitary tears that came on like dusk, as if rotting with pity amidst the cackling of the hens in the bedrooms aroused by that emergency love-making in the liquid glass air and the godforsaken August of three in the afternoon, my poor son. That state of scarcity was to last until the occupation forces left the country frightened off by an epidemic when they still needed so many years to fulfill the terms of the landing, they broke down the officers' residences into numbered pieces and packed them up in wooden crates, they dug up the blue lawns in one piece and carried them off all rolled up like carpets, they wrapped up the rubber cisterns with the sterile water sent from their country so that they would not be eaten up inside by the water worms of our streams, they took their white hospitals apart, dynamited their barracks so that no one would know how they were constructed, at the dock they left the old battleship from the landing and on the deck of which the ghost of a lost admiral strolled in the squall of June nights, but before bearing off that portable paradise of war in their flying trains they decorated him with the medal of the good neighbor, rendered him the honors of chief of state, and said to him aloud so that everybody could hear we leave you now with your nigger whorehouse so let's see how you shape things up without us, but they left, mother, God damn it, they've gone, and for the first time since his head-down days of occupation ox he went up the stairs giving orders in a loud voice and in person through a tumult of requests to reestablish cockfights, and he so ordered, agreed, that kite-flying be allowed again, and many other diversions that had been prohibited by the marines, and he so ordered, agreed, so convinced of being master of all his power that he inverted the colors of the flag and replaced the Phrygian cap on the shield with the invader's defeated dragon, because after all we're our own dogs now, mother, long live the plague. All her life Bendición Alvarado would remember those surprises of power and the other more ancient and bitter ones of poverty, but she never brought them back with so much grief as after the death farce when he was wallowing in the fen of prosperity while she went on lamenting to anyone who wanted to listen to her that it was no good being the president's mama with nothing else in the world but this sad sewing machine, she lamented, looking at him there with his gold-braided hearse, my poor son didn't have a hole in the ground to fall dead into after all those years of serving his country, lord, it's not fair, and she did not go on complaining out of habit or disillusionment but because he no longer made her a participant in his shake-ups nor did he hurry over as before to share the best secrets of power with her, and he had changed so much since the times of the marines that to Bendición Alvarado he seemed to be older than she, to have left her behind in time, she heard him stumble over words, his concept of reality became entangled, sometimes he drooled, and she was struck with the compassion that was not a mother's but a daughter's when she saw him arrive at the suburban mansion loaded down with packages and desperate to open them all at the same time, he cut the twine with his teeth, broke his fingernails on the hoops before she could get the scissors from her sewing basket, dug everything out from the underbrush of debris with flailing hands as he drowned in his high-flying anxiety, look at all this wonderful stuff, mother, he said, a live mermaid in a fishbowl, a lifesize wind-up angel who flew about the room striking the hour with its bell, a gigantic shell in which the listener didn't hear the sound of the waves and the sea wind but the strains of the national anthem, what fancy stuff, mother, now you can see how nice it is not to be poor, he said, but she couldn't feed his enthusiasm and began chewing on the brushes used to paint orioles so her son would not notice that her heart was crumbling with pity thinking back on a past that no one knew as well as she, remembering how hard it had been for him to stay in the chair he was sitting in, but not these days, lord, not these easy times when power was a tangible and unique matter, a little glass ball in the palm of the hand, as he said, but when he was a fugitive shad swimming around without god or law in a neighborhood palace pursued by the voracious swarm of the surviving leaders of the federalist war who had helped overthrow the general-poet Lautaro Muñoz, an enlightened despot whom God keep in His holy glory with his Suetonius missals in Latin and his forty-two pedigreed horses, and in exchange for their armed help they had taken over the ranches and live-stock of the outlawed former owners and had divided the country up into autonomous provinces with the unanswer-able argument that this is federalism general, this is what we have shed the blood of our veins for, and they were absolute monarchs in their territories, with their own laws, their personal patriotic holidays, their paper money which they signed themselves, their dress uniforms with sabers encrusted with precious stones and hussar jackets with gold frogs and three-cornered hats with peacock-tail plumes copied from ancient prints of viceroys of the country before them, and they were wild and sentimental, lord, they would come into the presidential palace through the main door, with no one's permission since the nation belongs to all general, that's why we've sacrificed our lives for it, they camped out in the ballroom with their respective harems and the farm animals which they demanded as tribute for peace as they went along everywhere so that they would always have something to eat, they brought along personal escorts of barbarian mercenaries who instead of boots used rags to clothe their feet and who could barely express themselves in Christian tongue but were wise in tricks of dice and ferocious and skilled in the manipulation of weap-ons of war, so that the house of power was like a gypsy encampment, lord, it had the thick smell of a river at flood-tide, the officers of the general staff had taken the furniture of the republic to their ranches, they played dominoes gam-bling away the privileges of government indifferent to the entreaties of his mother Bendición Alvarado who did not have a moment's rest trying to sweep up so much fair-ground garbage, trying to put just one little bit of order into that shipwreck, for she was the only one who had made any attempt to resist the irredeemable debasement of the

liberal crusade, only she had tried to drive them out with
her broom when she saw the house perverted by those
evil-living reprobates who fought over the large chairs of
the high command with playing-card altercations, she
watched them do sodomite business behind the piano, she
watched them shit in the alabaster amphoras even though
she told them not to, lord, they weren't portable toilets they
were amphoras recovered from the seas of Pantelleria, but
they insisted that they were rich men's pisspots, lord, it was
humanly impossible to stop General Adriano Guzmán from
attending the diplomatic party celebrating the tenth year of
my rise to power, although no one could have imagined
what awaited us when he appeared in the ballroom wearing
an austere linen uniform chosen especially for the occasion,
he came without weapons, just as he had promised me on
his word as a soldier, with his escort of escaped French
prisoners in civilian clothes and loaded down with goodies
from Cayenne which General Adriano Guzmán distributed
one by one to the wives of ambassadors and ministers after
asking permission from their husbands with a bow, for that
was what his mercenaries had told him was considered
proper in Versailles and so he went through it with the rare
genius of a gentleman, and then he sat in a corner of the
ballroom with his attention on the dance and nodding his
head in approval, very good, he said, these stuck-ups from
Europeland dance good, he said, to each his own, he said,
so forgotten in his easy chair that only I noticed that one
of his aides was filling his glass with champagne after each
sip, and as the hours passed he was becoming more tense
and flushed than he normally was, he opened a button on
his sweat-soaked tunic every time the pressure of a repressed belch came all the way up to eye level, he was
moaning with drowsiness, mother, and all of a sudden he
got up with difficulty during a pause in the dancing and
finally unbuttoned his tunic completely and then his fly and
he stood there wide open and staling away on the perfumed
décolletages of the ladies of the ambassadors and ministers
with his musty old hose of a buzzard's tool, with his sour
war-drunkard's urine he soaked the muslin laps, the gold

brocade bosoms, the ostrich-feather fans, singing impassively in the midst of the panic I'm the gallant swain who waters the roses of your bower, oh lovely rose in bloom, he sang on, with no one daring to control him, not even he, because I knew I had more power than any one of them but much less than two of them plotting together, still unaware that he saw the others just as they were while the others were never able to glimpse the hidden thoughts of the granite old man whose serenity was matched only by his smooth-sailing prudence and his immense disposition for waiting, we saw only his lugubrious eyes, his thin lips, the chaste maiden's hand which did not even tremble on the hilt of his saber that noon of horror when they came to him with the news general sir that General Narciso López high on green pot and anisette had hauled a cadet of the presidential guard into a toilet and warmed him up as he saw fit with the resources of a wild woman and then obliged him put it all into me, God damn it, that's an order, everything, my love, even your golden little balls, weeping with pain, weeping with rage, until he found himself vomiting with humiliation on all fours with his head stuck in the fetid vapors of the toilet bowl, and then he lifted the Adonic cadet up into the air and impaled him with a plainsman's lance onto the springtime tapestry of the audience room like a butterfly and no one dared take him down for three days, poor man, because all he did was keep an eye on his former comrades in arms so that they would not hatch plots but without getting enmeshed in their lives, convinced that they themselves would exterminate each other among themselves before they came to him with the news general sir that members of General Jesucristo Sánchez's escort had been forced to beat him to death with chairs when he had an attack of rabies that he got from a cat bite, poor man, he scarcely looked up from his domino game when they whispered in his ear the news general sir that General Lotario Sereno had been drowned when his horse had suddenly died under him as he was fording a river, poor man, he barely blinked when they came to him with the news general sir that General Narciso López had shoved a dyna-

47

mite stick up his ass and blown his guts out over the shame
of his unconquerable pederasty, and he said poor man as
if he had had nothing to do with those infamous deaths and
he issued the same decree of posthumous honors for all,
proclaiming them martyrs who had fallen in acts of service
and he had them entombed in the national pantheon with
magnificent pomp and all on the same level because a nation without heroes is a house without doors, he said, and
when there were only six combat generals left in all the land
he invited them to celebrate his birthday with a carousal of
comrades in the presidential palace, all of them together,
lord, even General Jacinto Algarabía who was the darkest
and shrewdest, who prided himself on having a son by his
own mother and only drank wood alcohol with gunpowder
in it, with no one else in the banquet hall like the good old
days general, all without weapons like blood brothers but
with the men of their escorts crowded into the next room,
all loaded down with magnificent gifts for the only one of
us who has been able to understand us all, they said, mean-
ing that he was the only one who had learned how to manage them, the only one who had succeeded in getting out
of the bowels of his remote lair on the highland plains the
legendary General Saturno Santos, a full-blooded Indian,
unsure, who always went around like the whore mother that
gave me birth with his foot on the ground general sir because we roughnecks can't breathe unless we feel the earth,
he had arrived wrapped in a cape with bright-colored prints
of strange animals on it, he came alone, as he always went
about, without an escort, preceded by a gloomy aura, with
no arms except a cane machete which he refused to take off
his belt because it wasn't a weapon of war but one for work,
and as a gift he brought me an eagle trained to fight in
men's wars, and he brought his harp, mother, that sacred
instrument whose notes could conjure up storms and has-
ten the cycles of harvest time and which General Saturno
Santos plucked with a skill from his heart that awoke in all
of us the nostalgia for the nights of horror of the war,
mother, it aroused in us the dog-mange smell of war, it
spun around in our souls the war song of the golden boat

that will lead us on, they sang it in a chorus with all their heart, mother, I sent myself back from the bridge bathed in tears, they sang, while they ate a turkey stuffed with plums and half a suckling pig and each one drank from his personal bottle, each one his own alcohol, all except him and General Saturno Santos who had never tasted a drop of liquor in all their lives, nor smoked, nor eaten more than what was indispensable for life, in my honor they sang in a chorus the serenade King David sang, with tears they wailed out all the birthday songs that had been sung before Consul Hanemann came to us with the novelty general sir of that phonograph with a horn speaker and its cylinder of happy birthday in English, they sang half-asleep, half-dead from drink, not worrying any more about the taciturn old man who at the stroke of twelve took down the lamp and went to inspect the house before retiring in accordance with his barracks-bred custom and he saw for the last time as he returned on his way through the banquet hall the six generals piled together on the floor, he saw them in embrace, inert and placid, under the protection of the five escort groups who kept watch among themselves, because even in sleep and in embrace they were afraid of each other almost as much as each one of them was afraid of him and as he was afraid of two of them in cahoots, and he put the lamp back on the mantel and closed the three locks, the three bolts, the three bars of his bedroom, and lay down on the floor face down, his right arm serving as a pillow at the instant that the foundations of the building shook with the compact explosion of all the escorts' weapons going off at the same time, one single time, by God, with no intermediate sound, no moan, and again, by God, and that was that, the mess was over, all that was left was a lingering smell of gunpowder in the silence of the world, only he remained safe forever from the anxieties of power as in the first mallow-soft rays of the new day he saw the orderlies on duty sloshing through the swamp of blood in the banquet hall, he saw his mother Bendición Alvarado seized by a dizzy spell of horror as she discovered that the walls oozed blood no matter how hard she scrubbed them with lye and

49

ash, lord, that the rugs kept on giving off blood no matter how much she wrung them out, and all the more blood poured in torrents through corridors and offices the more they worked desperately to wash it out in order to hide the extent of the massacre of the last heirs of our war who according to the official statement had been assassinated by their own maddened escorts and their bodies wrapped in the national flag filled the pantheon of patriots with a funeral worthy of a bishop, for not one single man of the escort had escaped alive from the bloody roundup, not one general, except General Saturno Santos who was armored by his strings of scapulars and who knew Indian secrets of how to change his form at will, curse him, he could turn into an armadillo or a pond general, he could become thunder, and he knew it was true because his most astute trackers had lost the trail ever since last Christmas, the best-trained jaguar hounds looked for him in the opposite direction, he had seen him in the flesh in the king of spades in his sibyls' cards, and he was alive, sleeping by day and traveling by night off the beaten track on land and water, but he kept leaving a trail of prayers that confused his pursuers' judgment and tired out the will of his enemies, but he never gave up the search for one instant day and night for years and years until many years later when he saw through the window of the presidential train a crowd of men and women with their children and animals and cooking utensils as he had seen so many times behind the troops in wartime, he saw them parading in the rain carrying their sick in hammocks strung to poles behind a very pale man in a burlap tunic who says he's a divine messenger general sir, and he slapped his forehead and said to himself there he is, God damn it, and there was General Saturno Santos begging off the charity of the pilgrims with the charms of his unstrung harp, he was miserable and gloomy, with a beat-up felt hat and a poncho in tatters, but even in that pitiful state he was not as easy to kill as he thought for he had decapitated three of his best men with his machete, he had stood up to the fiercest of them with such valor and ability that he ordered the train to stop opposite the cemetery on the plain where the messenger was preaching, and everybody drew apart in a stampede when the men of the presidential guard jumped out of the coach painted with the colors of the flag with their weapons at the ready, no one remained in sight except General Saturno Santos beside his mythical harp with his hand tight on the hilt of his machete, and he seemed fascinated by the sight of the mortal enemy who appeared on the platform of the coach in his denim suit with no insignia, without weapons, older and more remote as if it had been a hundred years since we saw each other general, he looked tired and lonely to me, his skin yellow from liver trouble and his eyes tending toward teariness, but he had the pale glow of a person who was not only master of his power but also the power won from his dead, so I made ready to die without resisting because it seemed useless to him to go against an old man who had come from so far off with no more motives or merits than his barbarous appetite for command, but he showed him the manta-ray palm of his hand and said God bless you, stud, the country deserves you, because it has always known that against an invincible man there is no weapon but friendship, and General Saturno Santos kissed the ground he had trod and asked him the favor of letting me serve you in any way you command general sir while I have the ability in these hands to make my machete sing, and he accepted, agreed, he made him his back-up man but only on the condition that you never get behind me, he made him his accomplice in dominoes and between the two of them they gave a four-handed skinning to many despots in misfortune, he would have him get barefoot into the presidential coach and take him to diplomatic receptions with that jaguar breath that aroused dogs and made ambassadors' wives dizzy, he had him sleep across the doorsill of his bedroom so as to relieve himself of the fear of sleeping when life became so harsh that he trembled at the idea of finding himself alone among the people of his dreams, he kept him close to his confidence at a distance of ten hands for many years until uric acid squeezed off his skill of making his machete sing and he asked the favor that you kill me yourself general sir so as not to leave someone else the pleasure of killing me when he has no right to, but he ordered him off to die on a good retirement pension and with a medal of gratitude on the byways of the plains where he had been born and he could not repress his tears when General Saturno Santos put aside his shame to tell him choking and weeping so you see general the time comes for the roughest of us studs to turn into fairies, what a damned thing. So no one understood better than Bendición Alvarado the boyish excitement with which he got rid of bad times and the lack of sense with which he squandered the earnings of power in order to have as an old man what he had lacked as a child, but it made her angry when they abused his premature innocence by selling him those gringo gewgaws which weren't all that cheap and didn't require as much ingenuity as the faked birds of which she had never managed to sell more than four, it's fine for you to enjoy it, she said, but think about the future, I don't want to see you begging hat in hand at the door of some church if tomorrow or later God forbid they take away the chair you're sitting in, if you only knew how to sing at least, or were an archbishop or a navigator, but you're only a general, so you're not good for anything except to command, she advised him to bury in a safe place the money you have left over from the government, where no one else could find it, just in case you have to leave on the run like those poor presidents of nowhere grazing on oblivion in the house on the reefs and begging a hello from ships, look at yourself in that mirror, she told him, but he didn't pay any attention to her except that he would ease her disconsolation with the magic formula of calm down mother, the people love me. Bendición Alvarado was to live for many years lamenting poverty, fighting with the maids over bills from the market and even skipping lunch in order to economize, and no one dared reveal to her that she was one of the richest women in the land, that everything he accumulated from government business he put in her name, that she was not only the owner of immeasurable land and uncountable livestock but also the local streetcars, the mails, the telegraph service, and the waters of the nation, so that every boat that plied the tributaries of the Amazon or the territorial seas had to pay her a rental fee which she never knew about down to the day she died, just as she was ignorant for so many years of the fact that her son was not so badly off as she supposed when he came to the suburban mansion and sank into the wonders of his old-age toys, for in addition to the personal tax that he collected for every head of cattle for the benefit of the country, in addition to payments for his favors and gifts which his partisans sent him to help their interests, he had conceived and had been putting to use for a long time an infallible system for beating the lottery. Those were the times following his false death, the noisy times, lord, and they weren't called that as many of us thought because of the underground boom that was felt all over the nation one Saint Heraclius Martyr night and for which there was never any sure explanation, but because of the constant noise of the projects begun that were proclaimed at their start as the greatest in the world and yet were never completed, a peaceful period during which he summoned councils of government while he took his siesta in the suburban mansion, he would lie in the hammock fanning himself with his hat under the sweet tamarind branches, with his eyes closed he would listen to the doctors with free-flowing words and waxed mustaches who sat around the hammock discussing things, pale from the heat inside their rough frock coats and celluloid collars, the civilian ministers he detested so much but whom he had appointed once more for convenience and whom he listened to as they argued over matters of state amidst the scandal of roosters chasing after the hens in the courtyard, and the continuous buzz of the cicadas and the insomnia-stricken gramophone in the neighborhood that was singing the song Susana come Susana, they suddenly fell silent, quiet, the general has fallen asleep, but he would roar without opening his eyes, without stopping his snoring, I'm not asleep you God-damned fools, go on, they went on, until he would feel his way out of the siesta cobwebs and declare that in all this damned-fool talk the only one who makes any

53

sense is my old friend the minister of health, by God, the mess was over, the whole mess was coming to an end, he chatted with his personal aides walking them back and forth while he ate with plate in one hand and spoon in the other, he said goodbye to them at the steps with an indifference of do what you think best because in the end I'm the one who gives the orders, God damn it, this farting around and asking whether they wanted to or didn't want to was over, God damn it, he cut inaugural ribbons, he showed himself large as life in public taking on the risks of power as he had never done in more peaceful times, what the hell, he played endless games of dominoes with my lifetime friend General Rodrigo de Aguilar and my old friend the minister of health who were the only ones who had enough of his confidence to ask him to free a prisoner or pardon someone condemned to death, and the only ones who dared ask him to receive in a special audience the beauty queen of the poor, an incredible creature from that miserable wallow we called the dogfight district because all the dogs in the neighborhood had been fighting for many years without a moment's truce, a lethal redoubt where national guard patrols did not enter because they would be stripped naked and cars were broken up into their smallest parts with a flick of the hand, where poor stray donkeys would enter by one end of the street and come out the other in a bag of bones, they roasted the sons of the rich general sir, they sold them in the market turned into sausages, just imagine, because Manuela Sánchez of my evil luck had been born there and lived there, a dungheap marigold whose remarkable beauty was the astonishment of the nation general sir, and he felt so intrigued by the revelation that if all this is as true as you people say I'll not only receive her in a special audience but I'll dance the first waltz with her, by God, have them write it up in the newspapers, he ordered, this kind of crap makes a big hit with the poor. Yet, the night after the audience, while they were playing dominoes, he commented with a certain bitterness to General Rodrigo de Aguilar that the queen of the poor wasn't even worth dancing with, that she was as common as so many other slum Manuela Sánchezes

54

with her nymph's dress of muslin petticoats and the gilt
crown with artificial jewels and a rose in her hand under the
watchful eye of a mother who looked after her as if she were
made of gold, so he gave her everything she wanted which
was only electricity and running water for the dogfight district, but he warned that it was the last time I'll ever receive
anybody on a begging mission, God damn it, I'm not going
to talk to poor people any more, he said, before the game
was over, he slammed the door, left, he heard the metal
tolling of eight o'clock, he gave the cows in the stables their
fodder, he had them bring up the cow chips, he inspected
the whole building eating as he walked with his plate in his
hand, he was eating stew with beans, white rice, and plantain slices, he counted the sentries from the entranceway to
the bedrooms, they were all there and at their posts, fourteen, he saw the rest of his personal guard playing dominoes at the post in the first courtyard, he saw the lepers
lying among the rosebushes, the cripples on the stairs, it
was nine o'clock, he put his unfinished plate down on a
window sill and found himself feeling around in the muddy
atmosphere of the sheds among the concubines who were
sleeping as many as three to a bed together with their
seven-month runts, he mounted a lump that smelled of
yesterday's stew and he separated two heads here six legs
and three arms there without ever asking who was who or
who was the one who finally suckled him without waking
up, without dreaming about him, or whose voice it had
been that murmured in her sleep from the other bed not
to get so excited general you'll frighten the children, he
went back inside the house, checked the locks on the
twenty-three windows, lighted the piles of cow chips every
twenty feet from the entranceway to the private rooms,
caught the smell of the smoke, remembered an improbable
childhood that might have been his and which he only
remembered at that instant when the smoke started up and
which he forgot forever, he went back turning out the lights
in reverse order from the bedrooms to the vestibule and
covering the cages of the sleeping birds whom he counted
before draping them with pieces of cloth, forty-eight, once

more he covered the whole house with a lamp in his hand, he saw himself in the mirrors one by one as up to fourteen generals walking with the lighted lamp, it was ten o'clock, everything in order, he went back to the sleeping quarters of the presidential guard, turned out their lights, good night gentlemen, he made a search of the public offices on the ground floor, the waiting rooms, the toilets, behind the curtains, underneath the tables, there was no one, he took out the bunch of keys which he was able to distinguish by touch one by one, he locked the offices, he went up to the main floor for a room-by-room search locking the doors, he took the jar of honey from its hiding place behind a picture and had two spoonfuls before retiring, he thought of his mother asleep in the suburban mansion, Bendición Alvarado in her drowsiness of goodbyes between the balm and the oregano with the bloodless hand of a birdwoman oriole painter as a dead mother on her side, have a good night, mother, he said, a very good night to you son Bendición Alvarado answered him in her sleep in the suburban mansion, in front of his bedroom he hung the lamp by its handle on a hook and he left it hanging by the door while he slept with the absolute order that it was never to be put out because it was the light for him to flee by, it struck eleven, he inspected the house for the last time, in the dark, in case someone had sneaked in thinking he was asleep, he went alone leaving a trail in the dust made by the star of his gold spur in the fleeting dawns of green flashes of the beams from the turns of the beacon, between two instants of light he saw an aimless leper who was walking in his sleep, he cut him off, led him through the shadows without touching him lighting the way with the lights of his vigilance, put him back among the rosebushes, counted the sentries in the darkness again, went back to his bedroom, seeing as he went past the windows a sea that was the same in every window, the Caribbean in April, he contemplated it twenty-three times without stopping and it was still as it always was in April like a gilded fen, he heard twelve o'-clock, with the last toll of the cathedral clappers he heard the twist of the thin whistle of his hernia, there was no other sound in the world, he alone was the nation, he lowered the three crossbars, locked the three locks, threw the three bolts in the bedroom, he urinated sitting down on the portable latrine, he urinated two drops, four drops, seven arduous drops, he fell face down on the floor, fell asleep immediately, did not dream, it was a quarter to three when he awoke drenched in sweat, shaken by the certainty that someone had been looking at him while he slept, someone who had had the ability to get in without taking off the crossbars, who's there, he asked, there was no one, he closed his eyes, again he felt he was watched, he opened his eyes to see with fright, and then he saw, God damn it, it was Manuela Sánchez who went across the room without opening the locks because she came and went as was her will by passing through the walls, Manuela Sánchez of my evil hour with her muslin dress and the hot coal of a rose in her hand and the natural smell of licorice of her breathing, tell me this delirium isn't true, he said, tell me it's not you, tell me that this deadly dizziness isn't the licorice stagnation of your breath, but it was she, it was her rose, it was her hot breath which perfumed the air of the bedroom like an obstinate downwind with more dominion and more antiquity than the snorting of the sea, Manuela Sánchez of my disaster, you who weren't written on the palm of my hand, or in my coffee grounds, or even in the death waters of my basins, don't use up my breathing air, my dreams of sleep, the confines of this room where no woman had ever entered or was to enter, extinguish that rose, he moaned, while he felt around for the light switch and found Manuela Sánchez of my madness instead of the light, God damn it, why do I have to find you since you haven't lost me, take my house if you want, the whole country with its dragon, but let me put the light on, scorpion of my nights, Manuela Sánchez of my rupture, daughter of a bitch, he shouted, thinking that the light would free him from the spell, shouting to get her out of here, get her off my back, throw her off a sea cliff with an anchor around her neck so that no one will ever suffer the glow of her rose, he went shrieking along the corridors, sloshing through the cow flops in the darkness, wondering in confusion what was going on in the world because it's going on eight and everybody's asleep in this house of scoundrels, get up, you bastards, he shouted, the lights went on, they played reveille at three o'clock, it was repeated at the harbor fort, the San Jerónimo garrison, in barracks all over the country, and there was the noise of startled arms, of roses that opened when there were still two hours left until dew time, of sleepwalking concubines who shook out rugs under the stars and uncovered the cages of the sleeping birds and replaced the flowers that had spent the night in the vases with last night's flowers, and there was a troop of masons who were building emergency walls and they disoriented the sunflowers by pasting gilt paper suns on the windowpanes so that it would not be noticed that it was still nighttime in the sky and it was Sunday the twenty-fifth in the house and it was April on the sea, and there was a hubbub of Chinese laundrymen who threw the last sleepers out of their beds to take away the sheets, premonitory blind men who announced love love where there was none, perverse civil servants who found hens laying Monday's eggs while yesterday's were still in the file drawers, and there was an uproar of confused crowds and dogfights in the councils of government urgently called together while he opened a way lighted by the sudden day through the persistent adulators who proclaimed him the undoer of dawn, commander of time, and repository of light, until an officer of the high command dared stop him in the vestibule and came to attention with the news general sir that it's only five after two, another voice, five after three in the morning general sir, and he fetched a ferocious clout with the back of his hand and howled with all his aroused chest so that the whole world would hear him, it's eight o'clock, God damn it, eight o'clock, I said, God's order. Bendición Alvarado asked him when she saw him enter the suburban mansion where are you coming from with that face that looks like a tarantula bit you, why are you holding your hand over your heart, she said to him, but he dropped into the wicker chair without answering her, changed the position of his hand, he had forgotten about her again when his mother pointed at him with the brush for painting orioles and asked in surprise whether he really believed in the Sacred Heart of Jesus with those languid eyes and that hand on his breast, and he hid it in confusion, shit mother, he slammed the door, left, kept walking back and forth at the palace with his hands in his pockets so that on their own they would not put themselves where they shouldn't be, he watched the rain through the window, he watched the water slipping across the cookie-paper stars and the silver-plated moons that had been placed on the windowpanes so that it would look like eight at night at three in the afternoon, he saw the soldiers of the guard numb with cold in the courtyard, he saw the sad sea, Manuela Sánchez's rain in your city without her, the terrible empty parlor, the chairs placed upside down on the tables, the irreparable loneliness of the first shadows of another ephemeral Saturday of another night without her, God damn it, if only I could get rid of what had been danced which is what hurts me most, he sighed, he felt ashamed on his state, he reviewed the places on his body where he could put his hand without its being on his heart, he finally put it on the rupture which had been eased by the rain, it was the same, it had the same shape, the same weight, it hurt the same, but it was even more atrocious like having your own living flesh heart in the palm of your hand, and only then did he understand why so many people in other times had said that the heart is the third ball general sir, God damn it, he left the window, he walked back and forth in the reception room with the unsolvable anxiety of a perpetual president with a fishbone driven through his soul, he found himself in the room of the council of ministers listening as always without understanding, without listening, suffering through a soporific report on the fiscal situation, suddenly something happened in the atmosphere, the treasury minister fell silent, the others were looking at him through the chinks of a cuirass cracked by pain, he saw himself defenseless and alone at the end of the walnut table with his face trembling from his pitiful state of a lifetime president with his hand on his chest having been revealed in broad daylight, his life was singed by the glacial hot coals of the tiny goldsmith eyes of my comrade the minister of health who seemed to be examining him inside as he fingered the chain of his small gold vest-pocket watch, careful, someone said, it might be a pang, but he had already put his siren's hand hardened by rage on the walnut table, he got his color back, along with the words he spat out a fatal wave of authority, you people probably hoped it was a pang, you bastards, go on, they went on, but they spoke without hearing themselves thinking that something serious must have happened to him if he flew into such a rage, they whispered it, the rumor went around, they pointed at him, see how depressed he is, he has to clutch his heart, he's coming apart at the seams, they murmured, the story went around that he had had the minister of health called urgently and that the latter had found him with his right arm laid out like a leg of lamb on the walnut table and he ordered him to cut it off for me, old friend, humiliated by his sad condition of a president bathed in tears, but the minister answered him no, general, I won't carry out that order even if you have me shot, he told him, it's a matter of justice, general, I'm not worth as much as your arm. These and many other versions of his state were becoming more and more intense while in the stables he measured out the milk for the garrisons watching Manuela Sánchez's Ash Tuesday rising in the sky, he had the lepers removed from the rose beds so that they would not stink up the roses of your rose, he searched out the solitary places in the building in order to sing without being heard your first waltz as queen, so you won't forget me, he sang, so you'll feel you're dying if you forget me, he sang, he plunged into the mire of the concubines' rooms trying to find relief from his torment, and for the first time in his long life of a volatile lover he turned his instincts loose, he lingered over details, he brought out sighs from the basest of women, time and again, and he made them laugh with surprise in the shadows doesn't it bother you general, at your age, but he knew only too well that that will to resist was a set of tricks he was playing on himself in order to waste time, that each step in his loneliness, each stumble in his breathing was bringing him remorselessly to the dog days of the unavoidable two o'clock in the afternoon when he went to beg for the love of God for the love of Manuela Sánchez in the palace of your ferocious dungheap kingdom of a dogfight district, he went in civilian clothes, without an escort, in the taxi which slipped away backfiring the smell of rancid gasoline through a city prostrate in the lethargy of siesta time, he avoided the Asiatic din of the commercial district alleys, he saw the great feminine sea of Manuela Sánchez of my perdition with a solitary pelican on the horizon, he saw the decrepit streetcars with frosted-glass windows with a velvet throne for Manuela Sánchez, he saw the deserted beach of your sea Sundays and he ordered them to build little dressing rooms and a flag with a different color according to the whims of the weather and a steel mesh fence around a beach reserved for Manuela Sánchez, he saw the manors with marble terraces and thoughtful lawns of the fourteen families he had enriched with his favors, he saw one manor that was larger with spinning sprinklers and stained glass in the balcony windows where I want to see you living for me, and they expropriated it forcibly, deciding the fate of the world while he dreamed with his eyes open in the back seat of the tin-can car until the sea breeze was gone and the city was gone and in through the chinks of the window came the satanic din of your dogfight district where he saw himself and did not believe it thinking mother of mine Bendición Alvarado look where I am without you, favor me, but no one recognized in the tumult the desolate eyes, the weak lips, the languid hand on his chest, the voice with the sleeping talk of a great-grandfather looking through a broken glass wearing a white linen suit and a foreman's hat and going around trying to find out where Manuela Sánchez of my shame lives, the queen of the poor, madam, the one with the rose in her hand, wondering in alarm where could you live in that turmoil of sharp bump backbones of satanic looks of bloody fangs of the string of fleeing howls with the tail between the legs of the butchery of dogs quartering each other as they exchanged nips in the mud puddles, where could the licorice smell of your breath be in this continuous thunder of whore-daughter loudspeakers you'll be the torture of my life of drunks booted out of slaughterhouse saloons, where could you have got lost in the endless binge of the fruits and the hodgepodge school of mullet and ray fish and a salami of penny-pitching and the black penny tossed of the mythical paradise of Black Adán and Juancito Trucupey, God damn it, which house do you live in in this clamor of peeling pumpkin yellow walls with the purple trim of a bishop's stole and green parrot windows with fairy blue partitions and columns pink like the rose in your hand, what time can it be in your life since these lowlifes don't know about my order that it's three o'clock now and not eight o'clock yesterday night as it seems to be in this hellhole, which one are you among these women who nod in the empty parlors and ventilate themselves with their skirts holding their legs apart in rocking chairs inhaling the heat from between their legs while he asked through the openings in the window where Manuela Sánchez of my rage lives, the one with the frothy dress with diamond spangles and the solid gold diadem he had given her on the first anniversary of her coronation, now I know who she is, sir, somebody in the tumult said, a big-assed teaty woman who thinks she's the gorilla's own mama, she lives there, sir, there, in a house like all the others, painted at the top of its lungs, with the fresh mark of someone who'd slipped on a lump of dog dirt and left a mosaic carlock, a poor person's house so different from Manuela Sánchez in the chair of the viceroys that it was hard to believe it was her, but it was her, mother of my innards Bendición Alvarado, give me your strength to go in, mother, because it was her, he'd gone around the block ten times to catch his breath, he'd knocked on the door with three knuckle-raps that were like three entreaties, he'd waited in the burning shadows of the entranceway without knowing whether the evil air he was breathing was perverted by the glare of the sun or by anxiety, he waited without even thinking of his own state until Manuela Sánchez's mother had him come into the cool fish

62

leftover smell of the shadows in the broad stark living room of a house asleep that was larger inside than out, he examined the scope of his frustration from the leather stool he had sat on while Manuela Sánchez's mother woke her from her siesta, he saw the walls and the dribbles of past raindrops, a broken sofa, two other stools with leather bottoms, a stringless piano in the corner, nothing else, shit, so much suffering for this trouble, he sighed, when Manuela Sánchez's mother came back with a sewing basket and sat down to make lace while Manuela Sánchez got dressed, combed her hair, put on her best shoes to attend with proper dignity the unexpected old man who wondered perplexed where can you be Manuela Sánchez of my misfortune that I came looking for you and cannot find you in this house of beggars, where is your licorice smell in this pesthole of lunch leftovers, where is your rose, where your love; release me from the dungeon of these dog doubts, he sighed, when he saw her appear at the rear door like the image of a dream reflected in the mirror of another dream wearing a dress of etamine that cost a penny a yard, her hair tied back hurriedly with a back comb, her shoes shabby, but she was the most beautiful and haughtiest woman on earth with the rose glowing in her hand, a sight so dazzling that he barely got sufficient control of himself to bow when she greeted him with her lifted head God preserve your excellency, and she sat down on the sofa opposite him, where the gush of his fetid body odor would not reach her, and then I dared to look at him face to face for the first time spinning the glow of the rose with two fingers so that he would not notice my terror, I pitilessly scrutinized the bat lips, the mute eyes that seemed to be looking at me from the bottom of a pool, the hairless skin like clods of earth tamped down with gall oil which became tighter and more intense on the right hand and the ring with the presidential seal exhausted on his knee, his baggy linen suit as if there were nobody inside, his enormous dead man's shoes, his invincible thought, his occult powers, the oldest ancient on earth, the most fearsome, the most hated, and the least pitied in the nation who was fanning himself with his foreman's hat contemplating me in silence from his other shore, good lord, such a sad man, I thought with surprise, and she asked without compassion what can I do for you your excellency, and he answered with a solemn air that I've only come to ask a favor of you, your majesty, that you accept this visit of mine. He visited her without cease month after month, every day during the dead hours of the heat when he used to visit his mother so that the security service would think he was at the suburban mansion, for only he was unaware of what everyone knew that General Rodrigo de Aguilar's riflemen were protecting him crouched on the rooftops, they raised hell with traffic, they used their rifle butts to clear the streets he would pass along, they put them off limits so that they would seem deserted from two until five with orders to shoot if anyone tried to come out onto a balcony, but even the least curious found some way to spy on the fleeting passage of the presidential limousine painted to look like a taxi with the canicular old man disguised as a civilian inside the innocent linen suit, they saw his orphan paleness, his face that had seen it dawn so many mornings, that had wept in secret, no longer bothered about what they might have thought of the hand on his chest, the archaic taciturn animal who went along leaving a trail of illusions of look at him go since he can't make it any more in the glassy heat of the forbidden streets, until the suspicions of strange illnesses became so loud and repeated they finally stumbled onto the truth that he was not at his mother's house but in the shadowy parlor of Manuela Sánchez's secret cove under the implacable vigilance of the mother who knitted without stopping to take a breath, because it was for her that he bought the ingenious machines that so saddened Bendición Alvarado, he tried to seduce her with the mystery of magnetic needles, the January snowstorms captive in quartz paperweights, apparatuses of astronomers and pharmacists, pyrographs, manometers, metronomes and gyroscopes which he kept on buying from anyone who would sell them against the advice of his mother, and in opposition to his own steely avarice, and only for the pleasure of enjoying them with Manuela Sánchez, he would put to her ear the patriotic shell that did not have the sound of the sea inside but the military marches that exalted his regime, he would bring the flame of a match close to the thermometers so you can see the oppressive mercury of what I think inside go up and down, he looked at Manuela Sánchez without asking her for anything, without expressing his intentions to her, but he would overwhelm her in silence with those demented presents to try to tell her with them what he was capable of saying, for he only knew how to show his most intimate urges with the visible symbols of his uncommon power as on Manuela Sánchez's birthday when he had asked her to open the window and she opened it and I was petrified with fright to see what they had done to my poor dogfight district, I saw the white wooden houses with canvas awnings and terraces with flowers, the blue lawns with their spinning sprinklers, the peacocks, the glacial insecticide wind, a vile replica of the former residences of the occupation officials which had been minutely reproduced at night and in silence, they had slit the throats of the dogs, they had removed the former inhabitants from their homes for they had no right to be the neighbors of a queen and sent them off to rot in some other dungheap, and in that way in a few furtive nights they had built the new district of Manuela Sánchez so you could see it from your window on your name day, there it is, queen, so that you may have many happy years to come, so see whether or not these displays of power were able to soften your courteous but unconquerable behavior, my mama is there with the fetters of my honor, and he drowned in his urges, swallowed his rage, drank with slow grandfather sips the cool soursop water of pity which she had prepared to give drink to the thirsty one, he bore up under the icy jabs in his temples so that the imperfections of age would not be revealed, so that you will not love me out of pity after he had exhausted all the resources for her to have loved him out of love, she left him in such a state of only when I'm with you I don't have the spirit even to be there, agonizing to stroke her if only with his breath before the human-size archangel should fly inside the house ringing the bell

65

of my fateful hour, and he got in one last sip of the visit while she put the toys away in their original cases so the sea rot would not turn them to dust, just one minute, queen, he got up from now until tomorrow, a lifetime, what a mess, he barely had an instant to take a last look at the untouchable maiden who with the step of the archangel had remained motionless with the dead rose in her lap while he took leave, he slipped into the first shadows trying to hide a shame which was in the public domain and which everyone commented upon on the street, it gave birth to an anonymous song which the whole country knew except him, even the parrots sang it in courtyards make way women there comes the general crying green with his hand on his chest, see how he goes he can't handle his power, he rules in his sleep, he's got a wound that won't close, wild parrots learned it from having heard it sung by tame parrots, budgies and mockingbirds learned it from them and they carried it off in flocks beyond his measureless realm of gloom, and in all the skies of the nation one could hear at dusk that unanimous voice of fleeting multitudes who sang there comes my ever-loving general giving off crap through his mouth and laws through his poop, an endless song to which everybody even the parrots added verses to mock the security services of the state who tried to capture it, military patrols in full battle dress broke down courtyard doors and shot down the subversive parrots on their perches, they threw whole bushels of parakeets alive to the dogs, a state of siege was declared in an attempt to extirpate the enemy song so that no one would discover that everybody knew that he was the one who slipped like a fugitive of dusk through the doors of the presidential palace, went through the kitchens and disappeared into the manure smoke of the private rooms until tomorrow at four o'clock, queen, until every day at the same hour when he arrived at Manuela Sánchez's house laden with so many unusual gifts that they had to take over the houses next door and knock down the intervening walls in order to have room for them, so that the original parlor had become an immense and gloomy shed where there were uncountable clocks from every period, there was every type of phonograph from primitive ones with cylinders to those with a mirror diaphragm, there were all sorts of sewing machines with cranks, pedals, motors, whole bedrooms full of galvanometers, homeopathic pharmaceuticals, music boxes, optical-illusion instruments, showcases of dried butterflies, Asiatic herbariums, laboratories for physiotherapy and physical education, machines for astronomy, orthopedics and natural sciences, and a whole world of dolls with hidden mechanisms for human traits, forbidden rooms where no one entered not even to sweep because the things stayed where they had been placed when they were brought, no one wanted to hear about them and Manuela Sánchez least of all because she did not wish to know anything about life ever since that black Saturday when the misfortune of being queen befell me, on that afternoon the world ended for me, her former suitors had died one after the other struck down by unpunished collapses and strange illnesses, her girl friends disappeared without a trace, she'd been moved without leaving her house into a district full of strangers, she was alone, watched over in her most intimate aims, the captive of a trap of fate in which she did not have the courage to say no nor did she have sufficient courage to say yes to an abominable suitor who besieged her with a madhouse love, who looked at her with a kind of reverential stupor fanning himself with his white hat, drenched in sweat, so far removed from himself that she had wondered whether he really was looking at her or whether it was only a vision of horror, she had seen him hesitating in broad daylight, she had seen him nibble at fruit juices, had seen him nod with sleep in the wicker easy chair with the glass in his hand when the copper buzz of the cicadas made the parlor shadows denser, she had seen him snore, careful your excellency, she had told him, he would wake up startled murmuring no, queen, I didn't fall asleep, I just closed my eyes, he said, without realizing that she had taken the glass from his hand so that he wouldn't drop it while he slept, she had amused him with subtle wiles until the incredible afternoon when he got to the house gasping with the news that today

I'm bringing you the greatest gift in the universe, a miracle of heaven that's going to pass by tonight at eleven-oh-six so that you can see it, queen, only so that you can see it, and it was the comet. It was one of our great moments of disappointment, because for some time a rumor had spread like so many others that the timetable of his life was not controlled by human time but by the cycles of the comet, that he had been conceived to see it once but that he was not to see it again in spite of the arrogant auguries of his adulators, so we had waited like someone waiting for the day when that secular November night is born on which joyous music was prepared, the bells of jubilation, the festival rockets which for the first time in a century did not burst to exalt his glory but to wait for the eleven metal rings of eleven o'clock which would signal the end of his years, to celebrate a providential event that he awaited on the roof of Manuela Sánchez's house, sitting between her and her mother, breathing strongly so that they would not notice the difficulties of his heart under a sky numb with evil omens, breathing in for the first time the nocturnal breath of Manuela Sánchez, the intensity of her inclemency, her open air, he heard on the horizon the conjure drums that were coming out to meet the disaster, he listened to distant laments, the sounds of the volcanic slime of the crowds who prostrated themselves in terror before a creature alien to their power who had preceded and who was to transcend the years of their age, he felt the weight of time, he suffered for an instant the misfortune of being mortal, and then he saw it, there it is, he said, and there it was, because he knew it, he had seen it when it had passed on to the other side of the universe, it was the same one, queen, older than the earth, the painful medusa of light the size of the sky which with every hand measure of its trajectory was returning a million years to its origins, they heard the buzzing of bits of tinfoil, they saw his afflicted face, his eyes overflowing with tears, the track of frozen poisons of its hair disheveled by the winds of space as it left across the world a trail radiant with star debris and dawns delayed by tarry moons and ashes from the craters of oceans previous to the origins

68

of earth time, there it is, queen, he murmured, take a good look at it because we won't see it again for another century, and she crossed herself in terror, more beautiful than ever under the phosphorous glow of the comet and with her head snowy from the soft drizzle of astral trash and celestial sediment, and it was then that it happened, mother of mine Bendición Alvarado, it happened that Manuela Sánchez had seen the abyss of eternity in the sky and trying to cling to life she had reached out her hand into space and the only thing she found to hang on to was the undesirable hand with the presidential ring, his hot stiff hand of rapine cooked in the embers of the slow fire of power. Very few were those who were moved by the biblical passage of the glowing medusa which frightened deer from out of the sky and fumigated the fatherland with a trail of radiant dust of star debris, for even the most incredulous of us were hanging on that uncommonly large death which was to destroy the principles of Christianity and implant the origins of the third testament, we waited in vain until dawn, we returned home more fatigued from waiting than from not sleeping through the post-party streets where the dawn women were sweeping up the celestial trash left by the comet, and not even then did we resign ourselves to believe that it was true that nothing had happened, but that on the contrary we had been the victims of another historic trick, for the official organs proclaimed the passage of the comet as a victory of the regime over the forces of evil, they took advantage of the occasion to deny the suppositions of strange diseases with unmistakable acts of vitality on the part of the man in power, slogans were renewed, a solemn message was made public in which he had expressed my unique and sovereign decision to be in my post of service to the nation when the comet passes again, but on the other hand he heard the music and the rockets as if they did not belong to his regime, he listened without emotion to the clamoring crowd gathered on the main square with large banners saying eternal glory to the most worthy one who will live to tell it, he was not concerned with the troubles of government, he delegated his authority to underlings tormented by the

memory of the hot coal that was Manuela Sánchez's hand
on his, dreaming of reliving that happy moment even if
nature's direction had to be turned off course and the universe be damaged, desiring it with such intensity that he
ended up beseeching his astronomers to invent him a fireworks comet, a fleeting morning star, a dragon made of
candles, any ingenious star invention that would be terrifying enough to cause a swoon of eternity in a beautiful
woman, but the only thing they could come up with in their
calculations was a total eclipse of the sun for Wednesday of
next week at four in the afternoon general sir, and he accepted it, all right, and it was such a true night in the middle
of the day that the stars lit up, flowers closed, hens went to
roost, and animals sought shelter with their best premonitory instincts, while he breathed in Manuela Sánchez's twilight breath as it became nocturnal and the rose languished
in her hand deceived by the shadows, there it is, queen, it's
your eclipse, but Manuela Sánchez did not answer, she did
not touch his hand, she was not breathing, she seemed so
unreal that he could not resist his urge and he stretched out
his hand in the darkness to touch her hand, but he could
not find it, he looked for it with the tips of his fingers in the
place where her smell had been, but he did not find it
either, he kept on looking for it through the enormous
house with both hands, waving his arms about with the
open eyes of a sleepwalker in the shadows, wondering with
grief where can you be Manuela Sánchez of my misfortune
as I seek you and cannot find you in the unfortunate night
of your eclipse, where can your inclement hand be, your
rose, he swam like a diver lost in a pool of invisible waters
in whose reaches he found floating the prehistoric crayfish
of the galvanometers, the crabs of the musical clocks, the
lobsters of your machines of illusory trades, but on the
contrary he did not even find the licorice breath of your
lungs, and as the darkness of the ephemeral night broke up
the light of truth grew brighter in his soul and he felt older
than God in the shadows of the six in the afternoon dawn
in the deserted house, he felt sadder, lonelier than ever in
the loneliness of this world without you, my queen, lost

forever in the enigma of the eclipse, nevermore, because never in the rest of the very long years of his power would he find Manuela Sánchez of my perdition again in the labyrinth of her house, she had disappeared in the night of the eclipse general sir, they told him that she'd been seen dancing the plena in Puerto Rico, there where they cut Elena general sir, but it wasn't her, that she'd been seen in the madness of Papa Montero's wake, tricky, lowlife rumba bunch, but it wasn't her either, that she'd been seen in the ticky-tacky of Barlovento over the mine, in the dance of Aracataca, in the pretty wind of the little drum of Panama, but none of them was her, general sir, she just blew the hell away, and if he did not abandon himself to the will of death at that time it was not because he lacked the rage to die but because he knew he was remorselessly condemned not to die of love, he had known it ever since one afternoon during the first days of his empire when he went to a sibyl for her to read to him in the water of her basins the keys to his fate which were not written in the palm of his hand, or in the cards, or in his coffee grounds, or in any other means of inquiry, only in that mirror of premonitory waters where he saw himself dead of natural causes during his sleep in the office next to the reception room, and he saw himself lying face down on the floor as he had slept every night of his life since birth, with the denim uniform without insignia, the boots, the gold spur, his right arm folded under his head to serve as a pillow, and at an indefinite age somewhere between 107 and 232 years.

THAT WAS HOW they found him on the even of his autumn, when the corpse was really that of Patricio Aragonés, and that was how we found him again many years later during a moment of such uncertainty that no one could give in to the evidence that the senile body there gouged by vultures and infested with parasites from the depths of the sea was his. The hand turned into a figurine by putrefaction gave no indication that it had ever been held on the chest because of the rebuffs of an improbable maiden during the noisy times, nor had we found any trace of his life that could have led us to the unmistakable establishment of his identity. It didn't seem strange to us, of course, that this should be so in our days, because even during his times of greatest glory there had been reasons to doubt his existence and his own henchmen had no exact notion of his age, for there were periods of confusion in which he seemed to be eighty years old at charity raffles, sixty at civil receptions and even under forty during the celebration of national holidays. Ambassador Palmerston, one of the last diplomats to present his credentials, told in his banned memoirs that it was impossible to conceive of old age as advanced as his or of a state of disorder and neglect as in that government house where he had to make his way through a dungheap of paper scraps and animal shit and the remains of the meals of dogs who slept in the halls, no one could give me any information about anything in tax bureaus or offices and I was forced to have recourse to the lepers and cripples who had already invaded the first part of the private quarters and who showed me the way to the reception room where the hens were pecking at the illusory wheat fields on the tapestries and a cow was pulling down the canvas with the portrait of an archbishop so she could eat it, and I realized at once that he was as deaf as a post not only because I would ask him about one thing and he would answer about another but also because it grieved him that the birds were not singing when in fact it was difficult to breathe with that uproar of birds which was like walking through the jungle at dawn, and he suddenly interrupted the ceremony of credentials with a lucid look and cupping his hand behind his ear he pointed out the window at the dusty plain where the sea had been and said in a voice to awaken the dead that I should listen to that troop of mules going along out there, listen my dear Stetson, it's the sea coming back. It was hard to admit that that broken-down old man was the same messianic figure who during the beginnings of his regime would appear in towns when least expected with no other escort but a barefooted Guajiro Indian with a cane-cutting machete and a small entourage of congressmen and senators whom he had appointed himself with his finger according to the whims of his digestion, he informed himself about the crop figures and the state of health of the livestock and the behavior of the people, he would sit in a reed rocking chair in the shadow of the mango trees on the square fanning himself with the foreman's hat he wore in those days, and even though he seemed to be dozing because of the heat he would not let a single detail go by without some explanation in his talks with the men and women he had called together using their names and surnames as if he had a written registry of inhabitants and statistics and problems of the whole nation inside his head, so he called me without opening his eyes, come here Jacinta Morales, he said to me, tell me what happened to the boy he had wrestled with himself and given a fall the year before so he would drink a bottle of castor oil, and you, Juan Prieto, he said to me, how is your breed bull that he had treated himself with prayers against sickness so the worms would drop out of his ears, and you Matilde Peralta, let's see what you're going to give me for bringing back that runaway husband of yours in one piece, there he is, pulled along with a rope around his neck and warned by him in person that he'd rot in the stocks the next time he tried to desert his legitimate spouse, and with the same sense of immediate governance he had ordered a butcher to cut off the hands of a cheating treasurer in a public spectacle and he would pick the tomatoes in a private garden and eat them with the air of a connoisseur in the presence of his agronomists saying that what this soil needs is a good dose of male donkey shit, it should be spread at government expense, he ordered, and he interrupted his civic stroll and shouted to me through the window breaking up with laughter aha Lorenza López how's that sewing machine he had given me as a present twenty years earlier, and I answered him that it had already given up the ghost, general, you have to remember that things and people we're not made to last a lifetime, but he answered just the opposite, the world is eternal, and then he set about dismantling the machine with a screwdriver and an oilcan indifferent to the official delegation that was waiting for him in the middle of the street, sometimes his desperation was evident from the bull snorts and even his face was daubed with motor oil, but after almost three hours the machine was sewing again as good as new, because in those days there was nothing contrary in everyday life no matter how insignificant which did not have as much importance for him as the gravest matter of state and he believed sincerely that it was possible to distribute happiness and bribe death with the wiles of a soldier. It was hard

to admit that that aged person beyond repair was all that
remained of a man whose power had been so great that
once he asked what time is it and they had answered him
whatever you command general sir, and it was true, for not
only did he alter the time of day as best suited his business
but he would change legal holidays in accordance with his
plans to cover the whole country from holiday to holiday
in the shadow of the barefoot Indian and the mournful-
looking senators and with the crates of splendid cocks who
faced the bravest there were in every village square, he
booked the bets himself, he made the foundations of the
cockpit shake with laughter because we all felt obliged to
laugh when he gave off his strange snare-drum guffaws that
rang out above the music and the rockets, we suffered when
he was silent, we would break out in an ovation of relief
when his birds struck ours with lightning ours having been
so well trained to lose that not a single one let us down,
except the cock of Dionisio Iguarán's misfortune who
struck down the gray one belonging to the power in an
attack so clean and sure that he was the first to cross the
ring and shake the winner's hand, you're a real man, he told
him with a pleasant manner, thankful that someone had
finally done him the favor of an innocuous defeat, how
much do you want for that red one, he said, and Dionisio
Iguarán answered him in a quavering voice it's yours general, my great honor, and he went home to the applause of
the excited people and the noise of the music and the
petards showing everybody the six pedigreed cocks he had
been given in exchange for the undefeated red one, but
that night he locked himself up in his bedroom and drank
a gourdful of cane liquor all by himself and hanged himself
with the rope from his hammock, poor man, for he was not
aware of the string of domestic disasters that his jubilant
appearances brought on, nor the trail of undesired deaths
he left behind, nor the eternal condemnation of comrades
in misfortune whom he called by the wrong name in front
of solicitous assassins who interpreted the mistake as a
deliberate sign of disfavor, he walked all across the country
with his strange armadillo step, his trail of strong sweat, his

tardy stubble of a beard, he would appear without notice in some kitchen with that air of a useful grandfather which made the people of the house tremble with fear, he would take a drink of water from the bucket with the calabash dipper, he would eat out of the stewpot itself picking up the chunks with his fingers, too jovial, too simple, not suspecting that that house was marked forever with the stigma of his visit, and he did not act that way out of any political calculation or the need for love as was the case in other times but because it was his natural way of being when power was still not the shoreless bog of the fullness of his autumn but a feverish torrent that we saw gush out of its spring before our very eyes so that all he had to do was point at trees for them to bear fruit and at animals for them to grow and at men for them to prosper, and he had ordered them to take the rain away from places where it disturbed the harvest and take it to drought-stricken lands, and that was the way it had been, sir, I saw it, because his legend had begun much earlier than he believed himself master of all his power, when he was still at the mercy of omens and the interpreters of his nightmares and he would suddenly cut short a trip he had just started because he had heard a bird sing above his head and he would change the date of a public appearance because his mother Bendición Alvarado had found an egg with two yolks, and he got rid of the retinue of solicitous senators and congressmen who went with him everywhere and delivered for him the speeches that he never dared deliver, he went without them because he saw himself in the big empty house of a bad dream surrounded by pale men in gray frock coats who were smiling and sticking him with butcher knives, they harried him with such fury that wherever he turned to look he found a blade ready to wound him in the face and eyes, he saw himself encircled like a wild beast by the silent smiling assassins who fought over the privilege of taking part in the sacrifice and enjoying his blood, but he did not feel rage or fear, rather an immense relief that grew deeper as his life trickled away, he felt himself weightless and pure, so he too smiled as they killed him, he smiled for them and

76

for himself in the confines of the dream house whose white-washed walls were being stained by my spattering blood, until someone who was a son of his in the dream gave him a stab in the groin through which the last bit of breath I had left escaped, and then he covered his face with the blanket soaked in his blood so that no one who had not been able to know him alive would know him dead and he collapsed shaken by such real death throes that he could not repress the urgency of telling it to my comrade the minister of health and the latter ended up by putting him in a state of consternation with the revelation that that death had already occurred once in the history of men general sir, he read him the story of the episode in one of the singed tomes of General Lautaro Muñoz, and it was identical, mother, so much so that in the course of its reading he remembered something that he had forgotten when he woke up and it was that while they were killing him all of a sudden and with no wind blowing all the windows in the presidential palace opened up and they were in fact the same number as the wounds in the dream, twenty-three, a terrifying coincidence which had its culmination that week with an attack on the senate and the supreme court by corsairs along with the cooperative indifference of the armed forces, the august home of our original patriotic forebears was burned to the ground and the flames could be séen until very late in the night from the presidential balcony, but he did not change his expression with the news general sir that they had not even spared the foundation stones, he promised us an exemplary punishment for the perpetrators of the attack who never appeared, he promised us that he would rebuild an exact replica of the house of our forebears but its blackened ruins remained down to our times, he did nothing to disguise the terrible exorcism of the bad dream but took advantage of the occasion to liquidate the legislative and judicial apparatus of the old republic, he heaped honors and fortune upon the senators and congressmen and magistrates whom he no longer needed to keep up the appearances of the beginning of his regime, he exiled them to happy and remote embassies and remained with no other retinue but the solitary shadow of the Indian with his machete who did not abandon him for an instant, who tasted his food and water, kept his distance, watched the door while he stayed in my house giving fuel to the story that he was my secret lover while in fact he visited me once or twice a month to consult me about the cards during those many years when he still thought himself mortal and had the virtue of doubt and knew how to make mistakes and trusted more in the deck of cards than in his rustic instincts, he still arrived as worried and as old as the first time he sat down opposite me and without saying a word stretched out to me those hands with palms as smooth and tight as the belly of a toad such as I had never seen or was ever to see again in my long life as an examiner of the destiny of others, he laid them both on the table at the same time almost like the mute begging of a hopeless case and he seemed so anxious to me and so without illusions that I was not so impressed by his arid palms as by his unalleviated melancholy, the weakness of his lips, his poor heart of an old man eaten by doubt whose fate was not only hermetic in his hands but in all the means of inquiry that we knew in those times, for as soon as he cut the cards they became pools of murky water, the coffee grounds became muddy in the bottom of the cup he had drunk from, the keys to everything that had to do with his personal future, his happiness and the destiny of his acts had been erased, but on the other hand they were crystal clear as concerned the destiny of anyone who had anything to do with him, so we saw his mother Bendición Alvarado painting birds with foreign names at such an advanced age that she could barely distinguish the colors in an air rarefied by a pestilential vapor, poor mother, we saw our city devastated by a hurricane so terrible that it did not deserve its woman's name, we saw a man with a green mask and a sword in his hand and he asked in anguish what part of the world he was in and the cards answered that every Tuesday he was closer to him than on other days of the week, and he said aha, and asked what color eyes he had, and the cards answered that one was the color of juice in the light and the other cane juice in the dark, and he said aha, and he asked what that man's intentions were, and that was the last time I revealed to him the truth of the cards to the very end because I answered him that the green mask was that of perfidy and treason, and he said aha, with a stress of triumph, I already know who he is, God damn it, he exclaimed, and it was Colonel Narciso Miraval, one of his closest aides who two days later put a bullet in his ear with no explanation, poor man, and that was how the destiny of the nation was arranged and its history anticipated according to the predictions of the cards until he heard tell of a singular sibyl who deciphered death in the error-free waters of her basins and he went to seek her out in secret along mule trails and with no other witness than the angel of the machete all the way up to the settlement on the plains where she lived with a great-granddaughter who had three children and was about to bear another by a husband dead the month before, he found her crippled and half blind in the back of a bedroom almost in darkness, but when she asked him to put his hands over the basin the waters became illuminated with a soft and clear interior glow, and then he saw himself, exactly as he was, lying face down on the floor, wearing a denim uniform without insignia, the boots and the gold spur, and he asked what place that was, and the woman answered examining the sleeping waters that it was a room not much larger than this with something that can be seen here that looks like a desk and an electric fan and a window facing the sea and these white walls with pictures of horses and a flag with a dragon on it, and again he said aha because he had recognized without any doubt the office next to the reception room, and he asked if it was to be in a bad way or from a bad illness, and she answered him no, it was to be during his sleep and without pain, and he said aha, and he asked her trembling when it was to be and she answered him that he could sleep peacefully because it would not take place before you reach my age, which was 107, but also not after 125 years more, and he said aha, and then he murdered the sick old woman in the hammock so that no one else would know the circumstances of his death, he strangled her with the strap from his gold spur, without pain, without a sigh, like a master executioner, in spite of the fact that she was the only being in this world, human or animal, whom he did the honor of killing with his own hand in peace or in war, poor woman. Similar evocations from his fasti of infamy did not twist his conscience during the nights of his autumn, on the contrary they served him as exemplary fables of what should have been done and what had not been, above all when Manuela Sánchez evaporated into the shadows of the eclipse and he wanted to feel himself in the full bloom of his barbarity once more so he could pluck out the rage of deception which was cooking his innards, he would lie down in the hammock under the tinkle bells of the wind in the tamarinds to think about Manuela Sánchez with a rancor that disturbed his sleep while the forces of land, sea and air sought her without any trace even in the unknown confines of the saltpeter deserts, where the fuck have you hidden yourself, he wondered, where the fuck do you think you can hide where my arm can't reach you so that you'll know who gives the orders, the hat on his chest quivered with the drive of his heart, he lay there ecstatic with rage and paying no attention to his mother's insistence as she tried to find out why you haven't spoken a word since the afternoon of the eclipse, but he wouldn't answer, he left, shit mother, he dragged his big orphan feet off bleeding drops of gall with his pride wounded by the irredeemable bitterness that all this trouble is happening to me because I've become such a horse's ass, because I haven't been the director of my destiny the way I was before, because I went into the house of a bitch with her mother's permission and not the way he had gone into the cool and quiet ranch house of Francisca Linero in Vereda de los Santos Higuerones when it was still he in person and not Patricio Aragonés who showed the visible face of power, he had gone in without even touching the door knocker in accordance with the pleasure of his will to the rhythm of the tolling of eleven o'clock on the grandfather clock and I heard the metal of the gold spur from the courtyard terrace and knew that those pile-driver steps with all that authority on the brick floor could not belong to

80

anyone else but him, I sensed him in the flesh before I saw
him appear in the doorway of the inner terrace where the
curlew was singing out eleven o'clock among the gold
geraniums, a troupial disturbed by the fragrant acetone of
the bunches of bananas hanging from the eaves, the light
of the ominous August Tuesday was taking its ease among
the new leaves of the plantain trees in the courtyard and the
carcass of the young buck which my husband Poncio Daza
had shot at dawn and hung by its hind legs to bleed beside
the bunches of bananas tiger-striped by their inner honey,
I saw him larger and more somber than in a dream his
boots dirty with mud and his khaki jacket soaked with sweat
and with no weapons on his belt but protected by the
shadow of the barefoot Indian who stood motionless behind him his hand resting on the hilt of his machete, I saw
the unavoidable eyes, the hand of a sleeping maiden that
plucked a banana from the nearest bunch and ate it with
anxiety his whole mouth making a swampy sound without
taking his eyes off the provocative Francisca Linero who
looked at him without knowing what to do in her modesty
of a newlywed because he had come to give pleasure to his
will and there was no power greater than his to stop him,
I barely felt the fearful breathing of my husband who sat
down beside me and we both remained motionless holding
hands and our two postcard hearts were frightened in uni-
son under the tenacious look of the unfathomable old man
who kept on eating one banana after another two steps
from the door and tossing the peels over his shoulder into
the courtyard without having blinked a single time after he
had begun to look at me, and only after he had eaten the
whole bunch and the bare stalk was left beside the dead
buck did he make a signal to the barefoot Indian and ordered Poncio Daza to go with my comrade the one with the
machete for a moment because he has some business and
although I was dying with fear I maintained enough lucidity
to realize that my only means of salvation was to let him do
everything he wanted to with me on the dinner table, even
more, I helped him find me among the lace of the petticoats
after he left me gasping for breath with his ammonia smell

81

and he tore off my drawers with a claw and looked for me
with his fingers where I wasn't while I thought in confusion
oh Blessed Sacrament such shame, such misfortune, because that morning I hadn't had time to wash myself being
involved with the buck, so he finally did his will after so
many months of siege, but he did it fast and poorly, as if
he had been older than he was, or much younger, he was
so upset that I scarcely noticed when he did his duty as best
he could and broke into sobbing with the hot urine tears
of a great and solitary orphan, weeping with such deep
affliction that not only did I feel pity for him but for every
man in the world and I began to rub his head with my
fingertips and console him with don't worry about it general, life is long, while the man with the machete took
Poncio Daza into the banana groves and cut him up into
such thin slices that it was impossible to put his body back
together again after it had been scattered by the hogs, poor
man, but there was no other way out, he said, because he
would have been a mortal enemy for the rest of his life.
They were images of his power which came to him from far
away and increased the bitterness over how much the brine
of his power had been watered down since it hadn't even
been of any use to conjure up the evil arts of an eclipse, he
was shaken by a thread of black bile at the domino table
across from the frozen realm of General Rodrigo de Aguilar who was the only man of arms in whom he had confided
his life since uric acid had crystallized the joints of the angel
with the machete, and yet he wondered if so much confidence and so much authority delegated to one single person might not have been the cause of his misfortune, if it
wasn't my lifetime comrade who had turned him into an ox
by trying to shear him of his natural fleece of a backlands
leader and convert him into a palace invalid incapable of
thinking up an order that hadn't already been carried out
ahead of time, by the unhealthy invention of showing in
public a face that wasn't his when the barefoot Indian of the
good old days had been sufficient and more than enough
all by himself to open a path with blows from his machete
through the crowds of people shouting make way you bas-

82

tards here comes the man in charge without being able to distinguish in that thicket of ovations who were the real patriots and who were the tricky ones because we still hadn't discovered that the shadiest ones were those who shout loudest long live the stud, God damn it, long live the general, and quite the opposite now the authority of his weapons wasn't even of any use to him to find the death-breeding queen who had made a mockery out of the unbreakable encirclement of his senile appetites, God damn it, he threw the pieces on the floor, left games half finished for no visible reason depressed by the sudden revelation that everyone ended up finding his place in the world, everyone except him, conscious for the first time that his shirt was soaked in sweat at such an early hour, conscious of the carrion stench that rose up from the vapors of the sea and the soft flute whistle of his rupture twisted by the dampness of the heat, it's the humid weather, he told himself without conviction at the window trying to decipher the strange state of the light of the motionless city where the only living beings seemed to be the flocks of vultures fleeing in fright from the cornices of the charity hospital and the blind man in the main square who sensed the trembling old man at the window of government house and made an urgent signal to him with his staff and shouted something that he couldn't make out and which he interpreted as one more sign in that oppressive feeling that something was about to happen, and yet he repeated to himself for the second time at the end of a long Monday of dejection that it's the humidity, he said that to himself and he fell asleep at once, lulled by the scratching of the drizzle on the frosted glass of the sleeping potion, but suddenly he awoke with a start, who's there, he shouted, it was his own heart oppressed by the strange silence of the cocks at dawn, he felt that the ship of the universe had reached some port while he was asleep, he was floating in a soup of steam, the animals of earth and sky who had the faculty to glimpse death beyond the clumsy omens and best-founded sciences of men were mute with terror, there was no more air, time was changing direction, and as he got up he felt his heart

83

swelling with every step and his eardrums bursting and some boiling matter was running out of his nose, it's death, he thought, his tunic soaked with blood, before realizing no general sir, it was the hurricane, the most devastating of all those that had broken the ancient compact realm of the Caribbean up into a string of scattered islands, a catastrophe so stealthy that only he had detected it with his premonitory instinct long before the panic of dogs and hens began, and so quick that there was scarcely time to find a woman's name for it in the disorder of terrified officials who came to me with the news that now yes it was true general sir, this country had gone to hell, but he ordered them to reinforce the doors and windows with long beams, they tied the sentries to their posts along the corridors, they locked up the hens and the cows in the offices on the first floor, they nailed everything down in place from the main square to the last border stone of his terrorized realm of gloom, the whole nation was anchored in place with the absolute order that with the first show of panic they would shoot twice in the air and the third time shoot to kill, and yet nothing could resist the passage of the tremendous blade of the spinning winds that cut a clean slice through the armored doors of the main entrance and carried off my cows into the air, but he did not realize it in the spell of the impact of where did it come from that roar of horizontal rain that scattered in its wake the volcanic grapeshot of the remains of balconies and beasts from the jungle and the bottom of the sea, nor was he lucid enough to think about the fearful proportions of the cataclysm but he walked about in the midst of the downpour wondering with an aftertaste of musk where can you be Manuela Sánchez of my bad saliva, God damn it, where can you have hidden yourself that this disaster of my vengeance hasn't reached you? In the peaceful pool that came after the hurricane he found himself alone with his closest aides floating in a rowboat in the stew of destruction that had been the reception room, they rowed out the coach house door without bumping into anything through the stumps of the palm trees and the downed lampposts of the main square, they went into the dead lagoon of the cathedral and for an instant he suffered the clairvoyant spark that he had never been nor would he ever be the master of all his power, he was still mortified by the irony of that bitter certainty while the rowboat ran into spaces of densities that differed according to the changes in color of the light from the stained glass in solid gold trim and the clusters of emeralds over the main altar and the gravestones of viceroys buried alive and archbishops dead of disenchantment and the granite promontory of the empty mausoleum for the admiral of the ocean sea with the profile of the three caravels which he had had built in case he wanted his bones to rest among us, we went out through the canal of the presbytery toward an inner courtyard converted into a luminous aquarium in the tiled depths of which schools of mojarra fish wandered among the stalks of spikenards and sunflowers, we cut through the gloomy streams of the cloister of the convent of Biscayan nuns, we saw the abandoned cells, we saw the harpsichord adrift in the intimate pool of the music room, in the depths of the sleeping waters of the refectory we saw the whole community of virgins drowned in their dinner places at the long table with the food served on it, and he saw as he went out through a balcony the broad lakelike expanse under a radiant sky where the city had been and only then did he believe that the news was true general sir that this disaster had happened all over the world only to free me from the torment of Manuela Sánchez, God damn it, how wild God's methods are when compared to ours, he thought smugly, contemplating the muddy swamp where the city had been and on whose limitless surface a world of drowned hens floated and all that rose up out of it were the steeples of the cathedral, the beacon of the lighthouse, the sun terraces of the stone and mortar mansions of the viceregal district, the scattered islands which had been the hills of the former slave port where the shipwrecked refugees from the cyclone were encamped, the last disbelieving survivors as we watched the silent passage of the rowboat painted with the colors of the flag through the sargasso of inert bodies of hens, we saw the sad eyes, the

faded lips, the pensive hand which was making the sign of the cross in a blessing so that the rains would cease and the sun shine, and he gave life back to the drowned hens, and ordered the waters to recede and they receded. In the midst of the jubilant bell-ringing, the festival rockets, the music of celebration with which the laying of the first stone of reconstruction was laid, and in the midst of the shouts of the multitude crowded into the main square to glorify the most worthy one who had put the hurricane dragon to flight, someone took him by the arm to lead him out onto the balcony because now more than ever the people needed his words of comfort, and before he could get away he heard the unanimous clamor which got into his innards like the wind of an evil sea, long live the stud, because ever since the first days of his regime he understood the unprotected state of being seen by a whole city at the same time, his words turned to stone, he understood in a flash of mortal lucidity that he did not have the courage nor would he ever have it to appear at full length before the chasm of a crowd, so on the main square we only caught sight of the usual ephemeral image, the glimpse of an ungraspable old man dressed in denim who imparted a silent blessing from the presidential balcony and immediately disappeared, but that fleeting vision was enough for us to sustain the confidence that he was there, watching over our waking and sleeping hours under the historic tamarinds of the suburban mansion, he was absorbed in thought in the wicker rocking chair, with the glass of lemonade untouched in his hand listening to the sound of the kernels of corn that his mother Bendición Alvarado was drying out in the calabash gourd, watching her through the quiver of the three o'clock heat as she grabbed a barred rock hen and stuck it under her arm and twisted its neck with a kind of tenderness while she told me with a mother's voice looking into my eyes you're getting consumptive from so much thinking and not eating well, stay for dinner tonight, she begged him, trying to seduce him with the temptation of the strangled hen that she was holding with both hands so that it would not get away from her in its death throes, and he said
86

all right, mother, I'll stay, he rested until sundown with his eyes closed in the wicker rocking chair, not sleeping, lulled by the soft smell of the hen boiling in the pot, hanging on the course of our lives, for the only thing that gave us security on earth was the certainty that he was there, invulnerable to plague and hurricane, invulnerable to Manuela Sánchez's trick, invulnerable to time, dedicated to the messianic happiness of thinking for us, knowing that we knew that he would not take any decision for us that did not have our measure, for he had not survived everything because of his inconceivable courage or his infinite prudence but because he was the only one among us who knew the real size of our destiny, and he had reached that point, mother, he had sat down to rest at the end of an arduous trip on the last historic stone on the remote eastern frontier where the name and dates of the last soldier killed in defense of the integrity of the nation were carved, he had seen the dismal and glacial city of the neighboring country, he saw the eternal drizzle, the morning mist with the smell of soot, the men in full dress on electric streetcars, the aristocratic funerals in gothic hearses with white Percherons with plumes on their heads, the children sleeping on the steps of the cathedral wrapped in newspapers, God damn it, what strange people, he exclaimed, they look like poets, but they weren't general sir, they're the Goths who hold power, they told him, and he had returned from that trip exalted by the revelation that there is nothing to equal this wind of rotten guavas and this clamor of a marketplace and this deep feeling of mournfulness at dusk in this homeland of misery whose frontiers he was never to cross, and not because he was afraid of moving from the seat where he was sitting, as his enemies said, but because a man is like a tree in the woods, mother, like the animals in the woods who never leave their lairs except to eat, he said, evoking with the mortal lucidity of siesta time the soporific August Thursday of so many years ago when he dared confess that he knew the limits of his ambition, he had revealed it to a warrior from other lands and other times whom he had received alone in the hot shadows of his office, he was a withdrawn

young man, troubled by haughtiness and always standing out from the rest with the stigma of solitude, and he had stood motionless in the doorway unable to decide to cross the threshold until his eyes grew accustomed to the half-light which was scented by a brazier of wisteria in all the heat and he was able to make him out sitting in the swivel chair with his fist motionless on the bare desk, so everyday and faded that there was nothing about him of his public image, without escort or weapons, his shirt soaked in the sweat of a mortal man and with salvia leaves stuck to his temples for his headache, and only when I was convinced of the incredible truth that this rusty old man was the same idol of our childhood, the purest incarnation of our dreams of glory, only then did he enter the office and introduce himself by name speaking with the clear firm voice of one who expects to be recognized because of his deeds, and he shook my hand with a soft and miserly hand, the hand of a bishop, and he paid startling attention to the fabulous dream of the foreigner who wanted arms and assistance for a cause which is also yours, excellency, he wanted logistical support and political aid for a war without quarter which would wipe out once and for all every conservative regime from Alaska to Patagonia, and he felt so moved by his vehemence that he had asked him why are you mixed up in this mess, God damn it, why do you want to die, and the foreigner had answered him without a trace of modesty that there was no higher glory than dying for one's country, excellency, and he replied smiling with pity don't be a horse's ass, boy, fatherland means staying alive, he told him, that's what it is, he told him, and he opened the fist that he had resting on the desk and in the palm of his hand showed him this little glass ball which is something a person has or doesn't have, but only the one who has it has it, boy, this is the nation, he said, while he sent him away with pats on the back and not giving him anything, not even the consolation of a promise, and he ordered the aide who closed the door that they were not to bother that man who has just left any more, don't even waste your time keeping him under surveillance, he said, he's got a fever in his
88

quills, he's no good for anything. We never heard that expression again until after the cyclone when he proclaimed a new amnesty for political prisoners and authorized the return of all exiles except men of letters, of course, them never, he said, they've got fever in their quills like thoroughbred roosters when they're moulting so that they're no good for anything except when they're good for something, he said, worse than politicians, worse than priests, just imagine, but let the others come back without distinction of color so that the rebuilding of the nation can be the task of all, so that nobody would be left without proof that he was once more the master of all his power with the fierce support of armed forces that had become once more the same as before since he had distributed the shipments of food and medicine and the material for public relief from foreign aid among the members of the high command, ever since the families of his ministers had Sunday outings at the beach with the Red Cross portable hospitals and field tents, they sold the shipments of blood plasma, the tons of powdered milk to the ministry of health and the ministry of health resold them to charity hospitals, the officers of the general staff gave up their ambitions in return for public works contracts and rehabilitation programs with the emergency loan granted by Ambassador Warren in exchange for unlimited fishing rights for vessels of his nation within our territorial waters, what the hell, only the one who has it has it, he said to himself, remembering the colored marble he had shown that poor dreamer who was never heard of again, so exalted with the reconstruction work that with his own voice and in person he worked on even the tiniest details as in the original days of his power, sloshing through the swamps in the streets with a hat and a pair of duck-hunter's boots so that a city different from the one he had conceived for his glory in his dreams of a solitary drowned man should be built, he ordered his engineers get rid of these houses here for me and put them over there where they won't be in the way, make that tower six feet taller so that people will be able to see the ships on the high seas, they raised it, reverse the course of this river for me, they reversed it, without any mistakes, without any signs of discouragement, and he went about so befogged with that feverish restoration, so absorbed in his task, and so far removed from other minor matters of state that he ran smack into reality when an absent-minded aide mentioned by mistake the problem of the children and he asked from his cloud what children, the children general sir, but which ones, God damn it, because up till then they had hidden from him the fact that the army was keeping in secret custody the children who picked the lottery numbers for fear they would tell why the presidential ticket always won, they told the parents who complained that it wasn't true while they made up a better answer, they told them they were rumors spread by traitors, lies of the opposition, and those who demonstrated in front of the barracks were repulsed with mortar fire and there was a public slaughter that we had also hidden from him so that you wouldn't be bothered general sir, because the fact was that the children were locked up in the dungeons of the harbor fort under the best of conditions, in excellent spirits and very good health, but the trouble is that now we don't know what to do with them general sir, and there were around two thousand of them. The infallible method for winning the lottery had occurred to him without his looking for it, observing the inlaid numbers on billiard balls, and it had been such a simple and dazzling idea that he himself couldn't believe it when he saw the anxious crowd that had overflowed the main square since noontime taking out their numbers in anticipation of the miracle under the broiling sun with a clamor of gratitude and signs painted with glory to the magnanimous one who distributes happiness, anachronistic wheels of fortune and faded animal lotteries, the rubble of other worlds and other times that pillaged in the realm of fortune in an attempt to thrive on the crumbs of so many illusions, they opened the balcony at three o'clock, they brought up the three children under the age of seven chosen at random by the crowd itself so that there would be no doubt concerning the honesty of the method, they gave each child a bag of a different color after showing trust-

worthy witnesses that there were ten billiard balls numbered from one to zero inside each bag, your attention,
ladies and gentlemen, the throng held its breath, each child
with his eyes blindfolded will take a ball from each bag, first
the child with the blue bag, then the one with the red, and
last the one with the yellow, one after the other the three
children put their hands into their bags, felt at the bottom
nine balls that were just alike and one that was ice-cold, and
following the orders we had given them in secret they chose
the ice-cold ball, showed it to the crowd, sang it out, and
in that way they drew out the three balls that had been kept
on ice for several days with the three numbers of the ticket
he had reserved for himself, but we never thought about
the children's telling it general sir, it occurred to us so late
that there was nothing else to do but hide them three by
three, and then five by five, and then twenty by twenty, just
imagine general sir, so pulling on the thread of the plot he
ended up discovering that all of the officers in the high
command of the land, sea and air forces were implicated in
the miraculous bounty of the national lottery, he found out
that the first children went up on the balcony with the
consent of their parents and even trained by them in the
illusory science of telling the numbers inlaid in ivory by
touch, but that the following ones were brought up by force
because the rumor had spread that once the children went
up they didn't come back down, their parents hid them,
they buried them alive while the raiding parties that sought
them in the middle of the night passed, the emergency
forces did not cordon off the main square to control the
public delirium as they had told him, but to hold at bay the
crowds that they herded like a drove of cattle with threats
of death, the diplomats who had asked for an audience to
mediate the conflict ran into the absurd tale that the func-
tionaries themselves told them that the legend of his
strange illnesses was true, that he couldn't receive them
because toads had proliferated in his belly, that he could
only sleep standing up so as not to injure himself with the
iguana crest that was growing along his spine, they had
hidden the messages of protest and entreaties from all over

the world from him, they had kept secret from him a telegram from the Supreme Pontiff in which our apostolic anguish over the fate of the innocents was expressed, there
was no room in jail for any more rebellious parents general
sir, there were no more children for the Monday drawing,
God damn it, what kind of a mess have we got into. In spite
of all, he did not measure the true depth of the abyss until
he saw the children like cattle in a slaughterhouse in the
inner courtyard of the harbor fort, he saw them come out
of the dungeons like a stampede of goats blinded by the
brilliance of the sun after so many months of nocturnal
terror, they were confused in the light, there were so many
at the same time that he didn't see them as two thousand
separate children but as a huge shapeless animal that was
giving off an impersonal stench of sun-baked skin and making a noise of deep waters and its multiple nature saved it
from destruction, because it was impossible to do away with
such a quantity of life without leaving a trace of horror that
would travel around the world, God damn it, there was
nothing to do, and with that conviction he called together
the high command, fourteen trembling commandants who
were never so to be feared because they had never been so
frightened, he took his time scrutinizing the eyes of each
one, one by one, and then he saw that he was alone against
them all, so he kept his head erect, hardened his voice,
exhorted them to unity now more than ever for the good
name and honor of the armed forces, absolved them of all
blame pounding his fist on the table so that they would not
see the tremor of uncertainty and ordered them as a consequence to continue at their posts fulfilling their duties with
the same zeal and the same authority as they had always
done, because my supreme and irrevocable decision is that
nothing has happened, meeting adjourned, I will answer
for it. As a simple means of precaution he took the children
out of the harbor fort and sent them in nocturnal boxcars
to the least-inhabited regions of the country while he confronted the storm unleashed by the official and solemn
declaration that it was not true, not only were there no
children in the power of the authorities but there was not

a single prisoner of any type in the jails, the rumor of the mass kidnapping was an infamous lie on the part of traitors to get people stirred up, the doors of the nation were open so that the truth could be established, let people come and look for it, they came, a commission from the League of Nations came and overturned the most hidden stones in the country and questioned all the people they wanted to and how they wanted to with such minute detail that Bendición Alvarado was to ask who were those intruders dressed like spiritualists who came into her house looking for two thousand children under the beds, in her sewing basket, in her paintbrush jars, and who finally bore public witness to the fact that they had found the jails closed down, the nation in peace, everything in place, and they had not found any indication to confirm the public suspicion that there had been or might have been a violation by intent or by action or by omission of the principles of human rights, rest easy, general, they left, he waved goodbye to them from the window with a handkerchief with embroidered edges and with the feeling of relief over something that was finished for good, goodbye, you horse's asses, smooth sailing and a prosperous trip, he sighed, the trouble's over, but General Rodrigo de Aguilar reminded him no, the trouble wasn't over because the children were still left general sir, and he slapped his forehead with the palm of his hand, God damn it, he'd forgotten completely, what'll we do with the children. Trying to free himself from that evil thought while a drastic formula was taking shape in his mind he had them take the children out of their hiding place in the jungle and carry them off in the opposite direction to the provinces of perpetual rain where there were no treasonous winds to spread their voices, where the animals of the earth rotted away as they walked and lilies grew on words and octopuses swam among the trees, he ordered them taken to the Andean grottoes of perpetual mists so that no one would find out where they were, for them to be transferred from the shady Novembers of putrefaction to the Februaries of horizontal days so that no one would know when they were, he sent them quinine tablets and wool blankets when he found out they were shivering with fever because for days and days they had been hidden in rice paddies with mud up to their necks so that the Red Cross airplanes wouldn't discover them, he had the light of the sun tinted red along with the glow of the stars to cure them of scarlet fever, he had them fumigated from the air with insecticides so that fat banana lice would not devour them, he sent them showers of candy and snowstorms of ice cream from airplanes and parachutes with loads of Christmas toys to keep them happy while a magical solution could occur to him, and in that way he was getting out of the reach of their evil memory, he forgot about them, he sank into the desolate swamp of the uncountable nights all the same of his domestic insomnia, he heard the metal blows strike nine o'clock, he took down the hens who were sleeping on the cornices of government house and took them to the chicken coop, he had not finished counting the creatures sleeping in the scaffolding when a mulatto servant girl came in to collect the eggs, he sensed the sunlight of her age, heard the sound of her bodice, he jumped on top of her, be careful general, she murmured trembling, you'll break the eggs, let them break, God damn it, he said, he threw her down with a cuff without undressing her or getting undressed himself disturbed by the anxiety to flee this Tuesday with its green-shit snow, sleeping creatures, he slipped, he fell into the illusory vertigo of a precipice cut by livid stripes of evasion and outpourings of sweat and the sighs of a wild woman and deceitful threats of oblivion, on the fallen woman he was leaving the curve of the urgent tinkle of the shooting star that was his gold spur, the trace of saltpeter from his wheeze of an urgent spouse, his dog whine, his terror of existing through the flash and the silent thunder of the instantaneous explosion of the deep spark, but at the bottom of the precipice there was the shitted slime again, the hens' insomniac sleep, the affliction of the mulatto girl who got up with her dress all smeared by the yellow molasses of the yolks lamenting now you see what I told you general, the eggs broke, and he muttered trying to tame the rage of another

94

love without love, write down how many they were, he told
her, I'll take it out of your wages, he left, it was ten o'clock,
he examined one by one the gums of the cows in the stables, he saw one of his women quartered by pain on the
floor of her hut and he saw the midwife who took from out
of her insides a steaming baby with the umbilical cord
wrapped around its neck, it was a boy, what name shall we
give him general sir, whatever you feel like, he answered,
it was eleven o'clock, as on every night during his regime
he counted the sentries, checked the locks, covered the
birdcages, put out the lights, it was twelve o'clock, the
nation was at peace, the world was asleep, he went to his
bedroom through the darkened building across the strips
of light from the fleeting dawns of the beacon turns, he
hung up the lamp for leaving on the run, he put up the
three bars, ran the three bolts, closed the three locks, sat
down on the portable latrine, and while he was passing his
meager urine he caressed the inclement child of a herniated
testicle until the twist was straightened out, it fell asleep in
his hand, the pain ceased, but it returned immediately with
a lightning flash of panic when in through the window there
came the lash of a wind from beyond the confines of the
saltpeter deserts which scattered about the bedroom the
sawdust of a song about tender-aged throngs who were
asking about a gentleman who went to war who were sighing what pain what grief who climbed up onto a tower to
see if he was coming who saw him coming back that he
came back that well in a velvet box what pain what mourning, and it was a chorus of such numerous and distant
voices that he could have gone to sleep with the illusion
that the stars were singing, but he got up irate, that's
enough, God damn it, he shouted, either them or me, he
shouted, and it was them, because before dawn he ordered
them to put the children in a barge loaded with cement,
take them singing to the limits of the territorial waters,
blow them up with a dynamite charge without giving them
time to suffer as they kept on singing, and when the three
officers who carried out the crime came to attention before
him with news general sir that his order had been carried

out, he promoted them two grades and decorated them with the medal of loyalty, but then he had them shot without honors as common criminals because there were orders that can be given but which cannot be carried out, God damn it, poor children. Experiences as harsh as that confirmed his very ancient certainty that the most feared enemy is within oneself in the confidence of the heart, that the very men he was arming and raising up so that they would support his regime will end up sooner or later spitting in the hand that feeds them, he wiped them out with one stroke, he took others out of nowhere, raised them to the highest ranks pointing at them according to the impulse of his inspiration, you to captain, you to colonel, you to general, and all the rest to lieutenant, what the hell, he watched them grow in their uniforms until they burst the seams, he lost sight of them, and a casual event like the discovery of two thousand sequestered children permitted him to discover that it was not just one man who had failed him but the whole supreme command of the armed forces who are only good for making me use up more milk and in times of trouble they shit in the plate they've just eaten out of, God damn it, I made them rich, he had won bread and respect for them, and yet he didn't have a moment's rest trying to keep clear of their ambition, he kept the most dangerous closest by to keep a better eye on them, the least bold he sent to frontier garrisons, because of them he had accepted the occupation by the marines, mother, not to fight yellow fever as Ambassador Thompson had written in the official communiqué, nor to protect him from public unrest, as the exiled politicians said, but to show our military men how to be decent people, and that's how it was, mother, to each his own, they taught them to walk with shoes on, to wipe themselves with paper, to use condoms, they were the ones who taught me the secret of maintaining parallel services to stir up distractive rivalries among the military, they invented for me the office of state security, the general investigation agency, the national department of public order, and so many other messes that I couldn't even remember them myself, identical organisms that he made look different in order to rule with more relaxation in the midst of the storm making them believe that some were being watched by others, mixing beach sand in with the gunpowder in the barracks and confusing the truth of his intentions with images of the opposite truth, and yet there were uprisings, he would storm into the barracks chewing the froth of his bile, shouting get out of the way you bastards here comes the one who gives the orders to the fright of the officers who were holding target practice with pictures of me, disarm them, he ordered without stopping but with so much authority that they disarmed themselves, take off those men's clothes you're wearing, he ordered, they took them off, the San Jerónimo base is in revolt general sir, he went in through the main gate dragging his huge feet of an old man in pain through a double file of mutinous guards who rendered him the honors of general supreme chief, he appeared in the post of the rebel command, without escort, without a weapon, but shouting with an explosion of power get down flat on the floor because the one who can do everything has arrived, on the floor, you bastards, nineteen officers of the general staff fell to the floor, face down, he paraded them eating dirt through the coastal villages so that the people could see how much a military man without a uniform is worth, sons of bitches, he heard over the other shouts in the aroused barracks his own irrevocable orders for the organizers of the revolt to be shot in the back, they displayed their corpses hanging by the heels in sun and dew so that nobody would fail to know how those who spit on God end up, tricky bastards, but the trouble didn't end with those bloody purges because with the least bit of carelessness he would find himself once more under the menace of that tentacular parasite he thought he had pulled out by the roots and which was proliferating again in the north winds of his power, in the shadow of the obligatory privileges and the crumbs of authority and the confidence of interest that he had to concede to the bravest officers even against his own will because it was impossible for him to maintain himself without them but also with them, condemned

97

forever to live breathing the same air which asphyxiated him, God damn it, it wasn't fair, as it wasn't possible either to live with the perpetual surprise of the pureness of my comrade General Rodrigo de Aguilar who had come into my office with the face of a dead man anxious to know what had happened to those two thousand children of my first prize because everybody says we drowned them in the sea, and he said without changing expression not to believe rumors spread by traitors, old friend, the children are growing up in God's peace, he told him, every night I can hear them singing over there, he said, pointing with a broad sweep of his hand to an indefinite place somewhere in the universe, and he left Ambassador Evans himself wrapped in an aura of uncertainty when he replied to him impassively I don't know what children you're talking about since your own country's delegate to the League of Nations has made a public statement that the children in the schools are all there and in good health, what the hell, the mess is over, and yet he could not stop them from waking him up in the middle of the night with the news general sir that the two largest garrisons in the country were in revolt and also the Conde barracks two blocks away from the presidential palace, an insurrection of the most dangerous kind led by General Bonivento Barboza who had dug himself in with fifteen hundred very well armed and well supplied troops with matériel obtained as contraband through consuls sympathetic to the opposition politicians, so things are in no shape for licking one's fingers general sir, now we really are fucked up. In other times that volcanic subversion would have been a stimulant for his passion for risks, but he knew better than anyone what the real weight of his age was, that he barely had enough will to resist the ravages of his secret world, that on winter nights he could not get to sleep without first placating the herniated testicle in the hollow of his hand with a coo of tenderness of sleep my sweet to the child of painful whistles, that his spirits were slipping away as he sat on the toilet pushing out his soul drop by drop as through a filter thickened by the mold of so many nights of solitary urination, that his memory was unraveling, that he

98

was not really sure he knew who was who, or from whom, at the mercy of an inescapable fate in that pitiful house which for some time he would have liked to exchange for another, far away from here, in some Indian settlement where no one would know that he had been the only president of the nation for so many and such long years that not even he himself had counted them, and still, when General Rodrigo de Aguilar offered himself as a mediator to negotiate a decorous compromise with the subversion he did not find himself in the presence of the dotty old man who would fall asleep at audiences but with the bison of old who without thinking about it for one instant answered not on your life, that he wasn't leaving, although it wasn't a question of leaving or not leaving but that everything is against us general sir, even the church, but he said no, the church is with the one in charge, he said, the generals of the high command having been meeting for forty-eight hours now already had not been able to reach an agreement, it doesn't matter he said, you'll see what they decide when they find out who pays them the most, the leaders of the civilian opposition have finally shown their faces and were conspiring openly in the street, all the better, he said, hang one from each lamppost on the main square so they'll know who the one is who can do anything, there's no way general sir, the people are with them, that's a lie, he said, the people are with me, so they won't get me out of here except dead, he decided, pounding the table with his rough maiden's hand as he only did in final decisions, and he slept until milking time when he found the reception room a shambles, because the insurrectionists in the Conde barracks had catapulted rocks which had not left one window intact in the eastern gallery and tallow balls which came in through the broken windows and kept the inhabitants of the building in a state of panic all through the night, if you could have seen general sir, we haven't closed an eye running back and forth with blankets and buckets of water to put out the puddles of fire that were lighting up in the least expected corner, but he scarcely paid any attention, I already told you not to pay them any heed, he said, dragging his graveyard feet along the corridors of ashes and scraps of carpets and singed tapestries, but they're going to keep it up, they told him, they had sent word that the flaming balls were just a warning, that the explosions will come after general sir, but he crossed the garden without paying attention to anyone, in the last shadows he breathed in the sound of the newborn roses, the disorders of the cocks in the sea wind, what shall we do general, I already told you not to pay any attention to them, God damn it, and as on every day at that hour he went to oversee the milking, so as on every day at that hour the insurrectionists in the Conde barracks saw the mule cart with the six barrels of milk from the presidential stable appear, and in the driver's seat there was the same lifetime carter with the oral message that the general sends you this milk even though you keep on spitting in the hand that feeds you, he shouted it out with such innocence that General Bonivento Barboza gave the order to accept it on the condition that the carter taste it first so that they could be sure it wasn't poisoned, and then they opened the iron gates and the fifteen hundred rebels looking down from the inside balconies saw the cart drive in to the center of the paved courtyard, they saw the orderly climb up onto the driver's seat with a pitcher and a ladle to give the carter the milk to taste, they saw him uncork the first barrel, they saw him floating in the ephemeral backwash of a dazzling explosion and they saw nothing else to the end of time in the volcanic heat of the mournful yellow mortar building in which no flower ever grew, whose ruins remained suspended for an instant in the air from the tremendous explosion of the six barrels of dynamite. That's that, he sighed in the presidential palace, shaken by the seismic wind that blew down four more houses around the barracks and broke the wedding crystal in cupboards all the way to the outskirts of the city, that's that, he sighed, when the garbage trucks removed from the courtyards of the harbor fort the corpses of eighteen officers who had been shot in double rows in order to save ammunition, that's that, he sighed when General Rodrigo de Aguilar came to attention before him with the news general sir that once again there was no more room in the jails for political prisoners, that's that, he sighed, when the bells began to peal in celebration, the festival rockets, the music of glory that announced the advent of another hundred years of peace, that's that, God damn it, the mess is over, he said, and he was so convinced, so careless about himself, so negligent about his personal safety that one morning he was crossing the courtyard on his way back from the milking and his instinct failed him as he did not see in time the bogus leper who rose up out of the rosebushes to cut off his path in the slow October drizzle and only too late did he see the sudden glimmer of the flourished revolver, the trembling index finger that began to squeeze the trigger when he shouted with his arms opened wide offering him his chest, I dare you you bastard, I dare you, dazzled by the surprise that his time had come contrary to the clearest forecasts of the basins, shoot if you've got any balls, he shouted, in the imperceptible instant of hesitation in which a pale star lighted up in the eyes of the attacker, his lips withered, his will trembled, and then he let go with both fists as hammers on his eardrums, he dropped him, he moved him on the ground with a pile-driver kick on the jaw, from another world he heard the uproar of the guard who came running to his shouts, he passed through the blue explosion of the continuous thunder of the five explosions of the false leper writhing in a pool of blood having shot himself in the stomach with the five bullets in his revolver so that he would not be taken alive by the fearsome interrogators of the presidential guard, he heard over the other shouts in the aroused building his own terminating orders that the body be quartered as a lesson, they sliced it up, they displayed the head smeared with rock salt in the main square, the right leg in the eastern confines of Santa María del Altar, the left one in the limitless saltpeter deserts of the west, one arm on the plains, the other in the jungle, the pieces of torso fried in hog fat and exposed to sun and dew until all that was left was naked bone as chancy and difficult as things were in this nigger whorehouse so that there would be no one who didn't know how those who raised their hands against their father ended up, and still green with rage he went among the rosebushes that the presidential guard had cleaned of lepers at bayonet point to see if at last they would show their faces, sneaky bastards, he went up to the main floor kicking aside the cripples to see if at last they would learn who it was who put their mothers to birth, sons of bitches, he went along the corridors shouting for them to get out of the way, God damn it, here comes the one who gives the orders in the midst of the panic of office workers and the persistent adulators who proclaimed him the eternal one, all through the house he left the rocky trail of his blacksmith-oven wheeze, he disappeared into the hearing room like a fugitive lightning flash toward the private quarters, he went into the bedroom, shut the three crossbars, the three bolts, the three locks, and with his fingertips he took off the pants he was wearing that were soaked in shit. He did not find a moment of rest as he sniffed round about to find the hidden enemy who had armed the bogus leper, for he felt that there was someone within reach of his hand, someone that close to his life who knew the hiding place of his honey, who had his eye at the keyholes and his ears at the walls every minute and everywhere just like my pictures, a voluble presence who whistled in the January trade winds and he recognized him in the jasmine embers on hot nights, one who had pursued him months on end in the fright of his insomnia dragging his fearful ghostly feet through the most hidden rooms of the darkened building, until one night at dominoes he saw the omen materialize in a pensive hand that finished the game with the double five, and it was as if an inner voice had revealed that that hand was the hand of treason, God damn it, it's him, he said to himself perplexed, and then he raised his eyes through the flow of light from the lamp hanging over the center of the table and met the handsome artilleryman's eyes of my soul comrade General Rodrigo de Aguilar, what a mess, his strong right arm, his sacred accomplice, it wasn't possible, he thought, all the more pained as he deciphered more deeply the weave of the false truths with which they had diverted his attention for so many years in order to hide the brutal truth that my lifetime comrade was in the service of politicians of fortune whom for convenience' sake he had taken from the darkest corners of the federalist war and had made them rich and had heaped fabulous privileges upon them, he had let himself be used by them, he had tolerated the fact that they were using him to rise up to a point that the old aristocracy swept away by the irresistible breath of the liberal whirlwind had never dreamed of and they still wanted more, God damn it, they wanted the place of the elect of God that he had reserved for himself, they wanted to be me, motherfuckers, with the way lighted by the glacial lucidity and the infinite prudence of the man who had managed to accumulate the most confidence and authority in his regime by taking advantage of the privileges of being the only person from whom he accepted papers to sign, he had him read aloud the executive orders and ministerial laws that only I could put through, he pointed out the amendments, he signed with his thumbprint and underneath he stamped it with the ring which he then put away in a strongbox whose combination only he knew, to your health, comrade, he always said to him when he handed him the signed papers, here's something to wipe yourself with, he told him laughing, and that was how General Rodrigo de Aguilar had succeeded in establishing another system of power within the power as widespread and as fruitful as mine, and not content with that in the shadows he had set up the mutiny of the Conde barracks with the complicity and unreserved assistance of Ambassador Norton, his buddy in matters of Dutch whores, his fencing master, the one who had smuggled in the ammunition in barrels of Norwegian cod under the protection of diplomatic immunity while he would use balm on me at the domino table with the incense candles saying there was no government more friendly, or just and exemplary than mine, and they were also the ones who had put the revolver in the hand of the false leper along with fifty thousand pesos in bills cut in half which we found buried at the attacker's home, and the other half of which was to be turned over after the crime by my own lifetime comrade, mother, what a bitter mess, and still they didn't resign themselves to failure but had ended up conceiving the perfect coup without shedding a drop of blood, not even yours general sir, because General Rodrigo de Aguilar had collected the most unimpeachable evidence that I spent my sleepless nights conversing with vases and oil paintings of patriots and archbishops in the darkened building, that I took the cows' temperature with a thermometer and gave them phenacetin to eat in order to bring down their fever, that I had had a tomb built for an admiral of the ocean sea who did not exist except in my feverish imagination when I myself with my own blessed eyes had seen the three caravels anchored across the harbor from my window, that I had squandered public funds on the irrepressible addiction of buying ingenious inventions and had even tried to get the astronomers to upset the solar system in order to please a beauty queen who had only existed in the visions of his delirium, and that during an attack of senile dementia had ordered two thousand children put on a barge loaded with cement that was dynamited at sea, mother, just imagine, what sons of bitches, and it was on the basis of that solemn testimony that General Rodrigo de Aguilar and the high command of the presidential guard in plenary session had decided to intern him in the asylum for illustrious old men on the reefs at midnight of March first next during the annual banquet in honor of the Holy Guardian Angel, the patron saint of bodyguards, or within three days general sir, just imagine, but in spite of the imminence and scope of the conspiracy he showed no sign that might have aroused the suspicion that he had uncovered it, but at the appointed hour as every year he received his personal guard as guests and had them sit at the banquet table for apéritifs until General Rodrigo de Aguilar arrived to make the toast of honor, he chatted with them, laughed with them, one after the other, the officers furtively looked at their watches, put them to their ears, wound them, it was five minutes to twelve and General Rodrigo de Aguilar hadn't arrived, it was as hot as a ship's boiler and there was a perfume of flowers, it smelled of gladioli and tulips, it smelled of live roses in the closed room, somebody opened a window, we breathe, we look at our watches, we feel a soft sea breeze with the smell of the delicate stew of a wedding feast, they were all sweating except him, we were all suffering from the drowsiness of the moment under the firm glow of the age-old animal who blinked with open eyes in a space of his own reserved in another age of the world, health, he said, the hand with no appeal like a languid lily raised again the glass with which he had toasted all evening without drinking, the visceral sound of watch works in the silence of a final abyss, it was twelve o'clock but General Rodrigo de Aguilar was not arriving, someone started to get up, please, he said, he turned him to stone with the fatal look of nobody move, nobody breathe, nobody live without my permission until twelve o'clock finished chiming, and then the curtains parted and the distinguished Major General Rodrigo de Aguilar entered on a silver tray stretched out full length on a garnish of cauliflower and laurel leaves, steeped with spices, oven brown, embellished with the uniform of five golden almonds for solemn occasions and the limitless loops for valor on the sleeve of his right arm, fourteen pounds of medals on his chest and a sprig of parsley in his mouth, ready to be served at a banquet of comrades by the official carvers to the petrified horror of the guests as without breathing we witness the exquisite ceremony of carving and serving, and when every plate held an equal portion of minister of defense stuffed with pine nuts and aromatic herbs, he gave the order to begin, eat hearty gentlemen.

HE HAD SKIRTED the reefs of so many earthly disorders, so many ominous eclipses, so many flaming tallow balls in the sky that it seemed impossible for someone from our time to trust still the prognostications of the cards regarding his fate. Yet, while the plans for reassembling and embalming the body went forward, even the most candid among us waited without so confessing for the fulfillment of ancient predictions, such as the one that said that on the day of his death the mud from the swamps would go back upriver to its source, that it would rain blood, that hens would lay pentagonal eggs, and that silence and darkness would cover the universe once more because he was the end of creation. It was impossible not to believe all of this since the few newspapers still publishing were still dedicated to proclaiming his eternity and counterfeiting his splendor with material from their files, every day they displayed him to us as during ecstatic times and on the front page in his tenacious uniform with the five sad pips of his days of glory, with more authority and diligence and better health than ever in spite of the fact that many years ago we had lost count of his age, in the usual pictures he was once more dedicating well-known monuments or public installations that no one knew about in real life, he presided over solemn ceremonies which they said had taken place yesterday but which had really taken place during the last century, even though we knew it wasn't true, because no one had seen him in public ever since Leticia Nazareno's atrocious death when he was left alone in that no man's land of a house while the daily affairs of government went along all by themselves and only through the momentum of his immense power over so many years, he locked himself up until death in the run-down palace from whose highest windows we were now watching with tight hearts the same gloomy sunset that he must have seen so many times from his throne of illusions, we saw the intermittent beacon of the lighthouse as it flooded the ruined salons with its green and languid waters, we saw the lamps of the poor inside the shell of what had once been the coral reefs of solar glass of the ministries which had been invaded by hordes of poor people when the multicolored huts on the harbor hills had been leveled by another of our numerous cyclones, we saw below the scattered, steamy city, the instantaneous horizon of pale lightning flashes in the crater of ashes of the sea that had been sold, the first night without him, his vast lakelike empire of malarial anemones, its hot villages on the deltas of muddy tributaries, the avid barbed-wire fences of his private provinces where there flourished without count or measure a new species of magnificent cows who were born with the hereditary presidential brand. Not only had we ended up really believing that he had been conceived to survive the third comet but that conviction had infused us with a security and a restful feeling that we tried to hide with all manner of jokes about old age, we attributed the senile characteristics of tortoises and the habits of elephants to him, in bars we told the story that someone had announced to the cabinet that he had died and that they had asked each other in fright who's going to tell him, ha, ha, ha, when the truth was that it wouldn't have mattered to him if he knew it or not or he himself wouldn't have been very sure whether that street joke was true or false, because at that time no one except him knew that all he had left in the pockets of his memory were a few odd scraps of the vestiges of the past, that he was alone in the world, deaf as a post, dragging his thick decrepit feet through dark offices where someone in a frock coat and starched collar had made an enigmatic signal to him with a handkerchief, hello, he said to him, the mistake became law, office workers in the presidential palace had to stand up with a white handkerchief when he passed, the sentries along the corridors, the lepers in the rose beds waved to him with a white handkerchief when he passed, hello general sir, hello, but he didn't hear, he had heard nothing since the sunset mourning rites for Leticia Nazareno when he thought that the birds in his cages were losing their voices from so much singing and he fed them his own honey so they would sing louder, he fed them Cantorina with an eyedropper, he sang them songs from a different age, bright January moon, he sang, for he had not realized that it was not the birds who were losing the strength of their voices but that it was he who was hearing less and less, and one night the buzzing in his eardrums broke all apart, it was over, it had been changed into an atmosphere of mortar through which only the farewell laments of the illusory ships from the shadows of power could pass, imaginary winds passed, the racket of inner birds which finally consoled him for the abyss of silence of the birds of reality. The few people who had access to government house then would see him in the wicker rocking chair enduring the drowsiness of two in the afternoon under the arbor of wild pansies, he had unbuttoned his tunic, had taken off his saber and the belt with the national colors, he had taken off his boots but left on the purple socks from the twelve dozen the Supreme Pontiff had sent him from his private sockery, the girls from a nearby school who would climb over the rear walls where the guard was less rigid had surprised him many times in that heavy insomnia, pale, with medicinal leaves stuck to his temples, tiger-striped by the bars of light from the arbor in the ecstasy of a manta ray lying face up at the bottom of a pool, old soursop, they would shout at him, he would see them distorted in the haze of the quivering heat, he would smile at them, wave at them with the hand without the velvet glove, but he couldn't hear them, he caught the shrimp-mud stench of the sea breeze, he caught the pecking of the hens on his toes, but he did not catch the luminous thunder of the cicadas, he couldn't hear the girls, he couldn't hear anything. His only contacts with the reality of this world were by then a few scattered scraps of his largest memories, only they kept him alive after he had been despoiled of the affairs of state and stayed swimming in a state of innocence in the limbo of power, only then did he confront the devastating winds of his excessive years when he wandered at dusk through the deserted building, hid in the darkened offices, tore the margins off ledgers and in his florid hand wrote on them the remaining residue of the last memories that preserved him from death, one night he had written my name is Zacarías, he read it again under the fleeting light of the beacon, he read it over and over and the name repeated so many times ended up seeming remote and alien to him, God damn it, he said to himself, tearing up the strip of paper, I'm me, he said to himself, and he wrote on another strip that he had turned a hundred around the time the comet had passed again although by then he wasn't sure how many times he'd seen it pass, and on another ledger strip he wrote from memory honor the wounded and honor the faithful soldiers who met death at foreign hands, for there were periods when he wrote down everything he thought, everything he knew, he wrote on a piece of cardboard and tacked it to the door of a toilet that it was fourbidden to do any dirty bizness in toylets because he had opened that door by mistake and had surprised a high-ranking officer squatting down and masturbating into the bowl, he wrote down the few things he remembered to make sure that he would never forget them, Leticia Nazareno, he wrote, my only and legitimate spouse who had taught him to read and write in the ripeness of his old age, he made an effort to bring back her public image, he

109

tried to see her again with her taffeta parasol with the colors of the flag and her first lady's fur piece of silver-fox tails, but all he could manage was to remember her naked at two in the afternoon under the flour-haze light of the mosquito netting, he remembered the slow repose of your soft and pale body surrounded by the hum of the electric fan, he felt your living teats your smell of a bitch in heat, the corrosive humors of your ferocious novice nun hands that curdled milk and rusted gold and withered flowers, but they were good hands for love, because only she had reached the inconceivable triumph of take your boots off so you don't soil my Brabant sheets, and he took them off, take off your saber, and your truss, and your leggings take everything off my love I can't feel you, and he took everything off for you as he had never done before and would never do again for any woman after Leticia Nazareno, my only and legitimate love, he sighed, he wrote down the signs on the yellowed ledger margins that he rolled like cigarettes and hid in the most unlikely chinks in the house where only he would be able to find them to remember who he was himself when he could no longer remember anything, where no one ever found them when even the image of Leticia Nazareno had finally slipped away down the drain of memory and all that remained was the indestructible memory of his mother Bendición Alvarado on the goodbye afternoons at the sub-urban mansion, his dying mother who had gathered the hens together by making noise with the kernels of corn in a calabash gourd so that he wouldn't notice that she was dying, who still brought him fruit drinks to the hammock hung between the tamarinds so that he wouldn't suspect that she could barely breathe because of her pain, his mother who had conceived him alone, who had borne him alone, who was rotting away alone until the solitary suffer-ing became so intense that it was stronger than her pride and she had to ask her son to look at my back to see why I feel this hot-ember heat that won't let me live, and she took off her blouse, turned around, and with silent horror he saw that her back had been chewed away by steaming ulcers in whose guava pulp pestilence the tiny bubbles of the first maggots were bursting. Bad times those general sir, there were no secrets of state that were not in the public domain, there was no order that was carried out with complete certainty ever since the exquisite corpse of General Rodrigo de Aguilar had been served up at the banquet table, but he didn't care, he didn't care about the stumbling of power during the bitter months in which his mother was rotting away in a slow fire in the bedroom next to his after the doctors most adept in Asiatic scourges decreed that her illness was not the plague, or scabies, or yaws, or any other Oriental pestilence, but some Indian curse that could only be cured by the one who had cast it, and he understood that it was death and he shut himself up to care for his mother with the abnegation of a mother, he stayed to rot with her so that no one would see her cooking in her stew of maggots, he ordered them to bring her hens to government house, they brought him the peacocks, the painted birds who wandered about at their pleasure through salons and offices so that his mother would not miss the rustic activities of the suburban mansion, he himself burned annato logs in the bedroom so that no one would catch the death stench of his dying mother, he himself with germicidal salves consoled the body that was red with Mercurochrome, yellow with picric, blue with methylene, he himself daubed with Turkish balms the steaming ulcers against the advice of the minister of health who was frightened to death of curses, what the hell, mother, it's better if we die together, he said, but Bendición Alvarado was aware of being the only one who was dying and she tried to reveal to her son the family secrets that she didn't want to carry to her grave, she told him how her placenta had been thrown to the hogs, lord, how it was that I could never establish which of so many back-trail fugitives was your father, she tried to tell him for history that she had conceived him standing up and with her hat on because of the storm of bluebottle flies around the wineskins of fermented molasses in the back room of a bar, she had given birth to him with difficulty in the entranceway to a convent, she had recognized him in the lights of the melancholy harps of the geraniums and his right testicle was the size of a fig and he relieved himself like a bellows and exhaled a bagpipe sigh with his breathing, she wrapped him up in the rags the novices had given her and she displayed him in marketplaces in case she might find someone who knew of a remedy that was better and above all cheaper than honey which was the only thing they recommended to her for his malformation, they consoled her with clichés, you can't get around fate, they told her, because after all the child was good for everything except playing wind instruments, they told her, and only a circus fortuneteller noticed that the newborn baby had no lines on the palm of his hand and that meant he had been born to be a king, and that's how it was, but he wasn't paying any attention to her, he begged her to go to sleep without digging up the past because it was more comfortable for him to believe that those stumbling blocks in national history were feverish deliriums, sleep, mother, he begged her, he wrapped her from head to toe in a linen sheet one of the many he had had made so as not to hurt her sores, he laid her down to sleep on her side with her hand on her heart, he consoled her with don't try to remember that sorry mess, mother, in any case I'm me, sleep softly. The many and ardent official attempts to calm the public rumors that the matriarch of the nation was rotting away in life had been useless, they published contrived medical reports, but the very couriers who carried the bulletins averred that what they themselves denied was true, that the air of corruption was so intense in the dying woman's bedroom that it had even frightened the lepers away, that they had butchered rams in order to bathe her in warm blood, that they took away sheets soaked in iridescent matter that flowed from her sores and no matter how much they washed them they were unable to return them to their original splendor, that no one had seen him again in the milking stalls or in the concubines' rooms where he had always been seen at daybreak even in the worst of times, the primate archbishop himself had offered to administer the last rites to the dying woman but he had left him standing at the door, no one's dying, father, don't believe rumors, he told him, he shared his meals with his mother on the same plate with the same spoon in spite of the pesthouse atmosphere in the room, he bathed her before putting her to bed with thankful-dog soap while his heart stood still with pity from the instructions she gave him with the last threads of her voice for the care of the animals after her death, that the peacocks should not be plucked to make hats, yes mother, he said, and he rubbed her body all over with creolin, don't let them make the birds sing at parties, yes mother, and he wrapped her in the sleeping sheet, they should take the hens out of their nests when there's thunder so they don't hatch basilisks, yes mother, and he laid her down with her hand on her heart, yes mother, sleep easy, he kissed her forehead, he slept the few hours remaining lying face down next to the bed, hanging on the drift of her sleep, hanging on the interminable delirium that was becoming more lucid as it approached death, learning with his accumulated rage gathered each night to bear up under the immense fury of the Monday of grief when the terrible silence of the world at dawn awoke him and it was that his mother of my life Bendición Alvarado had stopped breathing, and then he unwrapped the loathsome body and saw in the tenuous glow of the first cock's crow that there was another identical body with the hand on the heart painted in profile on the sheet, and he saw that the painted body had no plague wrinkles or ravages of old age but that it was firm and tight as if painted in oil on both sides of the shroud and it gave off a natural fragrance of young flowers that purified the hospital atmosphere of the bedroom and try as they might by rubbing with nitrate rock and boiling it in lye they could not erase it from the sheet because it was integrated front and back into the very material of the linen, and it was eternal linen, but he had not been calm enough to measure the scope of that miracle but had left the bedroom slamming the door with such rage that it sounded like a shot throughout the building, and then the bells in the cathedral began tolling and then those of every church in the nation which tolled without pause for one hundred days, and those who woke up to the bells understood with no illusions that he was once more the master of all his power and that the enigma of his heart oppressed by the rage over that death was rising up stronger than ever against the whims of reason and dignity and indulgence, because his mother of my life Bendición Alvarado had died on that early dawn of Monday February twenty-third and a new century of confusion and scandal was beginning in the world. None of us was old enough to have witnessed that death but the fame of the funeral ceremonies had come down to our times and we had trustworthy reports that he did not go back to being what he had been before for the rest of his life, no one had the right to disturb his orphan's insomnia for much more than the hundred days of official mourning, he was not seen again in the house of grief whose confines had been overflown by the immense resonances of the funeral bells, he had no time except for his mourning, he spoke to himself in sighs, the household guard went about barefoot as during the first years of his regime and only the hens could do what they wanted in the forbidden house whose monarch had become invisible, bleeding with rage in the wicker rocking chair while his mother of my soul Bendición Alvarado was going through those wastelands of heat and misery inside a coffin full of sawdust and chopped ice so that her body would not rot more than it had in life, for the body had been carried in a solemn procession to the least-explored corners of his realm so that no one would go without the privilege of honoring her memory, they carried it with hymns of black-ribbon winds to stations on the upland plains where it was received with the same mournful music by the same mournful throngs who in other days of glory had come to see the power hidden in the shadows of the presidential coach, they displayed the body in the convent of the Sisters of Charity where a wandering birdwoman at the beginning of time had given difficult birth to a no man's son who became king, they opened the large doors of the sanctuary for the first time in a century, mounted troops made a roundup of Indians in the villages, they herded them along, drove them with rifle butts into the vast nave of the church afflicted by the icy suns of the stained-glass windows where nine bishops in pontificals sang Tenebrae, rest in peace in your glory, the deacons sang, the acolytes, rest in your ashes, they sang, outside it was raining on the geraniums, the novices distributed cane juice and the bread of the dead, people sold spareribs, rosaries, flasks of holy water under the stone arcades of the courtyards, there was music in the sidewalk cafés, there was gunpowder, there was dancing in the entranceways, it was Sunday, now and forever, they were years of festivals along the escape trails and the foggy mountain passes where his mother of my death Bendición Alvarado had passed into life following the son who was making merry in the federalist whirlwind, for she had taken care of him during the war, she had kept the troops' mules from trampling him when he flopped onto the ground rolled up in a blanket, unconscious, talking nonsense because of tertian fever, she had tried to inculcate in him her ancestral fear of the dangers that lay in wait in the cities by the shadowy sea for people from the plains, she was afraid of the viceroys, the statues, the crabs that drink the tears of the newborn, she had trembled in terror before the majesty of the house of power which she first saw through the rain on the night of the attack without having imagined then that it was the house where she would die, the house of solitude where he was, where he asked himself in the heat of rage lying face down on the floor where the hell have you gone, mother, in what grubby mangrove swamp has your body got entangled, who shoos the butterflies from your face, he sighed, prostrate with grief, while his mother Bendición Alvarado floated along under a canopy of banana leaves through the nauseating vapors of the swamps to be displayed in backwoods public schools, in barracks on the saltpeter deserts, in Indian corrals, they displayed her in the main houses along with a picture of her when she was young, was languid, was beautiful, a diadem had been placed on her forehead, a lace gorget had been placed around her neck against her will, she had let them put powder on her face and lipstick on her mouth for just that one time, they put a silk tulip in her hand so that she would hold it that way, not like that, madam, like this, casually in her lap when the Venetian photographer of European monarchs took her official portrait as first lady as a final proof against any suspicion of substitution, and they were identical, for nothing had been left to chance, the body was being reconstructed in secret sessions as the cosmetics wore off and the skin wrinkled as the paraffin melted in the heat, they removed the mildew from her eyelids during the rainy season, army seamstresses kept her burial dress in shape as if it had been put on yesterday and they maintained in a state of grace the crown of orange blossoms and the veil of a virgin bride which she had never had during her lifetime, so that no one in this brothel of idolaters would ever dare repeat that you were different from your picture, mother, so that no one will forget who it is who rules till the end of time even in the poorest settlements on jungle sand dunes where after so many years of being forgotten at midnight they saw the return of the ancient riverboat with its wooden paddle wheel with all lights on and they received it with Easter drums thinking that the times of glory had returned, long live the stud, they shouted, blessed be the one who comes in the name of truth, they shouted, they jumped into the water with their fattened armadillos, with a pumpkin the size of an ox, they climbed over the carved wood railings to render the tribute of submission to the invisible power whose dice decided the fate of the nation and they stood breathless before the catafalque of chopped ice and rock salt which was multiplied by the startling glass of the mirrors in the presidential galley, exposed to public judgment under the fan blades in the archaic pleasure boat that traveled month after month among the ephemeral isles of the equatorial tributaries until it got lost in a nightmare age in which gardenias had the use of reason and iguanas flew about in the darkness, the world ended, the wooden wheel ran aground on sandbanks of gold, broke, the ice melted, the salt turned liquid, the swollen body remained floating adrift in a soup of sawdust, and yet it didn't rot, quite the contrary general sir, because then we saw her open her eyes and we saw that her pupils were bright and had the color of January wolfsbane and their usual quality of lunar stones, and even the most incredulous among us had seen the glass cover of the coffin fog over from the vapor of her breath and we had seen living and fragrant perspiration coming from her pores, and we saw her smile. You can't imagine what it was all like general sir, it was fantastic, we've seen mules give birth, we've seen flowers growing in the salt flats, we've seen deaf-mutes confused by the miracles of their own cries of miracle, miracle, miracle, they broke the glass of the coffin general sir and they were at the point of making mincemeat out of the corpse in order to distribute the relics, so we had to use a battalion of grenadiers to hold back the frantic mobs who were arriving in a tumult from the breeding ground of islands which is the Caribbean captivated by the news that the soul of your mother Bendición Alvarado had obtained from God the faculty of going against the laws of nature, they were selling shreds of the shroud, they were selling scapulars, waters from her body, cards with her picture as a queen, but it was such a huge and wild rabblement that it looked more like a torrent of untamed steers whose hoofs devastated everything they found in their path and they made an earthquake roar that even you yourself can hear from here if you listen carefully general sir, listen to it, and he cupped his hand behind his ear which was buzzing less, he listened carefully, and then he heard, mother of mine Bendición Alvarado, he heard the endless thunder, he saw the bubbling swamp of the vast crowd spreading out all the way to the horizon of the sea, he saw the torrent of lighted candles that brought out a different and even more radiant day within the radiant brightness of noon, for his mother of my soul Bendición Alvarado was returning to the city of her ancient terrors as she had arrived the first time with the turmoil of war, with the raw-meat smell of war, but free forever of the risks of the world because he had them tear the pages about the viceroys out of school primers so that they would not exist in history, he had forbidden the statues that disturbed your sleep, mother, so that now she was returning without her congenital fears on the shoulders of a peaceful multitude, she was returning without a coffin, under a clear sky, in an air forbidden to butterflies, overwhelmed by the golden weight of the religious offerings that had been hung on her during the interminable journey from the far reaches of the jungle across his vast and convulsed realm of sorrow, hidden under the pile of small gold crutches that recovered cripples had hung on her, the gold stars of shipwrecked sailors, the gold babies of incredulous barren women who had had to give emergency birth in the bushes, as in the war, general sir, drifting along in the center of the sweeping torrent of the biblical move of a whole nation which could not find a place to put down its kitchenware, its animals, the remains of a life with no more hope of redemption than the very secret prayers that Bendición Alvarado said during combat to turn the direction of the bullets shot at her son, how he had come in the tumult of the war with a red rag on his head shouting during the lull in fighting from the delirium of fever long live the liberal party, God damn it, long live victorious federalism, shitty Goths, even though really drawn along by the atavistic curiosity of knowing the sea, except that the misery-ridden crowd that had invaded the city with the corpse of his mother was more turbulent and frantic than any that had ravaged the country during the adventures of the federalist war, more voracious than that turmoil, more terrible than that panic, the most tremendous thing my eyes had seen in all the uncounted years of his power, the whole world general sir, look, what a wonder. Convinced by the evidence, he came out of the mist of his mourning, he came out pale, hard, with a black armband, resolved to make use of all the resources of his authority to attain the canonization of his mother Bendición Alvarado on the basis of the overwhelming proofs of her qualities as a saint, he sent his ministers of letters to Rome, once more he invited the apostolic nuncio for chocolate and cookies in the shafts of light under the pansy bower, he received him in a familiar way, he lying in his hammock, shirtless, fanning himself with his white hat, and the nuncio sitting opposite him with the cup of steaming chocolate, immune to the heat and the dust inside the lavender aura of his Sunday cassock, immune to the tropical languor, immune to the shitting of the dead mother's birds as they flew free through the puddlelike splotches of sun from the covering, he took measured sips of the vanilla chocolate, chewed the cookies with the modesty of a bride trying to delay the inevitable poison in the last sip, rigid in the wicker chair which he never let anyone sit in, only you, father, as on those mallow-mild afternoons of the days of glory when another old and innocent nuncio tried to convert him to the faith of Christ with Scholastic riddles from Thomas Aquinas, except that now I'm the one who is calling upon you to convert, father, that's the way the world turns, but I believe now, although in reality he didn't believe anything in this world or any other except that his mother of my life had a right to the glory of altars because of the very merits of her vocation for sacrifice and her exemplary modesty, so much so that he wasn't basing his request upon the public excitement over the fact that the north star moved along in the same direction as the funeral cortege and stringed instruments played all by themselves in their cabinets when they heard the corpse pass by but he based it on the virtue of this sheet which he unfurled full sail in the splendor of August so that the nuncio could see what indeed he did see printed on the texture of the linen, he saw the image of his mother Bendición Alvarado with no trace of old age or the ravages of disease lying on her side with her hand on her heart, he felt the dampness of eternal sweat on her fingers, he breathed in the fragrance of living flowers in the midst of the uproar of the birds roused up by the breath of the miracle, you can see what a wonder, father, he said, showing the sheet up and down and on both sides, even the birds recognize her, but the nuncio was absorbed in the cloth with an incisive attention that had been capable of discovering impurities of volcanic ash in the materials worked by the great masters of Christendom, he had known the cracks in character and even the doubts of a faith from the intensity of a color, he had suffered the ecstasy of the roundness of the earth lying face up under the dome of a solitary chapel in an unreal city where time did not pass but floated, until he got enough courage to take his eyes off the sheet and his deep contemplation and declared with a soft but irreparable tone that the body printed on the linen was not an act of Divine Providence to give us one more proof of His infinite mercy, not that or anything like it, your excellency, it was the work of a painter who was very skilled in the good and evil arts and who had abused your excellency's greatness of heart, because that wasn't oil paint it was house paint of the cheapest kind, for painting window frames, your excellency, beneath the smell of the natural resins that had dissolved in the paint the bastard dew of turpentine still remained, plaster crusts remained, a persistent dampness remained that was not the sweat of the last shudder of death as they had made him believe but the fake dampness of linen soaked in linseed oil and kept in dark places, believe me I'm terribly sorry, the nuncio concluded with genuine sadness, but he couldn't bring himself to say anything more as he faced the granite old man who was looking at him without blinking from the hammock, who had listened to him from the slime of his lugubrious Asiatic silences without even moving his mouth to contradict him in spite of the fact that no one knew better than he the truth of the secret miracle of the sheet in which I myself wrapped you with my own hands, mother, I was frightened with the first silence of your death which was as if the world had dawned at the bottom of the sea, I saw the miracle, God damn it, but in spite of his certainty he didn't interrupt the verdict of the nuncio, he only blinked a couple of times without closing his eyes, as iguanas do, he only smiled, it's all right, father, he finally sighed, it's probably the way you say, but I warn you that you carry the burden of your words, I'll repeat it letter by letter so that you won't forget it for the rest of your life you carry the burden of your words, father, I'm not responsible. The world remained in a lethargy during the week of evil omens in which he didn't get out of the hammock even to eat, he used the fan to shoo off the tame birds who alighted on his body, he shooed away the splotches of light coming through the pansies thinking they were tame birds, he received no one, he gave no orders, but the forces of public order remained aloof when the mobs of hired fanatics stormed the palace of the Apostolic Nunciature, sacked its museum of historic relics, surprised the nuncio taking his siesta outdoors in the peaceful backwaters of the inner garden, dragged him naked onto the street, shat on him general sir, just imagine, but he didn't move from the hammock, he didn't blink when they came to him with the news general sir that they were parading the nuncio through the business streets on a donkey under a downpour of dishwater thrown onto him from balconies, shouted pretty boy at him, miss vatican, suffer the little children to come unto me, and only when they left him half dead on the garbage heap in the public market did he get up out of the hammock waving the birds out of the way with his hands, appear in the hearing room waving away the cobwebs of mourning with the black armband and his eyes puffy from poor sleep, and then he gave orders for the nuncio to be placed on a life raft with provisions for three days and they cast him adrift on the lane that cruise ships took to Europe so that the whole world will know what happens to foreigners who lift their hands against the majesty of the nation, and the Pope will learn now and forever that he may be Pope in Rome with his ring on his finger sitting on his golden throne, but here I am what I am, God damn it, them and their shitty petticoats. It was an effective recourse, because before that year was out the process was initiated for the canonization of his mother Bendición Alvarado whose uncorrupted body was displayed for public veneration in the main nave of the cathedral, the Gloria was sung on altars, the state of war that he had declared against the Holy See was revoked, long live peace, the crowds on the main square shouted, long live God, they shouted, while in a solemn audience he received the auditor of the Sacred Congregation of the Rite and promoter and postulator of the faith Monsignor Demetrius Aldous, known as the Eritrene, to whom had been entrusted the mission of scrutinizing the life of Bendición Alvarado until not the slightest trace of doubt remained regarding the evidence of her sainthood, take as

long as you like, father, he said to him, holding his hand in
his, for he had an immediate confidence in that jaundiced
Abyssinian who loved life above all things, he ate iguana
eggs, general sir, he loved cockfights, the humor of mulatto
women, dancing the cumbia, just like us general sir, the
whole bag, and the most heavily guarded doors were
opened without restriction by his orders so that the scrutiny of the devil's advocate would not run into difficulties
of any kind, because there was nothing hidden just as there
was nothing invisible in his measureless nightmare realm
that wouldn't be an irrefutable proof that his mother of my
soul Bendición Alvarado was predestined to the glory of
altars, the nation is yours, father, here it is, and there he
had it, of course, the armed forces maintained order at the
palace of the Apostolic Nunciature across from which at
dawn could be seen the uncountable lines of restored lepers who came to show the newborn skin over their sores,
former victims of St. Vitus's dance came to thread needles
before the disbelieving, to display their fortunes came
those who had been enriched by the roulette table because
Bendición Alvarado had revealed the numbers in her
dreams to them, those who had had news of lost relatives
and friends, those who had found their drowned ones,
those who had had nothing and now had everything came,
paraded by without cease through the oven-hot office decorated with cannibal-killing muskets and prehistoric tortoises of Sir Walter Raleigh where the tireless Eritrene
listened to all without asking any questions, without inter-
rupting, soaked in sweat, alien to the plague of humanity
in decomposition that was accumulating in the office where
the air was rarefied by the smoke of his cigarettes which
were of the cheapest kind, he took detailed notes of the
declarations of the witnesses and had them sign here, with
your full name, or with an X, or like you general sir with
your fingerprint, in one way or another, but they signed,
the next one came in, just like the one before, I was consumptive, father, he said, I was consumptive, wrote the
Eritrene, and now listen to me, sign, I was impotent, father,
and now look how I can go all day long, I was impotent, he

wrote in indelible ink so that his careful writing would be safe from changes until the end of humanity, I had a live animal inside my belly, father, I had a live animal inside my belly, he wrote coldly, drunk with cheap bitter coffee, poisoned by the rancid tobacco of the cigarette that he lighted from the butt of the previous one, his collar unbuttoned like an oarsman's general sir, that's a real stud of a priest, yes sir, he said, a real stud, to each his own, working ceaselessly, not eating anything so as not to lose any time until well into the night, but even then he wouldn't take any rest but would appear freshly bathed in the dockside taverns in his rough patched cassock, he would arrive starving, sit down at the long plank table to share the bream stew with the longshoremen, he tore the fish apart with his fingers, he ground it right down to the bone with those Luciferine teeth that had their own glow in the dark, he drank his soup from the edge of the plate like a stevedore general sir, if you only could have seen him mingling with the human scum off the shabby sailing ships that weighed anchor loaded with fags and green bananas, loaded with shipments of unripe whores for the glass hotels of Curaçao, for Guantánamo, father, for Santiago de los Caballeros which doesn't even have a sea to get there by, father, for the saddest and most beautiful islands in the world that we go on dreaming about until the first light of dawn, father, remember how different we were when the schooners left, remember the parrot who could guess the future in the house of Matilde Arenales, the crabs that came walking out of the bowls of soup, the shark wind, the distant drums, life, father, bitchy life, boys, because he talks like us general sir, as if he'd been born in the dogfight district, he played ball on the beach, he learned to play the accordion better than the natives, he sang better than they, he learned the flowery language of the queens, he teased them in Latin, he got drunk with them in the fairy joints in the marketplace, he got into a fight with one of them because he said something bad about God, they started punching each other general sir, what shall we do, and he gave the order that nobody should separate them, they formed a circle around them, he won, the priest won general sir, I knew it, he said, pleased, he's a stud, and not as frivolous as everybody thought, because on those wild nights he found more truth than during the wearisome days in the palace of the Apostolic Nunciature, much more than in the shadowy suburban mansion that he had explored without permission one afternoon during a heavy rain when he thought he had tricked the sleepless vigilance of the presidential security services, he scrutinized it down to the last chink soaked by the interior rain from the roof gutters, trapped by the quicksands of malangas and the poisonous camellias of the splendid sleeping quarters that Bendición Alvarado had abandoned to the happiness of the servants, because she was good, father, she was humble, she put them to sleep on percale sheets while she slept on a bare mat on an army cot, she let them wear her first lady's Sunday clothes, they perfumed themselves with her bath salts, they frolicked naked with the orderlies in the colored bubbles in pewter bathtubs with lion's feet, they lived like queens while her life slipped past as she painted birds, cooked her vegetable mush on the wood fire, and cultivated medicinal plants for the emergencies of neighbors who would wake her up in the middle of the night with I've got a stomach spasm, ma'am, and she would give them watercress seeds to chew, that a godson was cross-eyed, and she would give him a worm remedy of epazote tea, I'm going to die, ma'am, but they didn't die because she held health in her hand, she was a living saint, father, she walked about in her own pure space through that mansion of pleasure where it had rained without pity ever since they took her by force to the presidential palace, it rained on the lotus blossoms on the piano, on the alabaster table in the sumptuous dining room which Bendición Alvarado never used because it's like sitting down to eat at an altar, just imagine, father, such a presentiment of sainthood, but in spite of the feverish testimony of the neighbors the devil's advocate found more traces of timidity than humility among the ruins, he found more proofs of poorness of spirit than abnegation among the ebony Neptunes and the pieces of native demons and warlike angels that were floating in the mangrove swamps of the former ballrooms, and on the other hand he did not find the slightest trace of that other difficult god, one and trine, who had sent him from the burning plains of Abyssinia in search of truth where it had never been, because he found nothing general sir, as he said nothing, what a mess. Yet Monsignor Demetrius Aldous was not satisfied merely with the scrutiny of the city but went up on muleback into the glacial limbo of the upland barrens trying to find the seeds of Bendición Alvarado's sainthood where her image might still not be perverted by the splendor of power, he rose out of the mist wrapped in a highwayman's cloak and wearing seven-league boots like a satanic apparition who at first aroused the fear and then the surprise and finally the curiosity of the uplanders who had never seen a human being of that color, but the astute Eritrene urged them to touch to convince themselves that he didn't give off tar, he showed them his teeth in the darkness, he got drunk with them eating cheese with his hand and drinking corn liquor out of the same gourd in order to win their trust in the gloomy little stores along the trails where at the dawn of other centuries they had known a striking birdwoman weighted down by her mad load of cages with chicks painted as nightingales, golden toucans, goatsuckers disguised as peacocks to trick mountain people on the funereal Sundays of upland fairs, she would sit there, father, in the glow of the bonfires, waiting for someone to do her the charity of going to bed with her on the wineskins full of molasses in the back of the store, in order to eat, father, only in order to eat, because no one was such a mountain hick as to buy those cheap goods of hers that faded with the first rain and fell apart when they walked, only she was so innocent, father, holy benediction of the birds, or of the barrens, as you wish, because no one knew for certain what her name was then or when she started calling herself Bendición Alvarado which couldn't have been her original name because it's not a name from these parts but for coastal people, what a mess, even that had been checked on by Satan's slippery prosecutor who was uncovering and digging out everything in spite of the presidential security thugs who tangled up the thread of the truth on him and put invisible barriers in his way, what do you think, general sir, they could hound him off a cliff like a deer, they could make his mule stumble on him, he stopped that with the personal order to watch him but to maintain his physical integrity repeat maintain physical integrity permitting absolute freedom all facilities fulfilling his mission by command without appeal from this highest authority obey carry out, signed I, and he repeated, I myself, conscious of the fact that with that decision he was taking on the terrible risk of learning the true image of his mother Bendición Alvarado during the forbidden times when she was still young, was languid, went about dressed in rags, barefoot, and had to use her lower parts in order to eat, but she was beautiful, father, and she was so innocent that she fitted out the cheapest lory parrots with tails from the finest cocks to make them pass for macaws, she repaired crippled hens with turkey-feather fans and sold them as birds of paradise, no one believed it, of course, no one was innocent enough to fall into the snare of the solitary birdwoman who whispered about in the mist of Sunday marketplaces to see who would say one and take her for nothing, because everybody on the barrens remembered her for her innocence and her poverty, and yet it seemed impossible to discover her identity because in the records of the monastery where she had been baptized her birth certificate could not be found and on the other hand they found three different ones for her son and on all three he was three times different, conceived three times on three different occasions, given a bad birth three times thanks to the artifices of national history which had entangled the threads of reality so that no one would be able to decipher the secret of his origins, the occult mystery which only the Eritrene managed to track down by removing the numerous falsehoods superimposed on it, because he had glimpsed it general sir, he had it within reach of his hand when there came the immense explosion that kept echoing along the gray ridges and deep canyons of the mountain range and one heard the endless wail of fright of the tumbling mule as it went on falling dizzily and endlessly from the peaks of perpetual snow through successive and instantaneous climes out of natural-history prints of the precipice and the birth trickle of great navigable waters and the high cornices up to which the learned doctors of the botanical expedition had climbed on Indian back with their herbal secrets, and the steppes of wild magnolias where warm-wooled sheep grazed the ones who give us generous sustenance and cover and good example and the mansions of the coffee plantations with their paper wreaths on solitary balconies and their endless invalids and the perpetual roar of the turbulent rivers of the great natural boundary lines where the heat began and at dusk there were pestilent waves from an old dead man dead from treachery dead all alone in the cacao groves with their great persistent leaves and scarlet blossoms and berry fruit whose seeds were used as the principal ingredient of chocolate and the motionless sun and the burning dust and the seed gourd and the honey gourd and the sad and skinny cows of the Atlantic province in the only charity school for two hundred leagues around and the exhalation of the still-living mule whose guts exploded like a succulent soursop among the banana trees and frightened pullets at the bottom of the abyss, God damn it, they deer-hunted him general sir, they had hunted him down with a jaguar rifle at the pass of the Solitary Soul in spite of the protection of my authority, sons of bitches, in spite of my strong telegrams, God damn it, but now they're going to find out who's who, he bellowed, chewing on his froth of gall not so much because of rage over the disobedience as over the certainty that they were hiding something big from him since they had dared go against the thunderbolts of his power, he carefully observed the breathing of those who gave him the information because he knew that only one who knew the truth would have the courage to lie to him, he scrutinized the secret intentions of the high command to see which of them was the traitor, you who I brought up out of nothing, you who I put to sleep in a golden bed after finding you on the ground, you whose life I saved, you who

127

I bought for more money than anyone else, all of you, you dirty mothers' sons, because only one of them would dare disregard a telegram signed with my name and countersigned with the wax of the ring of his power, so he assumed personal command of the rescue operation with the unrepeatable order that within a maximum of forty-eight hours you find him alive and bring him to me and if you find him dead bring him to me alive and if you don't find him bring him to me, an order so unmistakable and fearsome that before the time was up they came to him with the news general sir that they had found him in the underbrush of the precipice with his wounds cauterized by the golden flowers of the frailejone plant more alive than any of us general sir, safe and sound by virtue of his mother Bendición Alvarado who once more was giving a sign of her clemency and her power in the very person of the one who had tried to damage her memory, they brought him down along Indian trails on a hammock hung on a pole with an escort of grenadiers and preceded by a bullfight master on horseback who rang a high-mass bell so that everyone would know that this was a matter of the one who gives the orders, they put him in the bedroom for honored guests in the presidential palace under the immediate responsibility of the minister of health until he was able to bring to a close that terrible report written in his own hand and countersigned with his initials on the right-hand margin of every one of the three hundred and fifty folios of every one of these seven volumes which I sign with my name and my flourish and which I guarantee with my seal on this fourteenth day of the month of April of this year of Our Lord, I, Demetrius Aldous, auditor of the Sacred Congregation of the Rite, postulator and promoter of the faith, by the mandate of the Immense Constitution and for the splendor of justice of men on earth and the greater glory of God in the heavens I affirm and show this to be the only truth, the whole truth, and nothing but the truth, your excellency, here it is. There it was, indeed, captive in seven lacquered bibles, so unavoidable and brutal that only a man immune to the spell of glory and alien to the interests of his power

128

dared expose it in living flesh before the impassive old man who listened to him without blinking fanning himself in the wicker rocking chair, who only sighed after each mortal revelation, who only said aha, repeated it, using his hat to shoo away the April flies aroused by the luncheon leftovers, swallowing whole truths, bitter truths, truths which were like live coals that kept on burning in the shadows of his heart, because everything had been a farce, your excellency, a carnival apparatus that he himself had put together without really thinking about it when he decided that the corpse of his mother should be displayed for public veneration on a catafalque of ice long before anyone thought about the merits of her sainthood and only to contradict the evil tongues that said you were rotting away before you died, a circus trick which he had fallen into himself without knowing it ever since they came to him with the news general sir that his mother Bendición Alvarado was performing miracles and he had ordered her body carried in a magnificent procession into the most unknown corners of his vast statueless country so that no one should be left who did not know the worth of your virtues after so many years of sterile mortification, after so many painted birds without benefit, mother, after so much love without thanks, although it never would have occurred to me that the order was to be changed into the jape of the false dropsy victims who were paid to get rid of their water in public, they had paid two hundred pesos to a false dead man who arose from his grave and appeared walking on his knees through the crowd frightened by his ragged shroud and his mouth full of earth, they had paid eighty pesos to a gypsy woman who pretended to give birth in the middle of the street to a two-headed monster as punishment for having said that the miracles had been set up by the government, and that they had been, there wasn't a single witness who hadn't been paid money, an ignominious conspiracy that none the less had not been put together by his adulators with the innocent idea of pleasing him as Monsignor Demetrius Aldous had imagined during his first scrutinies, no, your excellency, it was a dirty piece of business on the part of your proselytes, the most scandalous and sacrilegious of all the things they had made proliferate in the shadow of his power, because the ones who had invented the miracles and backed up the testimonies of lies were the same followers of his regime who had manufactured and sold the relics of the dead bride's gown worn by his mother Bendición Alvarado, aha, the same ones who had printed the little cards and coined the medals with her portrait as a queen, aha, the ones who enriched themselves with curls from her head, aha, with the flasks of water drawn from her side, aha, with the shroud of diagonal cloth where they used door paint to sketch the tender body of a virgin sleeping in profile with her hand on her heart and which was sold by the yard in the back rooms of Hindu bazaars, a monstrous lie sustained by the supposition that the corpse remained uncorrupted before the avid eyes of the endless throng that filed through the main nave of the cathedral, when the truth was quite something else, your excellency, it was that the body of his mother was not preserved because of her virtues or through the repair work done with paraffin and the cosmetic tricks that he had decided upon out of pure filial pride but that she had been stuffed according to the worst skills of taxidermy just like the posthumous animals in science museums as he found out with my own hands, mother, I opened the glass casket as the funereal emblems fell apart with the air, I took the crown of orange blossoms from your moldy brow where the stiff filly-mane hairs had been pulled out by the roots strand by strand to be sold as relics, I pulled you out from under the damp gauze of your bridal veil and the dry residue and the difficult saltpeter sunsets of death and you weighed the same as a sun-dried gourd and you had an old trunk-bottom smell and I could sense inside of you a feverish restlessness that was like the sound of your soul and it was the scissor-slicing of the moth larvae who were chewing you up inside, your limbs fell off by themselves when I tried to hold you in my arms because they had removed the innards of everything that held together your live body of a sleeping happy mother with her hand on her heart and they had stuffed you up again with rags so that all that was left of what had been you was only a shell with dusty stuffing that crumbled just by being lifted in the phosphorescent air of your firefly bones and all that could be heard were the flea leaps of the glass eyes on the pavement of the dusk-lighted church, turned to nothing, it was a trickle of the remains of a demolished mother which the bailiffs scooped up from the floor with a shovel to throw it back any way they could into the box under the gaze of monolithic sternness from the indecipherable satrap whose iguana eyes refused to let the slightest emotion show through even when he was all alone in the unmarked berlin with the only man in this world who had dared place him in front of the mirror of truth, both looked out through the haze of the window curtains at the hordes of needy who were finding relief from the heat-ridden afternoon in the dew-cool doorways where previously they had sold pamphlets describing atrocious crimes and luckless loves and carnivorous flowers and inconceivable fruits that compromised the will and where now one only heard the deafening racket of the stalls selling false relics of the clothes and the body of his mother Bendición Alvarado, while he underwent the clear impression that Monsignor Demetrius Aldous had read his thoughts when he turned his sight away from the mobs of invalids and murmured that when all's said and done something good had come out of the rigor of his scrutiny and it was the certainty that these poor people love your excellency as they love their own lives, because Monsignor Demetrius Aldous had caught sight of the perfidy within the presidential palace itself, had seen the greed within the adulation and the wily servility among those who flourished under the umbrella of power, and he had come to know on the other hand a new form of love among the droves of needy who expected nothing from him because they expected nothing from anyone and they professed for him an earthly devotion that could be held in one's hands and a loyalty without illusions that we should only want for God, your excellency, but he did not even blink when faced with that startling revelation which in other times would have made his insides twist, nor did he sigh but meditated to himself with a hidden restlessness that this was all we needed, father, all we need is for nobody to love me now that you're going off to take advantage of the glory of my misfortune under the golden cupolas of your fallacious world while he was left with the undeserved burden of truth without a loving mother who could help him through it, more lonely than a left hand in this nation which I didn't choose willingly but which was given me as an established fact in the way you have seen it which is as it has always been since time immemorial with this feeling of unreality, with this smell of shit, with this unhistoried people who don't believe in anything except life, this is the nation they forced on me without even asking me, father, with one-hundred-degree heat and ninety-eight-percent humidity in the upholstered shadows of the presidential berlin, breathing dust, tormented by the perfidy of the rupture that whistled like a teakettle during audiences, no one to lose a game of dominoes to, and no one to believe his truth, father, put yourself in my skin, but he didn't say it, he just sighed, he just blinked for an instant and asked Monsignor Demetrius Aldous that the brutal conversation of that afternoon remain between ourselves, you haven't told me anything, father, I don't know the truth, promise me that, and Monsignor Demetrius Aldous promised him that of course your excellency doesn't know the truth, my word as a man. The cause of Bendición Alvarado was suspended for insufficient proof, and the edict from Rome was made public from pulpits with official permission along with the determination of the government to repress any protest or attempt at disorder, but forces of public order did not intervene when hordes of indignant pilgrims built bonfires on the main square with the large wooden doors of the cathedral and broke the stained-glass windows with angels and gladiators of the Apostolic Nunciature with stones, they demolished everything general sir, but he didn't move from the hammock, they laid siege to the convent of the Biscayan nuns to leave them to perish without food and water, they sacked churches, mission houses, they destroyed everything that had to do with priests general sir, but he remained motionless in the hammock under the cool shadows of the pansies until the commandants of his general staff in plenary session declared themsleves incapable of calming spirits and reestablishing order without the shedding of blood as had been resolved, and only then did he get up, appear in his office after so many months of indolence, and assume with his own voice and in person the solemn responsibility of interpreting the popular will through a decree which he conceived through his own inspiration and he proclaimed it on his own and at his own risk without advising the armed forces or consulting his ministers and in the first article of which he proclaimed the civil sainthood of Bendición Alvarado by the supreme decision of the free and sovereign people, he named her patroness of the nation, curer of the ill and mistress of birds and a national holiday was declared on her birthday, and in the second article and beginning with the promulgation of the present decree a state of war was declared between this nation and the powers of the Holy See with all the consequences which international law and all extant international treaties have established for such cases, and in the third article there was ordered the immediate, public and solemn expulsion of his grace the archbishop primate followed by that of bishops, apostolic prefects, priests, nuns and all persons native and foreign who had anything to do with the business of God in any condition and under any title within the borders of the country and up to fifty nautical leagues in territorial waters, and ordered in the fourth and last article was the expropriation of all goods of the church, its houses of worship, its convents, its schools, its arable lands with tools and animals thereon, its sugar plantations, factories and workshops and in the same manner everything which really belonged to it even though registered in the name of a third party, which goods would go to form part of the posthumous patrimony of Saint Bendición Alvarado of the Birds for the splendor of her cult and the grandeur of her memory from the date of the present decree promulgated orally and signed with the seal of the ring of this unappealable maximum authority of the supreme power, let it be obeyed and carried out. In the midst of the rockets of celebration, the bell-ringing of glory and the music of pleasure with which the event of the civil canonization was celebrated, he busied himself in person to see that the decree was carried out without any dubious maneuvers so as to be sure they would not make him the victim of new tricks, he picked up the reins of reality again with his firm velvet gloves as in the days of great glory when the people cut off his path on the stairs to beg him to restore horse racing in the streets and he so ordered, agreed, that sack races be revived and he so ordered, agreed, and he would appear in the most miserable of villages to explain how they should put hens in their nests and how calves should be gelded, because he had just been satisfied with his personal test of the minute details of the taking of inventory of church goods but he took charge of the formal ceremonies of expropriation so that there would be no chink between his will and the accomplished acts, he checked the facts on paper against the tricky facts of real life, he oversaw the expulsion of the larger communities to whom had been attributed the intent of smuggling out in bags with double bottoms and trick brassieres the secret treasures of the last viceroy which had been buried in pot- ter's field in spite of the bloodthirsty way in which the federalist leaders had searched for them during the long years of war, and not only did he order that no member of the church was to take with him any more baggage than a change of clothing but he decided beyond appeal that they be embarked naked as the day their mothers bore them, the rough village priests to whom it made no difference whether to wear clothes or go naked as long as they had a change of fortune, the prefects from mission lands who had been devastated by malaria, clean-shaven and dignified bishops, and behind them the women, the timid sisters of charity, the fierce missionary nuns accustomed to taming nature and making vegetables grow in the desert, and the slender Biscayan sisters who played the harpsichord, and the Salesian sisters with thin hands and bodies intact, be- cause even in the naked hide with which they had been thrown into the world it was possible to distinguish their high-class origins, the difference in their condition, and the inequality of their office as they filed past bundles of cacao and sacks of salted catfish in the huge customhouse shed, they went by in a whirling tumult of frightened sheep with their arms crossed over their breasts trying to hide the shame of the ones with that of the others before the old man who looked like stone under the fan blades, who looked at them without breathing, without taking his eyes off the fixed space through which the torrent of naked women would inexorably have to pass, he contemplated them impassively, without blinking, until there was not a single one left in all the national territory, for these were the last of them general sir, and yet he only remembered one whom he had separated with a simple touch of his glance from the troop of frightened novices, he distinguished her among the others in spite of the fact that she was no different, she was small and sturdy, robust, with opulent buttocks, large full teats, clumsy hands, protuberant sex, hair cut with pruning shears, spaced teeth firm as ax heads, snub nose, flat feet, a novice as mediocre as all of them, but he sensed that she was the only woman in the drove of naked women, the only one who on passing in front of him had left the obscure trail of a wild animal who carried off my vital air and he barely had time to change his imperceptible look to see her a second time forevermore when the officer from the identification services found her name in alphabetical order in the roster and shouted Nazareno Leticia, and she answered with a man's voice, present. That was how he had her for the rest of his life, present, until the last nostalgia trickled away through the fissures in his memory and all that remained was the image of her on the strip of paper where he had written Leticia Nazareno of my soul look what has become of me without you, he hid it in the cranny where he kept the honey, he would reread it when he knew he was not being observed, he would roll it up again after reliving for a fleeting instant the unforgettable afternoon of radiant rain on which they surprised him with the news general sir that they had repatriated you in fulfillment of his orders which he had not given, for all he had done was to murmur Leticia Nazareno while he contemplated the last ash barge as it sank below the horizon, Leticia Nazareno, he repeated aloud so as not to forget the name, and that had been enough for the presidential security services to kidnap her from the convent in Jamaica, gagged and in a strait jacket inside a pine box with metal hoops and black letters saying fragile and in English do not drop this side up and an export license in accordance with the necessary consular permission for the two thousand eight hundred champagne glasses of genuine crystal for the presidential wine cellar, for the return voyage they loaded her aboard among the ship's stores of a collier and they laid her naked and drugged on the columned bed in the bedroom for distinguished guests as he had remembered her at three in the afternoon under the flour-haze light of the mosquito netting, she had the restful look of sleep of so many other inert women who had served him without even awakening from the lethargy of the Luminal and tormented by a terrible feeling of abandonment and defeat, except that he did not touch Leticia Nazareno, he contemplated her in sleep with a kind of infantile amazement surprised at how much her nakedness had changed since he had seen her in the harbor shed, they'd curled her hair, they'd made her up right down to the most intimate nooks and crannies, and they'd put crimson polish on her fingernails and toenails and lipstick and rouge on her mouth and cheeks and mascara and she gave off a sweet fragrance that did away with your trace of a wild animal, Jesus, they'd ruined her trying to recreate her, they'd made her so different that he couldn't even see her underneath the clumsy cosmetics while he contemplated her naked in the ecstasy of the Luminal, he saw her come to the surface, he saw her wake up, he saw her see him, mother, it was her, Leticia Nazareno of my bewilderment petrified with terror before the stony old man who was contemplating her mercilessly through the tenuous mists of the netting, frightened with the unforeseeable aims of her silence because he couldn't imagine anything in spite of his uncountable years and his measureless power he was more frightened than she, more alone, more not knowing what to do, as confused and as defenseless as he had been the first time he was a man with a camp follower whom he had surprised in the middle of the night swimming naked in a river and whose strength and size he had imagined from her mare snorts after each dive, he heard her dark and solitary laugh in the darkness, he sensed the joy of her body in the darkness but he was paralyzed with fear because he was still a virgin even though he was already an artillery lieutenant in the third civil war, until the fear of losing the chance was more decisive than the fear of the attack, and then he jumped into the water with all his clothes on, boots, knapsack, cartridge belt, machete, carbine, buried under so many military encumbrances and so many secret terrors that the woman thought at first that he was someone who had ridden his horse into the water, but she realized immediately that he was only a poor frightened man and she gathered him into the lagoon of her pity, took him by the hand in the darkness of his confusion because he couldn't manage to find his way in the darkness of the lagoon, she indicated to him with a mother's voice in the darkness to get a good grip on my shoulders so the current won't knock you over, not to squat down in the water but to kneel firmly on the bottom breathing slowly so you'll have enough wind, and he did what she told him with a boyish obedience thinking mother of mine Bendición Alvarado why in hell do women do things as if they were inventing them, how can they be such men about it, he thought, while she was taking off the useless paraphernalia of other less fearful and desolate wars than that solitary war with the water up to his neck, he had died of fright under the protection of that body that smelled of pine soap when she finished unbuckling his two belts and unbuttoned his fly and I was twisted with terror because I couldn't find what I was looking for except for the enormous testicle swimming like a toad in the darkness, she let go of it with fright, go back to your mama and have her turn you in for another one, she told him, you're no good for anything, because he had been defeated by the same ances-

tral fear tht held him motionless before the nakedness of
Leticia Nazareno in whose river of unforeseeable waters
one was not to enter not even with everything he had on
until she could lend him the aid of her mercy, he himself
covered her with a sheet, played the song of poor Del-
gadina ruined by the love of her father on the gramophone
until the cylinder wore out, he had felt flowers put into the
vases so that they would not wilt like natural ones from the
evil touch of her hands, he did everything he could think of
to make her happy but he kept the rigors of captivity intact
and the punishment of nudity so that she would understand
that she would be well taken care of and well loved but that
she had no possibility of escaping that fate, and she understood so well that during the first truce of fear she ordered
him without saying please to open the window general so
that we could have a little air, and he opened it, to close it
again because the moon is hitting my face, he closed it, he
carried out her orders as if they were from love all the more
obedient and sure of himself the closer he got to the afternoon of radiant rain in which he slipped inside the mosquito netting and lay down with his clothes on beside her
without waking her up, he participated alone for nights on
end in the secret outflow of her body, he breathed in her
smell of a mountain bitch that grew warmer with the passage of months, the moss of her womb sprouted, she woke
up startled shouting get out of here general and he arose
with his heavy parsimony but lay down beside her again
while she was sleeping and in that way he enjoyed her
without touching her during the first year of captivity until
she grew accustomed to awakening beside him without understanding the direction of the currents of that indecipherable old man who had abandoned the flattery of power
and the enchantments of the world to devote himself to her
contemplation and service, she all the more disconcerted as
she came to know the afternoon of radiant rains when he
had gone into the water with everything on, the uniform
without insignia, the sword belts, the ring of keys, the leggings, the riding boots with the gold spur, a nightmare
attack that awakened her in terror trying to get out from

138

under that caparisoned charger, but he was so resolute that
she decided to gain time with the last recourse of take your
harness off general the buckles hurt my heart, and he took
it off, he should take off the spur general it injures my
ankles with its gold rowel, that he take off the clump of keys
from his belt they keep bumping into my hipbones, and he
ended up doing what she ordered although three months
were needed to get him to take off his sword belt which
hinders my breathing and another month for the leggings
which break my soul with their buckles, it was a slow and
difficult struggle in which she held him off without exas-
perating him and he ended up giving in so as to please her,
so neither of them ever knew how it was that the final
cataclysm occurred a short time after the second anniversary of the kidnapping when his aimless warm and tender
hands by chance came upon the hidden gems of the sleeping novice who awoke in shock with a pale sweat and a
death quiver and did not try to get away with either good
or evil arts from the uncouth animal she had on top of her
except that she shocked him by begging him to take off his
boots they were dirtying my Brabant sheets and he took
them off as best he could, take off your leggings, and pants,
and the truss, take it all off my life I can't feel you, until he
himself didn't know when he was left as only his mother had
known him in the light that filtered through the melancholy
harps of the geraniums, freed from fear, free, changed into
a battling bison who with the first charge demolished everything he found in his way and fell face down into an abyss
of silence where all that could be heard was the schooner-
beam creaking of the clenched back teeth of Nazareno Leticia, present, she had clutched all my hair in her fingers so
as not to die alone in the bottomless dizzy fall in which I
was already dying sought at the same time and with the
same drive by all the urgencies of the body, and none the
less he forgot about her, he was alone in the shadows looking for himself in the brackish water of his tears general, in
the gentle flow of the thread of his ox saliva general, in the
surprise of his surprise of mother mine Bendición Alvarado
how is it possible to have lived so many years without know-

ing this torment, he wept, disturbed by the anxiety of his kidneys, the artillery battery that was his intestines, the mortal tearing off of the tender tentacle that pulled his guts out by the roots and turned him into a beheaded animal whose tumbling death throes sprinkled the snowy sheets with a hot and sour matter that perverted in his memory the liquid glass air of the afternoon of radiant rains in the mosquito netting, because it was shit general, his own shit.

SHORTLY BEFORE NIGHTFALL, when we finished taking out the rotten husks of the cows and putting a little order into that fabulous disarray, we were still unable to tell if the corpse looked like its legendary image. We scraped it with fish scalers to get the deep-sea shark suckers off, we washed it down with creolin and rock salt to fix up the marks of putrefaction, we powdered his face with starch to hide the burlap repairs and paraffin stuffing that we had to use to restore the face that had been pecked away by dung-heap birds, we gave him back the color of life with woman's rouge and lipstick, but not even the glass eyes stuck into the empty sockets could give him the stamp of authority he needed if we were to put him on display for the masses. In the cabinet room meanwhile we called for the unity of all against the despotism of centuries so we could divide up the booty of his power in equal parts, because everyone had come home under the spell of the surreptitious news of his death that could not be contained, liberals and conservatives had returned in reconciliation with the embers of so many years of postponed ambitions, generals of the high command who had lost their compass of authority, the last three civilian ministers, the archbishop primate, all those whom he would not have wanted there were sitting around the long walnut table trying to come to an agreement on the manner in which the news of that enormous death was to be released so as to avoid the premature explosion of mobs in the street, first a bulletin number one at the start of the first night concerning a slight indisposition which had obliged him to cancel all of his excellency's public appearances and civilian and military audiences, then a second medical bulletin in which it was announced that the illustrious patient had been obliged to remain in his private quarters due to an indisposition in keeping with his years, and lastly, without any announcement, the heavy tolling of the cathedral bells on the radiant dawn of the hot August Tuesday of an official death which no one was ever to know for certain that really was his or not. We were defenseless against that evidence, compromised by a pestilential corpse that we were incapable of replacing in the world because he had refused in his senile insistence to take any decision concerning the destiny of the nation after he was gone, with the invincible stubbornness of an old man he had resisted all suggestions made to him ever since the government had been moved to the ministry buildings with their sun-drenched glass and he had stayed behind living alone in the deserted palace of his absolute power, we would find him walking about in dreams, waving his arms in the midst of the cows' destruction with no one to command except the blind men, the lepers and the cripples who were dying not from illness but from old age in the weeds of the rose garden, and yet he was so lucid and stubborn that we could only get evasive answers and postponements out of him every time we brought up the matter of putting his legacy in order, because he would say that thinking ahead about the world that's left after you've gone yourself was something made up of the same ashes as death itself, God damn it, because when I finally die the politicians will come back and divide up the mess the way it was during the times of the Goths, you'll see, he said, they'll go back to dividing everything up among the priests, the gringos and the rich, and nothing for the poor, naturally, because they've always been so fucked up that the day shit is worth money, poor people will be born without an asshole, you'll see, he said, talking to someone about his days of glory, even making fun of himself when he told us as he choked with laughter that for the three days he was going to be dead it wouldn't be worth the trouble taking him to Jerusalem and burying him in the Holy Sepulcher, and he put an end to all disagreement with the final argument that it didn't matter whether something back then was true or not, God damn it, it will be with time. He was right, because during our time there was no one who doubted the legitimacy of his history, or anyone who could have disclosed or denied it because we couldn't even establish the identity of his body, there was no other nation except the one that had been made by him in his own image and likeness where space was changed and time corrected by the designs of his absolute will, reconstituted by him ever since the most uncertain origins of his memory as he wandered at random through that house of infamy where no happy person had ever slept, as he tossed cracked corn to the hens who pecked around his hammock and exasperated the servants with orders he pulled out of the air to bring me a lemonade with chopped ice which he had left within reach of his hand, take that chair away from over there and put it over there, and they should put it back where it had been in order to satisfy in that minute way the warm embers of his enormous addiction to giving orders, distracting the everyday pastimes of his power with the patient raking up of ephemeral instants from his remote childhood as he nodded sleepily under the ceiba tree in the courtyard, he would wake up suddenly when he managed to grasp a memory like a piece in a limitless jigsaw puzzle of the nation that lay before him, the great, chimerical, shoreless nation, a realm of mangrove swamps with slow rafts and precipices that had been there before his time when men were so bold that they hunted crocodiles with their hands by placing a stake in their mouths, like that, he would explain to us holding his forefinger against his palate, he told us that on one Good Friday he had heard the hullabaloo of the wind and the scurf smell of the wind and he saw the heavy clouds of locusts that muddied the noonday sky and went along scissoring off everything that stood in their path and left the world all sheared and the light in tatters as on the eve of creation, because he had seen that disaster, he had seen a string of headless roosters hanging by their feet and bleeding drop by drop from the eaves of a house with a broad and crumbling sidewalk where a woman had just died, barefoot he had left his mother's hand and followed the ragged corpse they were carrying off to bury without a coffin on a cargo litter that was lashed by the blizzard of locusts, because that was what the nation was like then, we didn't even have coffins for the dead, nothing, he had seen a man who had tried to hang himself with a rope that had already been used by another hanged man from a tree in a village square and the rotted rope broke before it was time and the poor man lay in his death throes on the square to the horror of the ladies coming out of mass, but he didn't die, they beat him awake with sticks without bothering to find out who he was because in those days no one knew who was who if he wasn't known in the church, they stuck his ankles between the planks of the stocks and left him there exposed to the elements along with other comrades in suffering because that was what the times of the Goths were like when God ruled more than the government, the evil times of the nation before he gave the order to chop down all trees in village squares to prevent the terrible spectacle of a Sunday hanged man, he had prohibited the use of public stocks, burial without a coffin, everything that might awaken in one's memory the ignominious laws that existed before his power, he had built the railroad to the upland plains to put an end to the infamy of mules terrified by the edges of precipices as on their backs they carried grand pianos for the masked balls at the coffee plantations, for he had also seen the disaster of the thirty grand pianos destroyed in an abyss and of which they had spoken and written so much

even outside the country although only he could give truth-
ful testimony, he had gone to the window by chance at the
precise moment in which the rear mule had slipped and had
dragged the rest into the abyss, so that no one but he had
heard the shriek of terror from the cliff-flung mule train
and the endless chords of the pianos that fell with it playing
by themselves in the void, hurtling toward the depths of a
nation which at that time was like everything that had existed before him, vast and uncertain, to such an extreme
that it was impossible to know whether it was night or day
in the kind of eternal twilight of the hot steamy mists in the
deep canyons where the pianos imported from Austria had
broken up into fragments, he had seen that and many other
things in that remote world although not even he himself
could have been sure with no room for doubt whether they
were his own memories or whether he had heard about
them on his bad nights of fever during the wars or whether
he might have seen them in prints in travel books over
which he would linger in ecstasy for long hours during the
dead doldrums of power, but none of that mattered, God
damn it, they'll see that with time it will be the truth, he
would say, conscious that his real childhood was not that
crust of uncertain recollections that he only remembered
when the smoke from the cow chips arose and he forgot it
forever except that he really had lived it during the calm
waters of my only and legitimate wife Leticia Nazareno who
would sit him down every afternoon between two and four
o'clock at a school desk under the pansy bower to teach him
how to read and write, she had put her novice's tenacity
into that heroic enterprise and he matched it with his terrifying old man's patience, with the terrifying will of his limitless power, with all my heart, so that he would chant with
all my soul the tuna in the tin the loony in the bin the neat
nightcap, he chanted without hearing himself or without
anyone's hearing him amidst the uproar of his dead mother's aroused birds that the Indian packs the ointment in
the can, papa places the tobacco in his pipe, Cecilia sells
seals seeds seats seams scenes sequins seaweed and receiv-
ers, Cecilia sells everything, he would laugh, repeating

amidst the clamor of the cicadas the reading lesson that Leticia Nazareno chanted to the time of her novice's metronome, until the limits of the world became saturated with the creatures of your voice and in his vast realm of dreariness there was no other truth but the exemplary truths of the primer, there was nothing but the moon in the mist, the ball and the banana, the bull of Don Eloy, Otilia's bordered bathrobe, the rote reading lessons which he repeated at every moment and everywhere just like his portraits even in the presence of the treasury minister from Holland who lost the thread of an official visit when the gloomy old man raised the hand with the velvet glove on it in the shadows of his unfathomable power and interrupted the audience to invite him to sing with me my mama's a mummer, Ismael spent six months on the isle, the lady ate a tomato, imitating with his forefinger the beat of the metronome and repeating from memory Tuesday's lesson with a perfect diction but with such a bad sense of the occasion that the interview ended as he had wanted it to with the postponement of payment of the Dutch debts for a more propitious moment, for when there would be time, he decided, to the surprise of the lepers, the blind men, the cripples who rose up at dawn among the rosebushes and saw the shadowy old man who gave a silent blessing and chanted three times with high-mass chords I am the king and the law is my thing, he chanted, the seer has fear of beer, a lighthouse is a very high tower with a bright beam which guides sailors at night, he chanted, conscious that in the shadows of his senile happiness there was no time but that of Leticia Nazareno of my life in the shrimp stew of the suffocating gambols of siesta time, there were no other anxieties but those of being naked with you on the sweat-soaked mattress under the captive bat of an electric fan, there was no light but that of your buttocks, Leticia, nothing but your totemic teats, your flat feet, your ramus of rue as a remedy, the oppressive Januaries of the remote island of Antigua where you came into the world one early dawn of solitude that was furrowed by the burning breeze of rotted swamps, they had shut themselves up in the quarters for distinguished guests with the personal order that no one is to come any closer than twenty feet to that door because I'm going to be very busy learning to read and write, so no one interrupted him not even with the news general sir that the black vomit was wreaking havoc among the rural population while the rhythms of my heart got ahead of the metronome because of that invisible force of your wild-animal smell, chanting that the midget is dancing on just one foot, the mule goes to the mill, Otilia washes the tub, kow is spelled with a jackass k, he chanted, while Leticia Nazareno moved aside the herniated testicle to clean him up from the last love-making's dinky-poo, she submerged him in the lustral waters of the pewter bathtub with lion's paws and lathered him with Reuter soap, scrubbed him with washcloths, and rinsed him off with the water of boiled herbs as they sang in duet ginger gibber and gentleman are all spelled with a gee, she would daub the joints of his legs with cocoa butter to alleviate the rash from his truss, she would put boric acid powder on the moldy star of his asshole and whack his behind like a tender mother for your bad manners with the minister from Holland, plap, plap, as a penance she asked him to permit the return to the country of the communities of poor nuns so they could go back to taking care of orphan asylums and hospitals and other houses of charity, but he wrapped her in the gloomy aura of his implacable rancor, never in a million years, he sighed, there wasn't a single power in this world or the other that could make him go against a decision taken by himself alone and aloud, she asked him during the asthmas of love at two in the afternoon that you grant me one thing, my life, only one thing, that the mission territory communities who work on the fringes of the whims of power might return, but he answered her during the anxieties of his urgent husband snorts never in a million years my love, I'd rather be dead than humiliated by that pack of long skirts who saddle Indians instead of mules and pass out beads of colored glass in exchange for gold nose rings and earrings, never in a million years, he protested, insensitive to the pleas of Leticia Nazareno of my misfortune who had crossed her legs to ask him for the restitution of the confessional schools expropriated by the government, the disentailment of property held in mortmain, the sugar mills, the churches turned into barracks, but he turned his face to the wall ready to renounce the insatiable torture of your slow cavernous love-making before I would let my arm be twisted in favor of those bandits of God who for centuries have fed on the liver of the nation, never in a million years, he decided, and yet they did come back general sir, they returned to the country through the narrowest slits, the communities of poor nuns in accordance with his confidential order that they disembark silently in secret coves, they were paid enormous indemnities, their expropriated holdings were restored with interest and the recent laws concerning civil marriage, divorce, lay education were repealed, everything he had decreed aloud during his rage at the comic carnival of the process of the declaration of sainthood for his mother Bendición Alvarado may God keep her in His holy kingdom, God damn it, but Leticia Nazareno was not satisfied with all that but asked for more, she asked him to put your ear to the lower part of my stomach so that you can hear the singing of the creature growing inside, because she had awakened in the middle of the night startled by that deep voice that was describing the aquatic paradise of your insides furrowed by mallow-soft sundowns and winds of pitch, that interior voice that spoke to her of the polyps on your kidneys, the soft steel of your intestines, the warm amber of your urine sleeping in its springs, and to her stomach he put the ear that was buzzing less for him and he heard the secret bubbling of the living creature of his mortal sin, a child of our obscene bellies who would be named Emanuel, which is the name by which other gods know God, and on his forehead he will have the white star of his illustrious origins and he will inherit his mother's spirit of sacrifice and his father's greatness and his own destiny of an invisible conductor, but he was to be the shame of heaven and the stigma of the nation because of his illicit nature as long as he refused to consecrate at the altar what he had vilified in bed for so many years of sacrilegious concubinage, and then he opened a way through the foam of the ancient bridal mosquito netting with that snort of a ship's boiler coming from the depths of his terrible repressed rage shouting never in a million years, better dead than wed, dragging his great feet of a secret bridegroom through the salons of an alien house whose splendor of a different age had been restored after the long period of the shadows of official mourning, the crumbling holy-week crepe had been pulled from the cornices, there was sea light in the bedrooms, flowers on the balconies, martial music, and all of it in fulfillment of an order that he had not given but which had been an order of his without the slightest doubt general sir because it had the tranquil decision of his voice and the unappealable style of his authority, and he approved, agreed, and the shuttered churches opened again, and the cloisters and cemeteries were returned to their former congregations by another order of his which he had not given either but he approved, agreed, the old holy days of obligation had been restored as well as the practices of lent and in through the open balconies came the crowd's hymns of jubilation that had previously been sung to exalt his glory as they knelt under the burning sun to celebrate the good news that God had been brought in on a ship general sir, really, they had brought Him on your orders, Leticia, by means of a bedroom law which she had promulgated in secret without consulting anybody and which he approved in public so that it would not appear to anyone's eyes that he had lost the oracles of his authority, for you were the hidden power behind those endless processions which he watched in amazement through the windows of his bedroom as they reached a distance beyond that of the fanatical hordes of his mother Bendición Alvarado whose memory had been erased from the time of men, the tatters of her bridal dress and the starch of her bones had been scattered to the winds and in the crypt the stone with the upside-down letters had been turned over so that even the mention of her name as a birdwoman painter of orioles in repose would not endure till the end of time, and all of that by your orders, because

149

you were the one who had ordered it so that no other woman's memory would cast a shadow on your memory, Leticia Nazareno of my misfortune, bitch-daughter. She had changed it into an age in which no one changed unless it was to die, she had managed with bedroom wiles to do away with his puerile resistance of never in a million years, better dead than wed, she had made him put on his new truss listen to the way it sounds like the bell of a stray sheep in the dark, she made him put on your patent leather boots from the time he had danced the first waltz with the queen, the gold spur on his left heel which had been given him by the admiral of the ocean sea so that he would wear it unto death as a sign of the highest authority, your tunic with gold braid and tasseled ribbons and the statue epaulets which he had not worn since the times when his sad eyes could still be glimpsed, his pensive chin, the taciturn hand with the velvet glove behind the peepholes in the presidential coach, she made him put on his military saber, your man's perfume, your medals with the sash of the order of the knights of the Holy Sepulcher which the Supreme Pontiff sent you for having given back the church its expropriated possessions, you dressed me like a feast-day altar and you took me at early dawn on my own feet to the somber audience room which smelled of dead men's candles from the boughs of orange blossoms hung by the windows and the symbols of the nation hanging on the walls, without any witnesses, harnessed to the yoke of the novice who was stuccoed with a linen petticoat under the light breeze of muslin in order to smother the seven-month shame of hidden unrestraint, they were sweating in the lethargy of the invisible sea which sniffed restlessly about the gloomy ballroom to which access had been forbidden by his orders, the windows had been walled up, all trace of life in the building had been exterminated so that the world would not get even the slightest rumor of the monstrous hidden wedding, you could barely breathe in the heat because of the urgent pressure of the premature male who was swimming among the shadowy lichens on the dunes of your insides, for he had resolved that it would be a boy, and it was, he sang in the subsoil of your being with the same voice of an invisible spring with which the archbishop primate wearing pontificals sang glory to God on high so that the dozing sentries would not hear him, with the same terror of a lost diver with which the archbishop primate commended his soul to the Lord to ask the inscrutable old man what no one until then or ever after until the end of time had dared ask him do you take Leticia Mercedes María Nazareno as your wife, and he only blinked, agreed, on his chest the military medals gave a slight tinkle from the hidden pressure of his heart, but there was so much authority in his voice that the terrible creature in your insides rolled over completely in his equinox of thick waters, corrected his compass and found the direction of the light, and then Leticia Nazareno doubled over sobbing oh my father and my lord have pity on this your humble servant who has taken much pleasure in breaking your holy laws and accepts with resignation this terrible punishment, but biting her lace wristlet at the same time so that the sound of the disjointed bones of her waist would not reveal the dishonor held in by the linen petticoat, she squatted down, she fell to pieces in the steaming puddle of her own waters and withdrew from among the muslin folds the seven-month runt who had the same size and the same forlorn unboiled-animal look of a calf fetus, she lifted him up with both hands trying to recognize him in the dim light of the candles on the improvised altar, and she saw that he was a male, just as the general had decreed, a fragile and timid male who was to bear without honor the name Emanuel, as had been foreseen, and he was appointed a major general with effective jurisdiction and command from the moment he placed him on the sacrifice stone and cut his umbilical cord with the saber and recognized him as my only and legitimate son, father, baptize him for me. That unprecedented decision was to be the prelude of a new epoch, the first announcement of the evil times in which the army cordoned off the streets before dawn and made people close balcony windows and emptied the market with their rifle butts so that no one would see the fugitive passage of the flashy automobile with armored

plates of steel and the gold shackles of the presidential
squiry, and those who dared peek from the forbidden rooftops did not see as in other times the age-old military man
with his chin resting on the pensive hand with the velvet
glove through the peepholes edged with the colors of the
flag but the chubby former novice with her straw hat with
felt flowers and the string of blue foxes that hung around
her neck in spite of the heat, we would see her get out
across from the public market on Wednesdays at dawn
escorted by a patrol of combat soldiers leading by the hand
the tiny major general no more than three years old and
because of his grace and his languid air it was impossible
not to believe that it was a little girl dressed up as a soldier
in the dress uniform with gold braid which seemed to be
growing on his body, for Leticia Nazareno had put it on him
even before he grew his first teeth, when she would take
him in his baby carriage to preside over official acts as
representative of his father, she carried him in her arms
when he reviewed his troops, she would lift him over her
head to receive the cheers of the crowds in the ball park,
she would nurse him in the open car during parades on the
national holiday not concerned with the secret jokes
brought on by the public spectacle of a five-star general
clinging ecstatically to his mother's nipple like an orphaned
calf, he attended diplomatic receptions from the time he
was able to take care of himself, and then along with the
uniform he wore the military medals which he had chosen
himself from the jewel case full of decorations which his
father had given him to play with, and he was a strange,
serious child, he knew how to conduct himself in public
from the age of six holding in his hand the glass of fruit
juice instead of champagne as he spoke about grown-up
matters with a natural propriety and grace that he had not
inherited from anyone, although on more than one occasion a dark cloud would cross the ballroom, time would
stand still, the pale dauphin invested with the highest powers had fallen into a lethargy, silence, they whispered, the
little general is sleeping, his aides-de-camp would carry
him out in their arms through the crisp conversations of

high-class thugs and modest ladies who scarcely dared murmur repressing the laugh of embarrassment behind feathered fans, how awful, if the general only knew, because he let flourish the belief of his own invention that he was aloof from everything that happened in the world which was not up to the level of his grandeur and for that reason we had the public boldness of the only son he had accepted as his among the countless ones he had bred, or the widespread functions of my only and legitimate wife Leticia Nazareno who would arrive at the market at dawn on Wednesdays leading her toy general by the hand in the midst of the noisy escort of barracks maidservants and assault-troop orderlies who had been transfigured by that rare visible splendor of the awareness which precedes the imminent rising of the sun in the Caribbean, they would wade into the pestilential waters of the bay up to their waists to sack the sloops with patched sails that were anchored in the former slave port loaded with flowers from Martinique and ginger roots from Paramaribo, they swept away all the live fish in their path like a wartime mopping up, they fought over the hogs with rifle butts around the former slave platform still in use where on another Wednesday of another time in the nation before him they had sold at public auction a captive Senegalese woman who brought more than her own weight in gold because of her nightmare beauty, they wiped out everything general sir, it was worse than the locusts, worse than a hurricane, but he remained impassive at the growing scandal which had Leticia Nazareno bursting as he himself would not have dared into the motley gallery of the bird and vegetable market followed by the uproar of street dogs who barked in surprise at the astonished eyes of the blue foxes, she moved with the insolent domination of her authority through slender columns of ironwork with great yellow glass leaves, with pink glass apples, with fabulous cornucopias of riches amidst the blue glass flora of the gigantic dome of lights where she chose the most delicious fruits and the tenderest vegetables which would wither the instant she touched them, unaware of the evil virtue of her hands which made

mold grow on bread that was still warm and had blackened
the gold of her wedding ring, so that she heaped curses on
the vegetable women for having hidden their best wares
and for the house of power had only these miserable pig
mangoes left, sneak thieves, this pumpkin that sounds like
a musician's gourd inside, ill-born wenches, these shitty
ribs with wormy blood that a person can see a mile away
didn't come from a steer but a donkey dead from some
disease, by your evil mothers, she screamed, while the serving girls with their baskets and the orderlies with their
troughs cleaned out everything edible in sight, their corsair
shouts more strident than the clamor of the dogs maddened by the dampness of the snowy hideaways of the tails
of the blue foxes she had had brought alive from Prince
Edward Island, more cutting than the bloody reply of the
foul-mouthed macaws whose mistresses taught them in secret what they themselves could not have the pleasure of
shouting leticia larceny, whorehouse nun, they shrieked
roosting up on the iron branches of the dusty colored-glass
foliage of the dome of the market where they knew they
were safe from the devastating wind of that buccaneer zam-
bapalo dance which was repeated every Wednesday at
dawn during the turbulent childhood of the miniature hoax
of a general whose voice became more affectionate and his
manners sweeter the more he tried to look like a man with
the saber of a playing-card king that still dragged when he
walked, he would stand unperturbed in the midst of the
rapine, he would remain serene, haughty, with the inflexi-
ble decorum his mother had inculcated in him so that he
would deserve the flower of the bloodline that she herself
was squandering in the market with her drive of a furious
bitch and her Arab vendor's curses under the unaffected
look of the old black women in bright-colored rag turbans
who bore the insults and contemplated the sack fanning
themselves without blinking with the canyon-deep calm of
sitting idols, not breathing, ruminating wads of tobacco,
wads of coca leaves, the medicines of poverty which allowed them to live through so much ignominy as the ferocious assault of the whirlwind passed and Leticia Nazareno

opened a way with her vest-pocket officer through the frantic dogs whose hair stood on end along their spines and she would shout from the door send the bill to the government, as always, and they only sighed, oh Lord, if the general only knew, if there were only someone capable of telling him, fooled by the illusion that he would still be unaware until the hour of his death of what everyone knew to be the greatest scandal of his memory that my only and legitimate wife Leticia Nazareno had despoiled the Hindu bazaars of their terrible glass swans and mirrors with seashell frames and coral ashtrays, had stripped the Syrian shops of mortuary taffetas and carried off by the fistful the strings of little gold fish and the protective figs of the ambulant silversmiths in the business district who shouted to her face you're more of a fox than the blue leticias she wore around her neck, she carried off everything she found in her path to satisfy the only thing left from her former status as novice which was her childish poor taste and the vice of asking for something when there was no need, except that now she didn't have to beg in the name of God's love in the jasmine-scented doorways of the viceregal district but she carted off in army trucks everything that pleased her wishes without any more sacrifice on her part except the peremptory order of send the bill to the government. It was the same as saying collect from God, because no one knew for sure from then on whether he existed or not, he had become invisible, we could see the fortified walls on the knoll of the main square, the house of power with the balcony of legendary speeches and the windows with lace curtains and flower pots on the cornices and at night it looked like a steamboat sailing through the sky, not just from any spot in the city but also from seven leagues away at sea after they painted it white and lighted it with glass globes to celebrate the visit of the well-known poet Rubén Darío, although none of those signs indicated for certain that he was there, on the contrary, we thought with good reason that those signs of life were military tricks to try to give the lie to the widespread rumor that he had succumbed to a crisis of senile mysticism, that he had renounced the pomp and circumstance of

power and had imposed upon himself the penance of living
the rest of his life in a fearful state of prostration with hair
shirts of deprivation in his soul and all manner of irons of
mortification on his body, with nothing but rye bread to eat
and well water to drink, or nothing to sleep on except the
slabs of a bare cell from the cloisters of the Biscayan sisters
until he could expiate the horror of having possessed
against her will and having made pregnant with a male child
a forbidden woman who only because God is great had still
not taken her final vows, and yet nothing had changed in
his vast realm of gloom because Leticia Nazareno held the
keys to his power and all she needed to do was say that he
sent word to send the bill to the government, an ancient
formula that at first seemed very easy to evade but which
was getting more and more fearful, until a group of deter-
mined creditors dared present themselves after many years
with a suitcase full of pending bills at the pantry of the
presidential palace and we ran into the surprise that no one
said yes to us and no one said no but they sent us with a
soldier on duty to a discreet waiting room where we were
received by a friendly young naval officer with a calm voice
and a smiling face who offered us thin and fragrant coffee
from the presidential crop, he showed us the white, well-
lighted offices with metal screens on the windows and fans
on the ceiling, and everything was so bright and human that
one wondered in perplexity where the power of that air that
smelled of perfumed medicine was, where was the mean-
ness and the inclemency of power in the conscientiousness
of those clerks in silk shirts who governed without haste
and in silence, he showed us the small inner courtyard
where the rosebushes had been cut down by Leticia
Nazareno to purify the morning dew from the bad memory
of the lepers and the blind men and the cripples who were
sent off to die of oblivion in charity homes, he showed us
the former shed of the concubines, the rusty sewing machines, the army cots where the harem slaves had slept up
to groups of three in cells of shame which was going to be
torn down to build the private chapel in its place, he
showed us from an inside window the most intimate gallery

of government house, the pansy bower gilded by the four o'clock sun on the lattice screen with green stripes where he had just lunched with Leticia Nazareno and the child who were the only people allowed to sit at his table, he showed us the legendary ceiba tree in whose shadow they would hang the hammock with the colors of the flag where he took his siesta on the hottest days, he showed us the milking stables, the cheese vats, the honeycombs, and on coming back along the way he followed at dawn to oversee the milking he seemed to be struck by a bolt of revelation and he pointed out to us the mark of a boot in the mud, look, he said, it's his footprint, we were petrified as we looked at the imprint of a large, coarse sole which had the splendor and the dominion in repose and the stench of old mange of the track of a tiger accustomed to solitude, and in that footprint we saw the power, we felt the contact of his mystery with much more revealing force than when one of us was chosen to see him in person because the higher-ups in the army were beginning to rebel against the new-comer who had managed to accumulate more power than the supreme command, more than the government, more than he, for Leticia Nazareno had come so far with her airs of a queen that the presidential high command itself assumed the risk of opening the way to one of you, only one, in an attempt to have him get at least a tiny little idea of what's happening to the nation behind his back general sir, and that was how I got to see him, he was alone in the hot office with white walls and prints of English horses, he was stretched out in an easy chair, under the fan, in the wrinkled white drill uniform with copper buttons and no insignia of any kind, he had his right hand with the velvet glove on the wooden desk where there was nothing but three identical pairs of very small eyeglasses with gold rims, behind him he had a glass-enclosed case with dusty books that looked more like ledgers bound in human skin, on the right he had a large and open window, also with a metal screen, through which the whole city could be seen and all the sky without clouds or birds all the way to the other side of the sea, and I felt a great relief because he showed himself to be less conscious of his power than any of his partisans and he was more homey than in his photographs and also more worthy of compassion because everything about him was old and arduous and he seemed to be mined by an insatiable illness, so much so that he didn't have the breath to tell me to sit down but indicated it to me with a sad gesture of the velvet glove, he listened to my arguments without looking at me, breathing with a thin and difficult whistling, a mysterious whistling that left a dew of creosote in the room, concentrating deeply on the examination of the bills which I described with schoolboy examples because he couldn't grasp abstract notions, so I began by showing him that Leticia Nazareno owed us for an amount of taffeta twice the nautical distance to Santa María del Altar, that is, one hundred ninety leagues, and he said aha as if to himself, and I ended up by showing him that the total debt with the special discount for your excellency was equal to six times the grand prize in the lottery for ten years, and he said aha again and only then did he look at me directly without his glasses and I could see that his eyes were timid and indulgent, and only then did he tell me with a strange voice of harmony that our reasons were clear and just, to each his own, he said, have them send the bill to the government. That was what he was really like during the period in which Leticia Nazareno had remade him from the beginning without the backwoods difficulties of his mother Bendición Álvarado, she made him give up the habit of eating while walking with the plate in one hand and the spoon in the other and the three of them ate at a little beach table under the pansy bower, he opposite the child and Leticia Nazareno between the two teaching them the norms of good manners and good health in eating, she taught them to keep their spines against the chair back, the fork in the left hand, the knife in the right, chewing each mouthful fifteen times on one side and fifteen times on the other with the mouth closed and the head upright paying no attention to their protests that so many rules were like a barracks, after lunch she taught him to read the official newspaper in which he himself figured as patron and honorary editor, she would put it in his hands when she saw him lying in the hammock in the shade of the gigantic ceiba tree in the family courtyard telling him that it was inconceivable that a full-fledged chief of state should not be up on what was going on in the world, she would put his glasses on him and leave him splashing about in the reading of his own news while she trained the boy in the sport of novices which was throwing and catching a rubber ball, and he would come across himself in photographs so ancient that many of them were not of him but of a former double who had been killed by him and whose name he couldn't remember, he would find himself presiding over the Tuesday cabinet meetings which he hadn't attended since the time of the comet, he learned of historic phrases that his ministers of letters attributed to him, he would read as he nodded in the sultriness of the wandering clouds of August afternoons, he would sink little by little into the corn-soup sweat of his siesta muttering this paper is a piece of shit, God damn it, I can't understand how the people stand for it, he muttered, but something had to come out of that unpleasant reading because he would awaken from his short and tenuous sleep with some new idea inspired by the news, he would send orders to his ministers by Leticia Nazareno, they would answer him through her trying to get a glimpse of his thought, because you were what I wanted you to be the interpreter of my highest designs, you were my voice, you were my reason and my strength, she was his most faithful and attentive ear for the sound of the perpetual lava flows of the inaccessible world which besieged him, even though in reality the final oracles that governed his fate were the anonymous graffiti on the walls of the servants' toilets, in which he would decipher the hidden truths that no one would have dared reveal to him, not even you, Leticia, he would read them at dawn on his way back from the milking before the cleaning orderlies had erased them and he ordered the toilet walls whitewashed every day so that no one could resist the temptation to unburden himself of his hidden rancors, there he learned about the bitterness of the high command, the repressed intentions of those who prospered in his shadow and repudiated him behind his back, he felt master of all his power when he succeeded in penetrating an enigma of the human heart in the revealing mirror of the role of the rabblement, he sang again after so many years contemplating through the mist of the mosquito netting the morning beached whale's sleep of his only and legitimate wife Leticia Nazareno, get up, he sang, it's six o'clock in my heart, the sea is where it belongs, life goes on, Leticia, the unpredictable life of the only one of all his women who had got everything from him except the easy privilege of his awakening in bed with her, for he would leave after the last love, hang the runaway lamp by the door of his old bachelor's bedroom, fasten the three bars, the three locks, the three bolts, drop face down onto the floor, alone and with his clothes on, as he had done every night before you, as he did without you until the last night of his dreams of a solitary drowned man, he would return after the milking to your room with its smell of a beast of darkness to continue giving you whatever you wanted, much more than the incalculable inheritance of his mother Bendición Alvarado, much more than any human being had ever dreamed of on the face of the earth, not only for her but also for her inexhaustible relatives who kept arriving from the unknown keys of the Antilles with no other fortune but the flesh that covered them or any other title but their identity as Nazarenos, a harsh family of intrepid males and women who burned with the fever of greed who had taken by storm the monopolies of salt, tobacco, drinking water, the former perquisites with which he had favored the commanders of the various branches of the armed services so as to keep them away from other kinds of ambition and which Leticia Nazareno had been snatching away from them little by little through his orders which he did not give but approved, agreed, he had abolished the barbarous method of execution of being quartered by horses and had tried to put in its place the electric chair which had been given him by the commander of the landing forces so that we too could enjoy the more civilized method of killing, he had visited the horror laboratory at the harbor

fort where they chose the most run-down of political prisoners in order to get training in the manipulation of the
throne of death whose discharges absorbed the total electrical power of the city, we knew the exact moment of the
fatal experiment because we would be left in darkness for
an instant holding our breath in horror, we would observe
a minute of silence in the waterfront brothels and drink to
the soul of the condemned man, not once but several times,
because most of the victims remained hanging on the straps
of the chair with their bodies looking like a blood sausage
and sizzling like a roast but still panting with pain until
someone had the mercy to shoot them to death after several frustrated attempts, all in order to please you, Leticia,
for you had emptied the dungeons and authorized the
repatriation of his enemies once more and promulgated an
Easter edict that no one was to be punished for differences
of opinion or persecuted for matters of conscience, convinced in his heart in the fullness of his autumn that his
fiercest adversaries had a right to share in the tranquillity
which he enjoyed on engrossing January nights with the
only woman who had merited the glory of seeing him without a shirt and in his long drawers and the enormous rupture gilded by the moon on the terrace of government
house, together they looked at the mysterious willows that
they had been sent by the king and queen of Babylonia
around Christmas time so they could plant them in the rain
garden, they enjoyed the sun as it was broken up through
the perpetual waters, they took pleasure in the pole star
tangled in the branches, they scrutinized the universe on
the dial of the small radio through the interference of jeers
from fugitive planets, together they would listen to the
daily episode of the soap operas from Santiago de Cuba
which would leave in their hearts the feeling of a doubt of
whether we'll still be alive tomorrow to find out how this
misfortune is resolved, he would play with the child before
putting him to bed in order to teach him everything it was
possible to know about the use and maintenance of weapons of war which was the human science he knew better
than anyone, but the only advice he gave him was never

issue an order unless you're sure it's going to be carried out, he made him repeat it as many times as he thought necessary so that the boy would never forget that the only mistake that a man invested with authority and power cannot make even once in his lifetime is to issue an order which he is not sure will be carried out, more a piece of advice from a wary grandfather than from a wise father and which the child would never have forgotten even if he had lived as long as he because he taught it to him while he was preparing him to fire for the first time at the age of six a recoil cannon to whose catastrophic report we attributed the fearful dry storm of volcanic thunder and lightning and the awesome polar wind from Comodoro Rivadavia which turned the bowels of the sea upside down and carried off an animal circus set up on the square of the former slave port, we caught elephants in casting nets, drowned clowns, giraffes hanging on trapezes from the fury of the tempest which miraculously didn't sink the banana boat which arrived a few hours later bearing the young poet Félix Rubén García Sarmiento who was to become famous under the name of Rubén Darío, luckily the sea calmed down at four o'clock, the well-washed air filled with flying ants, and he looked out the bedroom window and saw to the lee of the harbor hills the little white ship listing to starboard and with its rigging dismantled sailing along out of danger in the backwaters of the afternoon that had been purified by the brimstone of the storm, he saw the captain on the quarterdeck directing the difficult maneuvers in honor of the illustrious passenger in a long dark coat and a checkered vest whom he had never heard of until the following Sunday night when Leticia Nazareno requested of him the inconceivable favor of accompanying her to an evening of poetry at the National Theater and he had accepted without blinking, agreed. We had been waiting for three hours standing in the steaming atmosphere of the orchestra seats suffocating in the full dress which had been required of us urgently at the last moment, when finally the national anthem began and we turned in applause toward the box marked with the national coat of arms where the chubby novice appeared in a hat with curling feathers and her nocturnal fox tails over a taffeta gown, she sat down without any greeting beside the young prince in an evening uniform who had answered the applause with the iris of the empty fingers of his velvet glove held in his fist as his mother had told him princes used to do in other days, we saw no one else in the presidential box, but during the two hours of the recital we bore the certainty that he was there, we felt the invisible presence that watched over our destiny so that it would not be altered by the disorder of poetry, he regulated love, he decided the intensity and term of death in a corner of the box in the shadows from where unseen he watched the heavy minotaur whose voice of marine lightning lifted him out of his place and instant and left him floating without his permission in the golden thunder of the trim trumpets of the triumphal arches of Marses and Minervas of a glory that was not his general sir, he saw the heroic athletes with their standards the black mastiffs of the hunt the sturdy war-horses with their iron hoofs the pikes and lances of the paladins with rough crests who bore the strange flag captive to honor arms that were not his, he saw the troop of fierce young men who had challenged the suns of the red summer the snows and winds of the icy winter night and dew and hatred and death for the eternal splendor of an immortal nation larger and more glorious than all those he had dreamed of during the long deliriums of his fevers as a barefoot warrior, he felt poor and tiny in the seismic thunder of the applause that he approved in the shadows thinking mother of mine Bendición Alvarado this really is a parade, not the shitty things these people organize for me, feeling diminished and alone, oppressed by the heavy heat and the mosquitoes and the columns of cheap gold paint and the faded plush of the box of honor, God damn it, how is it possible for this Indian to write something so beautiful with the same hand that he wipes his ass with, he said to himself, so excited by the revelation of written beauty that he dragged his great feet of a captive elephant to the rhythm of the martial beat of the kettledrums, he dozed off to the rhythm of the voices of glory of

the cadenced chant of the calorific choir that Leticia
Nazareno recited for him in the shade of the triumphal
arches of the ceiba tree in the courtyard, he would write the
lines on the walls of the toilets, he was trying to recite the
whole poem by heart in the tepid cowshit olympus of the
milking stables when the earth trembled from the dynamite
charge that went off ahead of time in the trunk of the
presidential automobile parked in the coach house, it was
terrible general sir, such a violent explosion that many
months later all over the city they were still finding twisted
pieces of the armored limousine that Leticia Nazareno and
the child would have used an hour later for their Wednesday marketing, because the attempt was against her life
general sir, without a doubt, and then he slapped his forehead, God damn it, how is it possible he didn't foresee it,
what had become of his legendary clairvoyance because for
so many months the graffiti in the toilets were not against
him, as always, or against any of his civilian ministers, but
were inspired by the audacity of the Nazarenos who had
reached the point of nibbling away at the sinecures reserved for the high command, or by the ambitions of
churchmen who were obtaining limitless and eternal favors
from the temporal power, he had observed that the innocent diatribes against his mother Bendición Alvarado had
become the curses of a macaw, broadsides of hidden rancor
which matured in the warm impunity of the toilets and
ended up coming out onto the streets as had happened so
many times with other minor scandals that he himself had
taken care to precipitate, although he had never thought or
would have been capable of thinking that they could have
been so ferocious as to place two hundred pounds of dynamite within the very confines of government house, sneaky
bastards, how is it possible that he was going around so
absorbed in the ecstasy of the triumphal bronzes that his
fine nose of a ravening tiger had not recognized the old and
sweet smell of danger in time, what a mess, he called an
urgent meeting of the high command, fourteen trembling
military men we were who after so many years of ordinary
behavior and secondhand orders were to see once more at

two fathoms distance the uncertain old man whose real existence was the simplest of his enigmas, he received us sitting on the thronelike seat in the hearing room with the uniform of a private soldier smelling of skunk piss and wearing small eyeglasses with solid gold frames which we had not seen even in his most recent portraits, and he was older and more remote than anyone had been able to imagine, except for the languid hands without the velvet gloves which did not look like his natural soldier's hands but those of someone much younger and more compassionate, everything else was dense and somber, and the more we recognized him the more obvious it was that he just barely had one last breath of life left, but it was the breath of authority without appeal, devastating, difficult even for him to keep in line like the restlessness of a mountain horse, not speaking, not even moving his head as we rendered him the honors of chief supreme general and finally sat down facing him in the easy chairs arranged in a circle, and only then did he take off his glasses and he began to scrutinize us with those meticulous eyes that knew the weasel hiding places of our second intentions, he scrutinized them without mercy, one by one, taking all the time he needed to establish with precision how much each one of us had changed since the afternoon in the mists of memory when he had promoted them to the highest ranks pointing to them according to the impulses of his inspiration, and as he scrutinized them he felt the certainty growing that among those fourteen hidden enemies were the authors of the assassination attempt, but at the same time he felt so alone and defenseless facing them that he only blinked, only lifted his head to exhort them to unity now more than ever for the good of the nation and the honor of the armed forces, he recommended energy and prudence to them and imposed on them the honorable mission of discovering without too much thought the authors of the attempt so that they could be submitted to the serene rigors of military justice, that's all gentlemen, he concluded, knowing full well that the author was one of them, or all of them, mortally wounded by the unavoidable conviction that Leticia Nazareno's life did not depend on God's will then but on the wisdom with which he could manage to preserve it from a threat that sooner or later would irremediably be fulfilled, damn it. He made her cancel her public appearances, he made her more voracious relatives get rid of all privileges that might run afoul of the armed forces, the most understanding were named consuls with a free hand and the most bloody were found floating in the mangrove swamps off the channels by the market, he appeared without prior announcement after so many years in his empty chair in the cabinet room ready to put a limit on the infiltration of the clergy into the business of state in order to keep you safe from your enemies, Leticia, and nevertheless he had made more deep soundings in the high command after the first drastic decisions and was convinced that seven of the commanders were unreservedly loyal to him in addition to the general in chief who was the oldest of his comrades, but still lacked power against the other six enemies who lengthened his nights with the unavoidable impression that Leticia Nazareno was already marked for death, they were killing her right in his hands in spite of the measures to have her food tested ever since the day they found a fish bone in the bread, they tested the purity of the air she breathed because he feared they had poisoned the Flit spray, he saw her looking pale at the table, he felt her become voiceless in the middle of love, he was tormented by the idea that they had put black vomit germs in her drinking water, vitriol in her eye drops, subtle and ingenious ways of death that embittered him at every moment during those days and would awaken him in the middle of his sleep with the vivid nightmare that Leticia Nazareno had been bled during her sleep by an Indian curse, upset by so many imaginary risks and real threats he forbade her to go out without the ferocious escort of presidential guards under instructions to kill without cause, but she did go out general sir, she took the child along, he controlled his feelings of evil omens to watch them get into the new armored limousine, he saw them off with signs of exorcism from an inner balcony begging mother of mine Bendición Alvarado protect them, make the bullets bounce off her brassiere, weaken the laudanum, mother, straighten twisted thoughts, without an instant of rest until he heard the sirens on the escort from the main square and saw Leticia Nazareno and the child crossing the courtyard with the first flashes from the lighthouse, she returned agitated, happy in the midst of the custody of warriors loaded down with live turkeys, orchids from Envigado, strings of little colored lights for Christmas nights already announced on the streets by signs made of luminous stars ordered by him to hide his anxiety, he would meet her on the stairs to feel you still alive in the naphthalene dew of the blue-fox tails, in the sour sweat of your tufts of invalid's hair, he helped you carry the gifts to the bedroom with the strange certainty that he was consuming the last crumbs of a condemned jubilation that he would have preferred never having known, all the more desolate as he became more convinced that every recourse he conceived of to alleviate that unbearable anxiety, every step he took to conjure it away brought him mercilessly closer to the frightful Wednesday of my misfortune when he took the tremendous decision of no more, God damn it, if it had to be let it be soon, he decided, and it was like an explosive order that he had not finished putting together when two of his aides burst into his office with the terrible news that Leticia Nazareno and the child had been torn to pieces and eaten by the stray dogs at the public market, they ate them alive general sir, but they weren't the same usual street dogs but hunting animals with frightened yellow eyes and the smooth skin of a shark that someone had set upon the blue foxes, sixty dogs all alike who nobody knew when leaped out from among the vegetable stands and fell upon Leticia Nazareno and the child without giving us time to shoot for fear of killing them who looked as if they were drowning along with the dogs in a hellish whirlpool, we could only see the instantaneous signs of some ephemeral hands reaching out to us while the rest of the body was disappearing into pieces, we saw fleeting and ungraspable expressions that sometimes were of terror, other times of pity, other times of jubilation until they finally sank into the whirlpool of the scramble and all that was left floating was Leticia Nazareno's hat with felt violets facing the impassive horror of the totemic vegetable women spattered with hot blood who prayed my God, this couldn't be possible unless the general wanted it, or at least unless he didn't know about it, to the eternal dishonor of the presidential guard who without firing a shot could only rescue the bare bones scattered among the bloody vegetables, nothing else general sir, the only thing we found were these medals that belonged to the boy, the saber without its tassels, Leticia Nazareno's cordovan shoes which no one knows why appeared floating in the bay about a league away from the market, the necklace of colored glass, the chain-mail purse which we deliver here to your own hand general sir, along with these three keys, the wedding ring of blackened gold and these fifty cents in ten-cent pieces which they put on the desk for him to count, and nothing else general sir, it was all that was left of them. It wouldn't have mattered to him if more had been left or less, if he had known then that the years he would need to erase down to the last vestige the memory of that inevitable Wednesday were not many or very difficult, he wept with rage, he woke up shouting with rage tormented by the barking of the dogs who spent the night chained in the courtyard while he decided what shall we do with them general sir, wondering in confusion whether killing the dogs might not be killing Leticia Nazareno and the child who were inside them all over again, he ordered them to tear down the iron cupola of the vegetable market and build in its place a garden with magnolias and quails and a marble cross with a light higher and brighter than the lighthouse to perpetuate in the memory of future generations until the end of time the remembrance of a historic woman whom he himself forgot about long before the monument was demolished by a nocturnal explosion that no one avenged, and the magnolias were eaten by hogs and the memorable garden changed into a dungheap of pestilential slime which he never came to know, not only because he had ordered the presidential chauffeur to avoid passing by the former vegetable market even if you have to travel around the world, but also because he never went out again after he sent the officers off to the solar glass windows of the ministries and kept just the minimal personnel to live in the run-down building where by his orders not the least visible vestige of your urges of a queen was left, Leticia, he kept wandering about the empty house with no known task except the eventual consultations with the high command or the final decision of a difficult cabinet meeting or the pernicious visits of Ambassador Wilson who was accustomed to spend time with him until well into the afternoon under the foliage of the ceiba tree and who brought him candy from Baltimore and magazines with color prints of naked women to try to convince him that he should give him the territorial waters on account for the enormous interest on the foreign debt, and he let him speak on, feigning to hear less or more than he really could hear according to his convenience, he defended himself from the wagging tongue by listening to the chorus of the petite painted bird perched on a lemon limb from the nearby girls' school, he would accompany him to the steps with the first shadows of evening trying to explain to him that he could take anything he wanted except the sea of my windows, just imagine, what would I do all alone in this big building if I couldn't look out now as always at this time at what looks like a marsh in flames, what would I do without the December winds that sneak in barking through the broken windowpanes, how could I live without the green flashes of the lighthouse, I who abandoned my misty barrens and enlisted in the agony of fever in the tumult of the federalist war, and don't you think that I did it out of patriotism as the dictionary says, or from the spirit of adventure, or least of all because I gave a shit about federal principles which God keep in his holy kingdom, no my dear Wilson, I did it all so that I could get to know the sea, so think about some other nuisance, he said, he took leave of him on the stairs with a pat on the shoulder, he went back lighting the lamps in the deserted salons of the former offices where on one of those afternoons he found a strayed cow, he chased her toward the stairs and the animal tripped on the patches in the rugs and fell on her back and tumbled down the stairs and broke her neck to the glory and sustenance of the lepers who fell upon her and carved her up, because the lepers had returned after the death of Leticia Nazareno and were there again along with the blind men and the cripples waiting for the salt of health from his hand in the wild rosebushes in the courtyard, he could hear them singing on starry nights, he would sing with them the song Susana come Susana from his times of glory, he would peek out of the skylight in the granary at five in the afternoon to watch the girls coming out of school and would grow ecstatic over their blue aprons, their knee socks, their braids, mother, we would run in fright from the consumptive eyes of the ghost who called to us from behind the iron bars with the torn fingers of his ragged glove, girl, girl, he would call to us, come let me feel you, he would watch them run off in fright thinking mother of mine Bendición Alvarado how young the young girls of today are, he would laugh at himself, but he would become reconciled with himself when his personal physician the minister of health would examine his retina with a magnifying glass every time he invited him to lunch, he would take his pulse, he tried to make me take some spoonfuls of candlewax to plug up the leaks in my memory, what a mess, spoonfuls of medicine for me who hasn't had any ailment in this life except the tertian fevers in the war, shit doctor, he sat eating alone at the single table with his back to the world as the erudite Ambassador Maryland had told him the kings of Morocco ate, he ate with knife and fork and his head erect in accordance with the strict norms of a forgotten teacher, he would go all over the building looking for the jars of honey whose hiding places he would forget after a few hours and he would find by mistake the rolls from the margins of ledgers where he had written in other times so as not to forget anything when he could no longer remember anything, he read on one that tomorrow is Tuesday, he read that there was an initial on your white handkerchief a red initial of a name that was not yours my master, he read intrigued Leticia Nazareno of my soul look what has become of me without you, he read Leticia Nazareno everywhere without being able to understand how anyone could be so unhappy to have left that flow of written sighs, and still it was my handwriting, the unique left-handed calligraphy that was found at that time on the walls of the toilets where he wrote to console himself long live the general, long live the general, God damn it, completely cured of the rage of having been the weakest military man on land sea and air because of a fugitive from the cloister of whom all that remained was the name written in pencil on strips of paper as he had resolved when he didn't even want to touch the things his aides put on his desk and he ordered without looking at them to take away those shoes, those keys, everything that might evoke the image of his dead, to put everything that belonged to them in the bedroom of his wild siestas and wall up the doors and windows with the final order not to enter that room even on my orders, God damn it, he survived the nocturnal shudders of the dogs chained in the courtyard for many months because he thought that any harm done to them might hurt his dead, he abandoned himself to his hammock, trembling with the rage of knowing who the assassins of his blood were and having to bear the humiliation of seeing them in his own house because at that moment he lacked power against them, he had been opposed to any kind of posthumous honors, he had forbidden visits of condolence, mourning, he was waiting for his moment rocking with rage in the hammock in the shade of the tutelary ceiba tree where my last comrade had expressed to him the pride of the high command over the serenity and order with which the people had withstood the tragedy and he gave a glimmer of a smile, don't be a horse's ass old friend, what serenity, what order, what's happening is that the people didn't give a shit for this misfortune, he went back and forth through the newspaper looking for something besides the news invented by his own press services, he had the little radio put within reach to listen to the same news item from Veracruz to Riobamba that the forces of law and order were close on the track of the authors of the attack, and he muttered of course, you sons of a tarantula, they had identified them beyond the slightest doubt, of course, they had them surrounded under mortar fire in a suburban house of ill repute, that's it, he sighed, poor devils, but he stayed in the hammock without displaying even a glimmer of his malice asking mother of mine Bendición Alvarado give me life for this challenge, don't let go of my hand, mother, give me inspiration, so sure of the efficacy of the plea that we found him recovered from his grief when we commanders of the general staff responsible for public order and state security came to give him the news that three of the authors of the crime had been killed in battle with public forces and the other two were awaiting your disposition general sir in the dungeons of San Jerónimo and he said aha, sitting in the hammock with the pitcher of fruit juice from which he poured each of us a glass with the calm pulse of a good marksman, wiser and more solicitous than ever, to the point that he guessed my anxiety to light a cigarette and gave me permission which until then he had never given to any officer on duty, under this tree we're all equals, he said, and he listened without rancor to the detailed report of the crime in the market, how from Scotland they had brought in separate shipments eighty-two newborn bulldogs of whom twenty-two had died in the course of their raising and sixty had been evilly taught to kill by a Scottish trainer who inculcated them with a criminal hatred not only for the blue foxes but for the very persons of Leticia Nazareno and the boy making use of these articles of clothing which they had slipped out little by little from the laundry services in government house, making use of Leticia Nazareno's brassiere, this handkerchief, these stockings, this complete uniform of the boy's which we displayed for him so that he would recognize them, but he only said aha, without looking at them, we explained to him how the sixty dogs had even been trained not to bark when they shouldn't, they were made accustomed to the taste of human flesh, they were kept locked up with no contact with the world for the difficult years of training on a former Chinese farm seven leagues from this capital city where they had life-size figures dressed in the clothing of Leticia Nazareno and the boy whom the dogs also knew from these original pictures and these newspaper clippings which we showed him pasted in an album so that you could get a better idea general sir of the perfection of the work those bastards did, if you could only say that for everybody, but he only said aha, without looking at them, we explained to him lastly that the accused had not been working on their own, of course, but were the agents of a subversive brotherhood with headquarters abroad whose symbol was this goose quill crossed over a knife, aha, all of them fugitives of military penal justice for other previous crimes against the security of the state, these three who are the dead ones whose pictures we showed him in the album with the respective police numbers hanging around their necks, and these two are the ones who are alive and in jail awaiting your final and unappealable decision general sir, the brothers Mauricio and Gumaro Ponce de León, twenty-eight and twenty-three years old, the first an unemployed army deserter with no fixed domicile and the second a ceramics teacher in the school of arts and crafts, and to whom the dogs gave such signs of familiarity and excitement that it alone would have been sufficient proof of guilt general sir, and he only said aha, but he cited with honors in the order of the day the three officers who brought the investigation of the crime to a conclusion and he awarded them the medal of military merit for services to the nation in the course of a solemn ceremony in which he named the summary court-martial which tried the brothers Mauricio and Gumaro Ponce de León and condemned them to be shot within the next forty-eight hours, unless they received the gift of your clemency general sir, you are in command. He remained in the hammock alone and absorbed, insensitive to the pleas for mercy from all over the world, on the radio he heard the sterile debate at the League of Nations, he heard insults from some neighboring countries and some distant support, he listened with equal attention to the timid reasons of the ministers in favor of clemency and the shrill motives of those in favor of punishment, he refused to see the apostolic nuncio with a personal message

173

from the Pope in which he expressed his pastoral concern for the fate of two errant members of the flock, he heard the reports on public order from all over the country which was upset by his silence, he heard the distant shooting, he felt the earth quake from the explosion without origin of a warship anchored in the bay, eleven dead general sir, eighty-two wounded and the ship out of commission, agreed, he said, looking out the bedroom window at the nocturnal bonfire in the cove of the harbor while the two condemned men began to live the night of their eve in the chapel at the San Jerónimo base which was set up as for a wake, he remembered them at that time as he had seen them in their pictures with the bushy eyebrows of their common mother, he remembered them trembling, alone, with the tags of successive numbers hanging around their necks under the always lighted bulb of the death cell, he felt sorry for them, he knew he was needed, required, but he had not made the least gesture that would let the direction of his will peep through when he finished repeating the routine acts of one or more day in his life and he took leave of the duty officer who was to remain on watch by his bedroom to carry the message bearing his decision at any moment he might make it before the first cockcrow, he took leave as he passed without looking at him, good night, captain, he hung the lamp on the door, fastened the three bars, the three locks, the three bolts, sank face down into an alert sleep through whose fragile thin walls he kept on hearing the anxious barking of the dogs in the courtyard, the sirens of the ambulances, the fireworks, the waves of music from some mistaken party in the intense night of the city huddling under the rigor of the sentence, he awoke with the twelve o'clock bells from the cathedral, he woke up again at two o'clock, he woke up again before three with the rattle of the drizzle on the window screens, then he got up off the floor with the arduous maneuvers of an ox first the haunches and then the hind legs and finally the confused head with a string of spittle from his snout and he ordered first to the officer of the guard that he take those dogs off where I won't hear them under the care of the government

until their natural demise, secondly he ordered the uncon-
ditional release of the soldiers from the escort for Leticia
Nazareno and the boy, and lastly he ordered that the brothers Mauricio and Gumaro Ponce de León be executed just
as soon as my supreme and unappealable decision is
known, but not at the execution wall, as had been called for,
but under the punishment that had fallen into disuse, that
of being quartered by horses and their parts exposed to
public indignation and horror in the most visible places of
his measureless realm of gloom, poor lads, while he
dragged his great feet of a badly wounded elephant begging with wrath mother of mine Bendición Alvarado, stay
with me, don't let go of my hand, mother, let me find the
man to help me avenge this innocent blood, a providential
man whom he had imagined in the delirium of his rancor
and whom he sought with an irresistible anxiety in the
depths of the eyes he found in his path, he tried to find him
crouching in the most subtle registers of voices, in the
beating of his heart, in the least used crannies of his memory, and he had lost the illusion of ever finding him when
he discovered himself fascinated by the most dazzling and
haughty man my eyes have ever seen, mother, dressed like
the Goths of yesteryear in a Henry Pool jacket with a gardenia in the buttonhole, with Pecover trousers and a brocade
vest of silver highlights that he had worn with his natural
elegance in the most difficult salons of Europe holding the
leash of a taciturn Doberman the size of a young bull with
human eyes, José Ignacio Saenz de la Barra, at your excellency's service, he introduced himself, the last scion of our
aristocracy which had been demolished by the federalist
leaders, wiped off the face of the nation with their arid
dreams of grandeur and their vast and melancholy mansions and their French accents, a splendid tailend of a
breed with no other fortune but his thirty-two years, seven
languages, four records in trapshooting at Deauville, solid,
slender, the color of iron, half-breed hair with the part in
the middle and a dyed white lock, the linear lips of eternal
will, the resolute look of the providential man who pretended to be playing cricket with a cherrywood cane so they

could take his picture in color with the backdrop of idyllic springtimes of the tapestries in the ballroom, and the instant he saw him he let out a sigh of relief and said to himself that's the one, and that he was. He entered his service under the simple condition that you give me a budget of eight hundred fifty million without my having to give an accounting to anyone and with no authority over me but that of your excellency and in the course of two years I will deliver to you the real assassins of Leticia Nazareno and the child, and he accepted, agreed, convinced of his loyalty and his efficiency after so many difficult tests to which he had submitted him in order to scrutinize the byways of his soul and learn the limits of his will and the chinks in his character before deciding to place in his hands the keys to his power, he submitted him to the ultimate test of the inclement domino games in which José Ignacio Saenz de la Barra assumed the temerity of winning without permission, and he won, because he was the bravest man my eyes had ever seen, mother, he had a patience without pause, he knew everything, he was familiar with seventy-two ways of making coffee, he could distinguish the sex of shellfish, he could read music and Braille, he would stand looking into my eyes without speaking, and I didn't know what to do opposite that indestructible face, those listless hands on the nub of the cherrywood cane with a morning-water stone on the ring finger, that huge dog lying by his feet watchful and ferocious inside the live velvet wrapping of his sleeping skin, that fragrance of bath salts of a body immune to tenderness and death belonging to the most handsome man and the one with the most control my eyes had ever seen when he had the courage to tell me that I was only a military man out of convenience, because military men are just the opposite of you, general, they're men of quick and easy ambition, they like command better than power and they're not in the service of something but of someone, and that's why it's so easy to make use of them, he said, especially one against the other, and all I could think of to do was smile persuaded that he couldn't have hidden his thoughts from that dazzling man to whom he had given more power than anyone he ever had under his regime since my comrade General Rodrigo de Aguilar whom God keep at his holy right side, he made him absolute master of a secret empire within his own private empire, an invisible service of repression and extermination that not only lacked an official identity but was even difficult to conceive of in its real existence, because no one was responsible for its acts, nor did it have a name or a location in the world, and yet it was a fearsome truth that had been imposed by terror over other organs of repression of the state for a long time before its origins and its unfathomable nature had been established in all certainty by the high command, not even you yourself foresaw the reach of that machine of horror general sir, nor could I myself suspect that at the instant in which he accepted the agreement I was at the mercy of the irresistible charm and the tentacular drive of that barbarian dressed like a prince who sent to me at the presidential palace a fiber sack that seemed to be full of coconuts and he ordered them to put it over there in a closet for file papers built into the wall where it would be out of the way, he forgot about it and after three days it was impossible to breathe because of the stench of carrion that penetrated the walls and fogged the mirrors over with a pestilential mist, we looked for the stink in the kitchen and we found it in the stables, we chased it out of the offices with incense and it came out to meet us in the hearing room, with its outpouring of rotted roses it saturated the most hidden crannies where even concealed in other fragrances the tiniest breath of the nighttime plague air mange had reached, and yet it was where we had looked for it least in the sack of seeming coconuts that José Ignacio Saenz de la Barra had sent as the first fruit of the agreement, six heads with the corresponding death certificates, the head of the blind stone-age founding father Don Nepomuceno Estrada, age ninety-four, last veteran of the great war and founder of the Radical Party, dead according to the accompanying certificate on May 14 as the consequence of a senile collapse, the head of Dr. Nepomuceno Estrada de la Fuente, son of the first, age fifty-seven, homeopathic physician, dead according to the accompanying certificate on the same date as his father as the consequence of a coronary thrombosis, the head of Eliécer Castor, age twenty-one, student of letters, dead according to the accompanying certificate as a consequence of various stab wounds from a barroom fight, the head of Lídice Santiago, age thirty-two, clandestine activist, dead according to the certificate as the consequence of an induced abortion, the head of Roque Pinzón, alias Jacinto the Invisible, age thirty-eight, manufacturer of colored globes, dead on the same date as the previous as a consequence of ethyl alcohol intoxication, the head of Natalicio Ruiz, secretary of the clandestine October 17 Movement, age thirty, dead according to the accompanying certificate as a consequence of a pistol shot in the palate because of a broken love affair, six in all, and the corresponding receipt which he signed with his bile all bubbling because of the smell and the horror thinking mother of mine Bendición Alvarado this man is a beast, who would have imagined that with his airs of a mystic and the flower in his buttonhole, he ordered don't send me any more chops, Nacho, your word is enough, but Saenz de la Barra answered that it was a matter between men, general, if you haven't got the stomach to look truth in the face here's your gold and we're the same friends we were before, what a mess, for much less than that he would have had his own mother shot, but he bit his tongue, it's all right, Nacho, he said, do your duty, so the heads kept on coming in those shadowy fiber sacks that looked like bags of coconuts and with his innards all twisted he ordered them taken far away from here while he forced himself to read the details of the death certificates in order to sign the receipts, agreed, he had signed for nine hundred eighteen heads of his fiercest enemies the night he dreamed that he saw himself changed into an animal with only one finger which went along leaving a trail of fingerprints on a plain of fresh concrete, he woke up with a dampness of bile, he eluded his bad dawn mood by taking a head count in the dungheap of sour memories of the milking stalls, so abstracted in his old-man ponderings that he confused the buzzing in his eardrums

178

with the sound of the insects in the rotten hay thinking
mother of mine Bendición Alvarado how is it possible that
there are so many of them and they still haven't got to the
ones who are really guilty, but Saenz de la Barra had made
him note that with every six heads sixty enemies are produced and for every sixty six hundred are produced and
then six thousand and then six million, the whole country,
God damn it, we'll never end, and Saenz de la Barra answered him impassively to rest easy, general, we'll finish
with them when they're all finished, what a barbarian. He
never had an instant of doubt, he never left a chink for an
alternative, he relied on the hidden strength of the Doberman lying in wait eternally who was the only witness to the
audiences in spite of the fact that he tried to stop it from
the first time he saw José Ignacio Saenz de la Barra leading
the animal with mercurial nerves who only obeyed the imperceptible mastery of the most dashing but also the least
accommodating man my eyes have ever seen, leave that
dog outside, he ordered, but Saenz de la Barra answered
him no, general, there's no place in the world where I can
enter where Lord Köchel doesn't enter, so he entered, he
remained asleep at his master's feet while they took the
routine account of the severed heads but he got up with a
throbbing anxiousness when the accounting became harsh,
his feminine eyes made it hard for me to think, his human
breath made me shudder, I saw him lift up his steaming
snout suddenly with the bubbling of a saucepan when he
pounded on the table with rage because in the sack he had
found the head of a former aide who had also been his
domino crony for many years, God damn it, that's the end
of this mess, but Saenz de la Barra always convinced him,
not so much with arguments as with his soft inclemency of
a trainer of wild dogs, he reproached himself for his submission to the only mortal who dared treat him like a vassal,
alone he rebelled against his domination, he decided to
shake himself loose of that servitude which was slowly satu-
rating the space of his authority, this mess is all over right
now, God damn it, he would say, because when all's said
and done Bendición Alvarado didn't give birth to me to

take orders but to give them, but his nighttime decisions fell apart the moment Saenz de la Barra came into the office and he would succumb to the dazzle of his soft manners the natural gardenia his pure voice aromatic salts emerald cufflinks the waxed head his serene walking stick the serious beauty of the most attractive and most unbearable man my eyes had ever seen, it's all right, Nacho, he would repeat, do your duty, and he kept on receiving the sacks of heads, he signed the receipts without looking at them, he sank with nothing to grasp on to into the quicksands of his power wondering with every passage of every dawn of every sea what's happening in the world it's going on eleven o'clock and there isn't a soul in this cemetery house, who's there, he asked, only he, where am I that I can't find myself, he said, where are the teams of barefoot orderlies who unload the donkeys with their greens and chicken cages in the passageways, where are the puddles of dirty water of my foul-mouthed women who replaced the night flowers with fresh ones in the vases and washed the cages and shook rugs off the balconies singing to the rhythm of their dry reed brooms the song Susana come Susana I want to enjoy your love, where are my skinny seven-month runts who shat behind the doors and drew dromedaries in piss on the walls of the hearing room, what happened to my uproar of clerks who found hens laying in the file drawers, my traffic of whores and soldiers in the toilets, the rampaging of my street dogs who ran about barking at diplomats, who has taken my cripples away from the stairs again, my lepers from the rose beds, my insistent adulators from everywhere, he could barely catch a glimpse of his last comrades of the high command behind the compact fence of the new ones responsible for his personal security, he barely had occasion to participate in the meetings of new cabinet members named at the instance of someone who was not he, six doctors of letters in funereal frock coats and wing collars who anticipated his thoughts and decided on matters of government without consulting me about them and I am the government after all, but Saenz de la Barra explained to him impassively that you aren't the government, general, you are the power, he grew bored on domino nights even when he faced the sharpest opponents because try as he might to set up the best traps against himself he couldn't lose, he had to submit to the designs of the testers who dunked into his meals an hour before he could eat them, he couldn't find the honey in its hiding places, God damn it, this isn't the power I wanted, he protested, and Saenz de la Barra answered that there isn't any other, general, it was the only power possible in the lethargy of death which in other times had been his paradise and when he had no other chore except to wait for four o'clock to listen to the radio and the daily episode of the soap opera with its sterile loves on the local station, he would listen to it in the hammock with his pitcher of fruit juice untouched in his hand, he would remain floating in the emptiness of suspense his eyes moist with tears over the anxiety to know whether that girl who was so young was going to die or not and Saenz de la Barra would ascertain yes, general, the girl is going to die, then she's not to die, God damn it, he ordered, she's going to keep on living to the end and get married and have children and get old like everybody else, and Saenz de la Barra had the script changed to please him with the illusion that he was giving the orders, so no one died again by his orders, engaged couples who didn't love each other got married, people buried in previous episodes were resuscitated and villains were sacrificed ahead of time in order to please him general sir, everybody was to be happy by his orders so that life would seem less useless when he inspected the building to the metallic clangs of eight o'clock and he found that someone ahead of him had changed the cows' fodder, the lights had been turned off in the barracks of the presidential guard, the personnel were asleep, the kitchens were in order, the floors clean, the butcher blocks scrubbed with creolin without a trace of blood had a hospital smell about them, someone had drawn the bars on the windows and had locked the offices in spite of the fact that it was he and he alone who had the ring of keys, the lights were going out one by one before he touched the switches from the first vestibule down to his

181

bedroom, he was walking in the dark dragging his thick feet of a captive monarch past the darkened mirrors with the single spur wrapped in velvet so that nobody could follow his trail of gold shavings, he went along seeing as he passed the same sea through the windows, the Caribbean in January, he looked at it without stopping twenty-three times and it was the same as always in January like a flowering swamp, he looked into Bendición Alvarado's room to see that her legacy of lemon balm was still in its place, the cages of dead birds, the bed of pain where the mother of her country bore her rotting old age, have a good night, he murmured, as always, even though no one had answered him for such a long time a very good night to you son, sleep with God, he headed toward his bedroom with the runaway lamp when he felt the shiver of the astonished hot coals that were Lord Köchel's eyes in the dark, caught a fragrance of man, the thickness of his dominion, the glow of his disdain, who goes there, he asked, although he knew who it was, José Ignacio Saenz de la Barra in full dress who was coming to remind him that it was an historic night, August 12, general, the immense date on which we were celebrating the first centenary of his rise to power, so that visitors had come from all over the world captivated by the announcement of an event which it was possible to witness only once in the passage of the longest of lives, the nation was celebrating, everybody in the nation except him, since in spite of the insistence of José Ignacio Saenz de la Barra that he live that memorable night in the midst of the clamor and fervor of his people, earlier than ever he drew the three bars of his sleeping dungeon, threw the three bolts, the three locks, he lay face down on the bare bricks with his rough denim uniform without insignia, the boots, the gold spur, and the right arm bent under his head to serve as a pillow as we were to find him pecked away by the vultures and infested with animals and flowers from the bottom of the sea, and through the mist of the sleeping potions he perceived the remote rockets of the celebration without him, he perceived the joyful music, the bells of pleasure, the torrent of slime of the crowds who had come to exalt a glory that was not theirs, while he murmured more absorbed than sad mother of mine Bendición Alvarado of my destiny, a hundred years already, God damn it, a hundred years already, the way time passes.

THERE HE WAS, then, as if it had been he even though it might not be, lying on the banquet table in the ballroom with the feminine splendor of a dead pope amidst the flowers in which he would not have recognized himself in the display ceremony of his first death, more fearsome dead than alive, the velvet glove stuffed with cotton on a chest armored with false medals of imaginary victories in chocolate wars invented by his persistent adulators, the thunderous full-dress uniform and the patent leather boots and the single gold spur that we found in the building and the ten sad pips of general of the universe to which he was promoted at the final moment to give him a rank higher than that of death, so immediate and visible in his new posthumous identity that for the first time it was possible to believe in his real existence without any doubt whatsoever, although in reality no one looked less like him, no one was so much the opposite of him as that showcase corpse which was still cooking in the middle of the night on the slow fire of the tiny space of the little room where he was laid out with candles while in the cabinet room next door we were discussing the final bulletin with the news that no one dared believe word by word when we were awakened by the noise of the trucks loaded with troops in battle gear whose stealthy patrols had been occupying public buildings since before dawn, they took up prone positions under the arcades of the main commercial street, they hid in doorways, I saw them setting up tripod machine guns on the roofs of the viceregal district when I opened the balcony of my house at dawn looking for a place to put the bouquet of wet carnations I had just cut in the courtyard, beneath the balcony I saw a patrol of soldiers under the command of a lieutenant going from door to door ordering people to close the doors of the few shops that were beginning to open on the commercial street, today is a national holiday they shouted, orders from higher up, I threw them a carnation from the balcony and I asked what was going on with so many soldiers and so much noise of weapons everywhere and the officer caught the carnation in midair and replied to me just imagine girl we don't know ourselves either, the dead man must have come back to life, he said, dying with laughter, because nobody dared think such an earthshaking event could have happened, rather, on the contrary, we thought that after so many years of negligence he had picked up the reins of his authority again and was more alive than ever, once more dragging his great feet of an illusory monarch through the house of power where the globes of light had gone on again, we thought that he was the one who had put out the cows as they frisked about over the cracks in the paving on the main square where the blind man sitting in the shade of the dying palm trees mistook the hoofs for military boots and recited those lines of poetry about the happy warrior who came from afar in a conquest of death, he recited them with full voice and his hand outstretched toward the cows who climbed up to eat the balsam apple garlands on the bandstand with their habit of going up and down stairs to eat, they stayed on to live among the ruins of the muses crowned with wild camellias and the monkeys hanging from the lyres of the rubble of the National Theater, dying with thirst and with the clatter of broken pots of spikenards they went into the cool shadows of entranceways in the viceregal district and sank their burning snouts into the pools in inner courtyards and no one dared molest them because we recognized the congenital brand of the presidential iron which the females bore on their flanks and the males on their necks, they were untouchable, even the soldiers made way for them on the narrow turns of the commercial street which had lost its former clamor of an infernal Moorish bazaar, all that was left was a rubble pile of broken ship frames and pieces of rigging in the puddles of burning sludge where the public market had been when we still had the sea and the schooners lay aground among the vegetable stands, there were empty spaces where the Hindu bazaars had stood in his times of glory, because the Hindus had left, they didn't even say thank you to him general sir, and he shouted what the hell, confused by his last senile tantrums, let them go clean up Englishmen's shit, he shouted, they all left, in their place street vendors of Indian amulets and snakebite cures rose up, the frantic seedy jukebox bars with beds for rent in the rear which the soldiers wrecked with their rifle butts while the iron bells of the cathedral announced the mourning, everything had come to an end before he did, we had even extinguished the last breath of the hopeless hope that someday the repeated and always denied rumor that he had finally succumbed to some one of his many regal illnesses would be true, and yet we didn't believe it now that it was, and not because we really didn't believe it but because we no longer wanted it to be true, we had ended up not understanding what would become of us without him, what would become of our lives after him, I couldn't conceive of the world without the man who had made me happy at the age of twelve as no other man was ever to do again since those afternoons so long ago when we would come out of school at five o'clock and he would be lying in wait by the skylights of the stables for the girls in blue uniforms with sailors' collars and a single braid thinking mother of mine Bendición Alvarado how pretty women look to me at my age, he would call to us, we would see his quivering eyes, the hand with the glove with torn fingers which tried to entice us with the candy rattle from Ambassador Forbes, they all ran off frightened, all except me, I stood alone on the street by the school when I knew that no one was watching me and I tried to reach the candy and he grabbed me by the wrists with a gentle tiger's claw and lifted me painlessly up into the air, took me through the skylight with such care that not a pleat in my dress was wrinkled and he laid me down on the hay that was scented with rancid urine trying to tell me something that wouldn't come out of his arid mouth because he was more frightened than I, he was trembling, you could see his heart beating under his jacket, he was pale, his eyes were full of tears as no other man ever had them in all of my life in exile, he touched me in silence, breathing unhurriedly, he tempted me with a male tenderness which I never found again, he made my little buds stand out on my breasts, he put his fingers underneath the edge of my panties, he smelled his fingers, he made me smell them, smell it, he told me, it's your smell, I didn't need Ambassador Baldrich's candy any more to climb through the stable skylight to live the happy hours of my puberty with that man of a healthy and sad heart who waited for me sitting in the hay with a bag containing things to eat, he used bread to soak up my first adolescent sauce, he would put things there before eating them, he gave them to me to eat, he put asparagus stalks into me to eat them marinated with the brine of my inner humors, delicious, he told me, you taste like a port, he dreamed about eating my kidneys boiled in their own ammonia stew, with the salt of your armpits, he dreamed, with your warm urine, he sliced me up from head to toe, he seasoned me with rock salt, hot pepper and laurel leaves and left me to boil on a hot fire in the incandescent fleeting mallow sunsets of our love with no future, he ate me from head to toe with the drive and the generosity of an old man which I never found again in so many hasty and greedy men who tried to make love to me without managing to for the rest of my life without him, he talked to me about himself during the slow digestions

of love while we pushed away from us the snouts of the
cows who were trying to lick us, he told me that not even
he himself knew who he was, that he was up to his balls with
general sir, he said it without bitterness, without any reason, as if talking to himself, floating in the continuous buzzing of an inner silence that could only be broken with
shouts, no one was more gracious or wiser than he, no one
more of a man, he had become the only reason for my life
at the age of fourteen when two military men of the highest
rank appeared at my parents' home with a suitcase bulging
with solid gold doubloons and in the middle of the night
they put me aboard a foreign ship along with my whole
family and orders never to return to the national territory
for years and years until the news burst in the world that
he had died without having known that I had spent the rest
of my life dying for him, I would go to bed with strangers
off the street to see if I could find one better than he, I
returned aged and embittered with this drove of sons by
different fathers with the illusion that they were his, and on
the other hand he had forgotten her the second day he
didn't see her climb in through the skylight of the milking
stables, he replaced her with a different one every afternoon because by then he couldn't distinguish very well who
was who among the troop of schoolgirls in identical uniforms who stuck out their tongues at him and shouted old
soursop when he tried to entice them with candy from
Ambassador Rumpelmayer, he called them without distinction, without ever wondering if today's had been the same
one as yesterday's, he received them all equally, he thought
of them all as the same one while he listened half-asleep in
the hammock to the always identical arguments of Ambassador Streimberg who had given him an ear trumpet just
like the one with the dog of his master's voice with an
electrical amplifying device so that he could listen once
more to the insistent plan to carry off our territorial waters
as surety for the interest on the foreign debt and he repeated the same as always never in a million years my dear
Stevenson, anything except the sea, he would disconnect
the electric hearing aid so as not to continue listening to

that loud voice of a metallic creature who seemed to be turning the record over to explain to him once more what had been explained to me so many times by my own experts without any dictionary tricks that we're down to our skins general sir, we had used up our last resources, bled by the age-old necessity of accepting loans in order to pay the interest on the foreign debt ever since the wars of independence and then other loans to pay the interest on back interest, always in return for something general sir, first the quinine and tobacco monopolies for the English, then the rubber and cocoa monopoly for the Dutch, then the concession for the upland railroad and river navigation to the Germans, and everything for the gringos through the secret agreements that he didn't find out about until after the sudden downfall and public death of José Ignacio Saenz de la Barra whom God keep roasting on an open flame in the cauldrons of his deep hell, we didn't have anything left general, but he had heard the same thing said by all of his treasury ministers ever since the difficult days when a moratorium was declared on the obligation contracted from the bankers of Hamburg, the German fleet had blockaded the port, an English warship had fired a warning shot that opened a breach in the cathedral tower, but he shouted I shit on London's king, better dead than sold down the river, he shouted, death to the Kaiser, saved at the last moment by the good offices of his domino companion Ambassador Charles W. Traxler whose government underwrote a guarantee of the European agreements in exchange for a right of lifetime exploitation of our subsoil and ever since then we've been the way we are owing everything down to the drawers we're wearing general sir, but he took the eternal five o'clock ambassador to the stairs and took leave of him with a pat on the shoulder, never in a million years my dear Baxter, I'd rather be dead than without a sea, overwhelmed by the desolation of that cemetery house where one could walk without running into anyone as if one were under water ever since the evil times of that José Ignacio Saenz de la Barra of my mistake who had cut off the heads of the whole human species except those he was

189

supposed to cut off, those of the authors of the assassination of Leticia Nazareno and the child, the birds refused to sing in their cages no matter how many drops of Cantorina he put in their beaks, the girls in the school next door no longer sang their recess song about the petite painted bird perched on the green lemon limb, life had been going off for the impatient wait to be with you in the stables, my child, with your little palm-nut teats and your clam of a thing, he ate alone under the pansy bower, he floated in the quivering two o'clock heat pecking at his siesta sleep so as not to lose the thread of the television movie in which everything happened according to his orders and completely the opposite of life, because the all-worthy who knew everything never knew that ever since the times of José Ignacio Saenz de la Barra we had first installed an individual transmitter for the soap operas on the radio and then a closed-circuit television system so that only he would see the movies arranged to his taste in which no one died except the villains, love prevailed over death, life was a breath of fresh air, we made him happy with the trick as he had been so many afternoons of his old age with the girls in uniform who would have pleased him until his death if he had not had the bad luck to ask one of them what do they teach you in school and I told him the truth that they don't teach me anything sir, what I am is a waterfront whore, and he made her repeat it in case he hadn't understood well what he had read on my lips and I repeated it letter by letter that I'm not a student sir, I'm a waterfront whore, the sanitation service had bathed her in creolin and rinsed her off, they told her to put on this sailor suit and these nice-girl's stockings and go along this street every afternoon at five, not just me but all the whores of my age recruited and bathed by the sanitary police, all with the same uniform and the same men's shoes and these horsehair braids which look you can put on and take off like a comb, they told us don't be afraid he's a poor foolish old grandfather who isn't even going to lay you but will give you a doctor's examination with his finger and suck on your titties and put things to eat in your pussies, well, everything you do to me when

I come, all we had to do was close our eyes in pleasure and say my love my love which is what you like, they told us that and they even made us rehearse and repeat everything from the beginning before they paid us, but I think it's too much of a drag all those ripe bananas in the twitty-twat and all those parboiled malangas up the behind for the four consumptive pesos we've got left after deducting the sanitation tax and the sergeant's commission, God damn it, it's not right to ruin all that food down below if a person doesn't have anything to eat up above, she said, wrapped in the lugubrious aura of the unfathomable old man who listened to the revelation without blinking as he thought mother of mine Bendición Alvarado why do you send me this punishment, but he didn't give any sign that would reveal his desolation taking care rather in every kind of stealthy investigation until he discovered that the girls' school next door had in fact been closed for many years general sir, his own minister of education had provided the funds in an agreement with the archbishop primate and the heads of family association to construct a new three-story building on the shore where the princesses of families of great conceit were safe from the ambushes of the sunset seducer whose body of a beached shad face up on the banquet table began to stand out against the pale mallow of the moon-crater horizon of our first dawn without him, he was under the protection of everything among the snowy African lilies, free at last of his absolute power at the end of so many years of reciprocal captivity in which it was difficult to distinguish who was the victim of whom in that cemetery of living presidents which they had painted tomb-white inside and out without consulting me about it but rather they ordered him around without recognizing him don't come in here sir you'll dirty our whitewash, and he didn't go in, stay up on the second floor sir a scaffold might fall on you, and he stayed there, confused by the noise of the carpenters and the rage of the masons who shouted at him get away from here you old fool you'll get the mixture all shitty, and he got away, more obedient than a soldier during the harsh months of a renovation done without consulting him which opened new windows to the sea, more alone than ever under the fierce vigilance of an escort whose mission didn't seem to be to protect him but to watch over him, they ate half of his meal to avoid his being poisoned, they changed the hiding place of his honey, they put his gold spur on up where a fighting cock has his so it wouldn't bell-ring when he walked, God damn it, a whole string of cowboy tricks that would have made my comrade Saturno Santos die of laughter, he lived at the mercy of eleven flunkies in jacket and tie who spent the day doing Japanese acrobatics, they brought in an apparatus with green and red lights that went on and off when someone within a radius of two hundred feet was carrying a weapon, and we went through the streets like fugitives in seven identical cars which kept changing places, some getting ahead of others along the way so that even I didn't know which one I'm riding in, God damn it, a useless waste of gunpowder on buzzards because he'd pushed the blinds aside to see the streets after so many years of confinement and he saw that no one was reacting to the stealthy passage of funereal limousines of the presidential caravan, he saw the cliffs of solar glass of the ministries that rose up higher than the towers of the cathedral and had cut off the colorful promontories of the Negro shacks on the harbor hills, he saw a patrol of soldiers erasing a sign recently painted with a broad brush on a wall and he asked what it had said and they answered eternal glory to the maker of the new nation although he knew it was a lie, of course, if not they wouldn't have been erasing it, God damn it, he saw an avenue with coconut palms six lanes wide with flower beds down to the sea where the bogs had been, he saw a suburb with villas replete with Roman porticoes and hotels with Amazonian gardens where the public market dump had been, he saw cars moving like tortoises along the serpentine labyrinths of the urban freeways, he saw the crowds dulled by the dog-days sun of high noon on the sun-baked sidewalk while on the opposite side there was no one but the unofficial collectors of the tax for the right to walk in the shade, but no one trembled that time with the omen of hidden power in the refrigerated coffin of a presidential limousine, no one recognized the disillusioned eyes, the anxious lips, the useless hand that kept giving undestined waves amidst the shouting of vendors of newspapers and amulets, the ice cream carts, the three-numbered lottery signs, the everyday clamor of the street world alien to the intimate tragedy of the solitary military man who was sighing with nostalgia thinking mother of mine Bendición Alvarado what has happened to my city, where is the alley of misery of women without me who came out naked at dusk to buy blue corvinas and red snappers and exchange mother curses with the vegetable women while their clothes were drying on the balconies, where are the Hindus who shat by the doors of their stalls, where are their pale wives who soften death with songs of pity, where is the woman who was changed into a scorpion for having disobeyed her parents, where are the mercenaries' bars, their brooks of fermented urine, the everyday look of the pelicans around the corner, and, suddenly, alas, the waterfront, where is it because it used to be here, what happened to the smugglers' schooners, the iron scarp from the marines' landing, my smell of shit, mother, what was going on in the world that no one recognized the fugitive lover's hand in the oblivion as it left a wake of useless waves of the hand from the opened panes of the window of an inaugural train that whistled through fields planted with aromatic herbs where the swamps with strident malaria birds in the rice paddies had been, it passed along through the unlikely plains of blue grazing land frightening herds of cattle marked with the presidential brand and inside the railroad car of responses to my irrevocable fate padded with ecclesiastical plush he went along wondering where was my little old four-legged train, damn it, my boughs with anacondas and poisonous balsam apples, my uproar of monkeys, my birds of paradise, the whole nation with its dragon, mother, where is it all because there used to be stations here with taciturn Indian women in derbies who sold candy animals through the windows, they sold mashed potatoes, mother, they sold hens boiled in yellow lard under the arches of a sign made out of flowers eternal glory to the all-worthy that nobody knows where he is, but whenever he protested that that life of a fugitive was worse than being dead they answered no general sir it was peace within order, they told him, and he ended up accepting it, agreed, dazzled one more time by the personal fascination of José Ignacio Saenz de la Barra of my unmothering whom he had degraded and spat upon so many times in the rage of his sleeplessness but he would succumb again to his charms as soon as he entered the office with the light of day leading that dog with the look of human people whom he doesn't leave even to urinate and who has a person's name besides Lord Köchel, and once more he would accept his formulas with a meekness that rose up against himself, don't worry Nacho, he would give in, do your duty, so that José Ignacio Saenz de la Barra would go back once more with his powers intact to the torture he had set up less than five hundred yards from the presidential palace in the innocent colonial masonry building which had been the Dutch insane asylum, a house as large as yours general sir, hidden in an almond grove and surrounded by a field of wild violets, the first floor of which was reserved for the identification and registry services of the civil state and where in the rest of the building the most ingenious and barbarous machines of torture that the imagination could conceive of were installed, so terrible that he hadn't wanted to know about them but advised Saenz de la Barra you keep on doing your duty as best suits the interests of the nation with the only condition that I know nothing and I haven't seen anything and I've never been in that place, and Saenz de la Barra pledged his word of honor to serve you, general, and he had kept it, just as he followed his orders not to go back to martyrizing children under the age of five with electric wires on their testicles in order to force their parents to confess because he was afraid that the infamy might repeat itself during the insomnia of all those nights the same as during the days of the lottery, although it was impossible for him to forget about that workshop of horror because it was such a short distance from his bedroom and on nights of a quiet moon he would be awakened by the fleeting train music of Bruckner thunder dawns that brought on ruinous floods and left a desolation of tattered gowns of dead brides on the branches of the almond trees at the former Dutch lunatic asylum all so that the shrieks of terror and pain of those dying would not be heard on the street, and all of that without collecting a cent general sir, because José Ignacio Saenz de la Barra used his salary to buy the clothing of a prince, shirts of natural silk with his monogram on the chest, kid shoes, boxes of gardenias for his lapel, lotions from France with the family crest printed on the original label, but he didn't have a woman that anybody knew of and no one said he's a fairy and he doesn't have a single friend or a house of his own to live in, nothing general sir, the life of a saint, slaving away at the torture factory until fatigue made him drop onto the couch in the office where he slept as best he could but never at night and never more than three hours at a time, with no guard at the door, no weapon within reach, under the tense protection of Lord Köchel who was bursting his skin from the anxiety caused by eating the only thing they say he eats, that is, the hot guts of the beheaded people, making that boiling-pot sound to awaken him as soon as his look of a human person sensed through the walls that someone was approaching the office, no matter who it is general sir, that man doesn't even trust mirrors, he would make his decisions without consulting anyone after listening to the reports of his agents, nothing went on in the country and no exile in any part of the planet could so much as sigh without José Ignacio Saenz de la Barra's knowing about it immediately thanks to the threads of the invisible web of informers and bribery with which he had covered the whole orb of the earth, that's what he spent his money on general sir, because it wasn't true that the torturers received the salary of ministers as people said, on the contrary, they volunteered for nothing to show that they were capable of quartering their mothers and throwing the pieces to the pigs without any change in their voice, instead of letters of recommendation and certificates of good conduct, they offered testimony of atrocious antecedents so they would be given work under the guidance of French torturers who are rationalists general sir, and consequently are methodical in cruelty and resistant to compassion, they were the ones who made progress within order possible, they were the ones who anticipated conspiracies long before they started incubating in people's thoughts, the distracted customers who were enjoying the coolness of the fan blades in ice cream parlors, those reading the newspaper in Chinese lunchrooms, those who slept in the movies, those who gave their seats on the bus to ladies, those who had learned to be electricians and plumbers after having passed half a lifetime as nocturnal muggers and bandits of the byways, the casual boyfriends of servant girls, the whores on ocean liners and in international cocktail lounges, the promoters of tourist trips from Miami to the paradises of the Caribbean, the private secretary of the Belgian minister of foreign affairs, the tenured chambermaid of the fourth floor of the International Hotel in Moscow, and so many others that no one knows to what far corner of the earth they reach, but you can sleep peacefully general sir, because the good patriots of the nation say that you know nothing, that all of this is going on without your consent, that if general sir knew it he would have sent Saenz de la Barra to push up daisies in the renegades' cemetery at the harbor fort, because every time they learned of a new act of barbarism they would sigh inside if the general only knew, if we could only make him know, if there were some way to see him and he ordered the one who had told him never to forget that the truth is I don't know anything, I haven't seen anything, I haven't talked about these things with anyone, and in that way he regained his calm, but so many sacks of severed heads kept arriving that it seemed inconceivable to him that José Ignacio Saenz de la Barra was daubing himself with blood up to his tonsure without some benefit from it because people are dumb bastards but not that dumb, nor did it seem reasonable to him that whole years could pass without the commanders of the three services protesting over their subordinate status, nor did they ask for a raise in salary, nothing, so he had made soundings on his own to try to establish the causes of military compliance, he wanted to find out why they weren't trying to rebel, why they accepted the authority of a civilian, and he had asked the most greedy of them if they didn't think it was time to trim the crest of the bloodthirsty upstart who was tarnishing the merits of the armed forces, but they answered him of course not general sir, it's nothing serious, and since then I no longer know who is who, or who is with whom or against whom in this snare of progress within order that's starting to smell to me like someone playing possum like that other time I don't care to recall with the poor children and the lottery, but José Ignacio Saenz de la Barra calmed his drives with his suave domination of a trainer of wild dogs, sleep in peace, general, he told him, the world is yours, he made him believe that everything was so simple and so clear that he left him again in the shadows of that no man's house which he would cover from one end to the other asking himself with great shouts who the hell am I because I feel as if the reflection in the mirrors is reversed, where the hell am I because it's going on eleven o'clock in the morning and there isn't a single hen even a stray one in this desert, remember the way it was before, he shouted, remember the uproar of the lepers and the cripples as they fought with the dogs over food, remember that slippery chute of animal shit on the stairs and that hullabaloo of patriots who wouldn't let me walk with their begging throw the salt of health on my body general sir, baptize my body to see if he can get rid of his diarrhea because they all said my laying on of hands had binding virtues more effective than green bananas, put your hand here to see if my palpitations die down because I don't feel like living any more with this eternal earth tremor, fix your eyes on the sea general sir to send the hurricanes away, look up to the skies to make eclipses repent, look down to the earth to drive off the plague because they said I was the all-worthy one who filled nature with respect and straightened the order of the universe and had taken Divine Providence down a peg, and I gave them what they asked of me and bought everything they wanted to sell me not because he was soft-hearted as his mother Bendición Alvarado said but because a person needed an iron liver to refuse a favor to someone who was singing his praises, and now on the contrary there was no one to ask him for anything, no one to say to him at least good morning general sir, did you have a good night, he didn't even have the consolation of those nocturnal explosions that woke him up with a hail of broken glass and blew the doors off their hinges and sowed panic among the troops but which at least let him feel he was alive and not in this silence that buzzes inside my head and wakes me up with its noise, all I am now is a fright painted on the wall of this horror show where it was impossible for him to give an order that hadn't been carried out long before, he found his most intimate desires satisfied in the official newspaper which he still read in the hammock at siesta time from front to back including the advertisements, there was no impulse of his feelings or design of his will which did not appear in print in large letters with the photograph of the bridge he had not ordered built because he'd forgotten, the opening of the school to teach sweeping, the milk cow and the breadfruit tree with a photograph of him with other inaugural ribbons from the times of glory, and yet he couldn't find peace, he dragged his great feet of a senile elephant looking for something that hadn't been lost to him in his house of solitude, he found that someone before him had covered the cages with mourning cloths, someone had contemplated the sea from the windows and had counted the cows before him, everything was complete and in order, he went back to the bedroom with the candle when he recognized his own amplified voice in the quarters of the presidential guard and he looked in through the half-open window and saw a group of officers dozing in the smoke-filled room opposite the sad glow of the television screen and there he was on the screen thinner and trimmer, but it was me, mother, sitting in the office where he was to die with the coat of arms of the nation behind him and three pairs of gold eyeglasses on the desk, and he was reciting from memory an analysis of the nation's finances with the words of a sage that he never would have dared repeat, damn it, it was a more upsetting sight than that of his dead body among the flowers because now he was seeing himself alive and listening to himself speak with his own voice, I myself, mother, I who never had been able to bear the embarrassment of appearing on a balcony and had never overcome the shyness about speaking in public, and there he was, so genuine and mortal that he stood perplexed by the window thinking mother of mine Bendición Alvarado how is this mystery possible, but José Ignacio Saenz de la Barra remained impassive facing one of the few explosions of rage that he permitted himself in the uncountable years of his regime, it's nothing, general, he said with his softest emphasis, we had to use this illicit recourse to keep the ship of progress within order from running aground, it was a divine inspiration, general, thanks to it we have succeeded in conjuring away the uncertainty of the people over a flesh and blood power who on the last Wednesday of every month rendered a soothing report on the acts of his government on the state radio and television, I assume all responsibility, general, I put this vase with six microphones in the shape of sunflowers here and they recorded the thoughts you had aloud, I was the one who asked the questions he answered during Friday audiences without suspecting that his innocent answers were the fragments of the monthly speech addressed to the nation, because he'd never used an image that wasn't his or a word that he wouldn't have said as you yourself can see with this record that Saenz de la Barra put on the desk beside these films and this letter in my own hand which I sign in your presence, general, so that you may decide my fate as you see fit, and he looked at him disconcertedly because suddenly he came to the realization that Saenz de la Barra was without the dog for the first time, defenseless, pale, and then he sighed, it's all right, Nacho, do your duty, he said, with an air of infinite fatigue, sitting back in the swivel chair with his gaze fixed on the accusing eyes of the portraits of the founding fathers, he was older than ever, gloomier and sadder, but with the same expression of unforeseeable designs that Saenz de la Barra was to recognize two weeks later when he entered the office again without an appointment almost dragging the dog by the leash and with the urgent news of an armed insurrection that only his intervention could stop, general, and finally he discovered the imperceptible crack he had been seeking for so many years in that obsidian wall of fascination, mother of mine Bendición Alvarado of my revenge, he said to himself, this poor bastard is shitting in his pants with fear, but he didn't make a single gesture that would let his intentions show but wrapped Saenz de la Barra in a maternal aura, don't worry, Nacho, he sighed, we've got plenty of time to think without anyone's disturbing us where the hell was the truth in that bog of contradictory truths that seem less true than if they were lies, while Saenz de la Barra checked his pocket watch to see that it was going on 7 P.M., general, the commanders of the three branches were finishing dinner at their respective homes with their wives and children, so not even they could suspect his plans, they will leave dressed in civilian clothes without an escort through the service entrance where a taxi called by phone awaits them to trick the vigilance of our men, they won't see any, of course, but there they are, general, the drivers, but he said aha, he smiled, don't worry so much, Nacho, explain to me instead how we have lived up till now with our skins intact since according to your figures of severed heads we've had more enemies than we had soldiers, but Saenz de la Barra was only sustained by the tiny throb of his pocket watch, there were less than three hours left, general, the commander of the land forces was on his way at that moment to the Conde barracks, the commander of the naval forces to the harbor fort, the commander of the air forces to the San Jerónimo base, it was still possible to arrest them because a state security van loaded with vegetables was following them at a short distance, but he didn't change his expression, he felt that the growing anxiety of Saenz de la Barra was freeing him from the punishment of a servitude that had been more implacable than his appetite for power, calm down, Nacho, he said, explain to me rather why you haven't bought a mansion as big as an ocean liner, why you work like a mule since money doesn't matter to you, why you live like a monk when the tightest women get all loosened up with the thought of getting into your bedroom, you're more of a priest than any priest, Nacho, but Saenz de la Barra was suffocating in a cold sweat that he was unable to hide with his matchless dignity in that crematory oven of an office, it was eleven o'clock, it's too late now, he said, a coded message began to circulate at that time over the telegraph wires to the various garrisons of the country, the rebel commanders were pinning decorations onto their parade uniforms for the official portrait of the new government junta while their aides were transmitting the final orders of a war without enemies whose only battles were reduced to the control of the centers of communication and public services, but he didn't even blink at the eager throbbing of Lord Köchel who had stood up with a thread of drivel that looked like an endless tear, don't be afraid, Nacho, explain to me rather why you are so afraid of death, and José Ignacio Saenz de la Barra with one tug pulled off the celluloid collar softened by sweat and his baritone face was soulless, it's quite natural, he answered, a fear of death is the ember of happiness, that's why you don't feel it, general, and he stood up counting out of pure habit the bells of the cathedral, it's twelve o'clock, he said, you haven't got anyone left in the world, general, I was the last one, but he didn't move in the big chair until he perceived the underground thunder of the tanks on the main square, and then he smiled, don't be mistaken, Nacho, I still have the people, he said, the poor people as always who before dawn took to the streets instigated by the unpredictable old man who over the state radio and television addressed all patriots of the nation without distinction of any kind and with the most vivid historical emotion to announce that the commanders of the three branches of the service inspired by the unchanging ideals of the regime, under my personal direction and interpreting as always the will of the sovereign people had put an end on this glorious midnight to the apparatus of terror of a bloodthirsty civilian who had been punished by the blind justice of the mob, for there was José Ignacio

Saenz de la Barra, beaten to a pulp, hanging by his feet from a lamppost on the main square with his own genitals stuck in his mouth, just as you had foreseen general sir when you gave us orders to cordon off the streets to the embassies to stop him from seeking asylum, the people had stoned him general sir, but first we had to riddle with bullets the butcher dog who sucked the guts out of four civilians and left seven of our soldiers badly wounded when the people attacked his living quarters and threw out of the window two hundred brocade vests with the price tags still on them, they threw out some three thousand pairs of Italian boots that had never been worn, three thousand general sir, that's what the government money was being spent on, and I don't know how many boxes of buttonhole gardenias and all the Bruckner records with their respective conductor's scores annotated in his own hand, and they also freed the prisoners in the dungeons and set fire to the torture chambers in the old Dutch insane asylum with shouts of long live the general, long live the stud who finally discovered the truth, because they all say that you didn't know anything general sir, that they kept you in limbo abusing your good heart, and even at this moment they're hunting the state security torturers down like rats since we left them without military protection in accordance with your orders so the people can relieve themselves of so much pent-up rage and so much terror, and he approved, agreed, moved by the bells of jubilation and the music of freedom and the shouts of gratitude from the crowds massed on the main square with large signs saying God keep the magnificent one who redeemed us from the shadows of terror and in that fleeting replica of the times of glory he had the cadet officers who had helped him take off his own chains of a galley slave of power gather in the courtyard and pointing to us according to the impulses of his inspiration he used us to fill in the last high command of his decrepit regime in replacement of the authors of the death of Leticia Nazareno and the child who were captured in their bedclothes when they tried to find asylum in foreign embassies, but he barely recognized them, he'd forgotten their names, he searched in his heart for the burden of hatred he'd tried to keep alive until his death and all he found were the ashes of a wounded pride which was no longer worth maintaining, get them away from here, he ordered, they put them on the first ship to weigh anchor for a place where no one would ever remember them again, poor bastards, he presided over the first cabinet meeting of the new government with the clear impression that those exemplaries chosen from a new generation of a new century were once again the usual civilian ministers with dusty frock coats and weak guts, except that these were more avid for honors than power, more jittery and servile and more useless than all the previous ones in the face of a foreign debt more costly than anything that could be sold in his ravished realm of gloom, because there was nothing to do general sir, the last train on the upland barrens had fallen down an orchid-covered precipice, leopards were sleeping on the velvet seats, the carcasses of the paddle-wheelers were sunk in the swamps of the rice paddies, the news was rotting in the mailbags, the pairs of manatees tricked by the illusion that they were engendering mermaids among the shadowy irises of the round mirrors in the presidential stateroom, and only he was unaware of it, naturally, he had believed in progress within order because at that time the only contact he had with real life was the reading of the government newspaper which they printed only for you general sir, a whole edition of one single copy with the news you liked to read, with the photographs you expected to find, with advertisements that made him dream of a world different from the one they had given him for his siesta, until I myself was able to ascertain with these incredulous eyes of mine that behind the solar glass windows of the ministries still intact were the colors of the Negro shacks on the harbor hills, they had built the palm-lined avenues to the sea so that I wouldn't notice that behind the Roman villas with identical porticoes the miserable slums devastated by one of our many hurricanes were still there, they had sown aromatic herbs on both sides of the railroad tracks so that from the presidential car the world seemed

magnified by the venal waters his mother of my insides
Bendición Alvarado used for painting orioles, and they
were not deceiving him in order to please him as had been
done in the later years of his times of glory by General
Rodrigo de Aguilar, or to keep useless annoyances from
him as Leticia Nazareno used to do more out of pity than
love, but to keep him the captive of his own power in the
senile backwater of the hammock under the ceiba tree in
the courtyard where at the end of his years even the schoolgirl chorus of the petite painted bird perched on a green
lemon limb wasn't to be real, what a mess, and yet the trick
didn't affect him but rather he tried to reconcile himself
with reality through the recovery by decree of the quinine
monopoly and that of other potions essential to the well-
being of the state, but truth came back to surprise him with
the news that the world was changing and life was going on
behind the back of his power, because there wasn't any
more quinine, general, there's no more cocoa, there's no
more indigo, general, there wasn't anything, except his
personal fortune which was uncountable and sterile and
threatened by idleness, and still he wasn't upset by such
dire news but sent a message of challenge to old Ambassador Roxbury in hopes they might find some formula of
relief over the domino table, but the ambassador answered
him in his own style of never in a million years, your excellency, this country isn't worth a plug nickel, except for the
sea, of course, which was diaphanous and succulent and all
it needed was a flame underneath to cook the great clam
chowder of the universe in its own crater, so think about it,
your excellency, we'll accept it on account for the interest
of that debt which is in arrears and which won't be paid off
even with a hundred generations of leaders as diligent as
your excellency, but he didn't even take him seriously that
first time, he accompanied him to the stairs thinking
mother of mine Bendición Alvarado look at these gringo
barbarians, how is it possible that they can only think of the
sea as food, he sent him off with the usual pat on the
shoulder and he was alone with himself again feeling
around among the wisps of illusory mist on the barren

plains of power, because the crowds had abandoned the main square, they took away the repetitious placards and put away the rented signs for other identical celebrations in the future as soon as the stimulus of things to eat and drink that the troops distributed during breaks in the ovations was exhausted, they had left the salons deserted and sad again in spite of his order not to close the main doors at any hour so that anyone who wants to can come in, as before, when this wasn't a house of the dead but a palace for the neighborhood, and yet the only ones who stayed were the lepers general sir, the blind men and the cripples who had remained for years and years in front of the building just as Demetrius Aldous had seen them gilding themselves in the sun by the gates of Jerusalem, destroyed and invincible, certain that sooner or later they would come in again to receive from his hands the salt of health because he was to survive all the reverses of adversity and the most inclement passions and the worst attacks of oblivion, because he was eternal, and so it was, he found them again on his way back from the milking as they boiled cans of kitchen leftovers on the brick fireplaces improvised in the courtyard, he saw them stretched out with their arms crossed on the mats devastated by the sweat of their ulcers in the fragrant shadows of the rose beds, he had a common fireplace built for them, he bought them new mats, and he had a palm-branch shelter built for them in the rear of the courtyard so that they wouldn't have to take shelter inside the building, but four days didn't pass without his finding a pair of lepers sleeping on the Oriental rugs in the ballroom or a blind man lost in the offices or a cripple broken on the stairs, he had the doors closed so that they wouldn't leave a trail of open sores on the walls or stink up the air of the building with the smell of the carbolic acid with which the sanitary services fumigated them although no sooner did he get them out of one place than they appeared in another, tenacious, indestructible, clinging to their old fierce hope when nobody hoped for anything any more from that useless old man who had written reminders in the cracks in the wall and felt his way along like a sleepwalker through the winds he found in the misty swamps of memory, he spent hours of insomnia in the hammock wondering how the hell am I going to get around the new ambassador Fischer who proposed to me to disclose the existence of a plague of yellow fever in order to justify a landing of marines in accordance with the mutual assistance treaty for as many years as would be necessary to bring new breath into the dying nation, and he replied immediately never in a million years, fascinated by the evidence that he was living in the origins of his regime when he had taken advantage of the same solution to assume the exceptional powers of martial law in the face of a serious threat of civil uprising, he had declared a state of plague by decree, he planted the yellow flag on the pole of the lighthouse, he closed the port, Sundays were suppressed, it was forbidden to weep for the dead in public and to play music that would make them be remembered and he made use of the armed forces to police the enforcement of the decree and to dispose of those infested according to his will, so that troops with sanitary armbands held public executions of people of the most diverse stations in life, they would mark a red circle on the doors of houses suspected of nonconformity with the regime, they put a branding iron to the foreheads of the lesser lawbreakers, dikes and fags while a sanitary mission urgently summoned from his government by Ambassador Mitchell took charge of keeping the contagion from the occupants of the presidential palace, they gathered up the runt poo from the floor to analyze it with magnifying glasses, they threw disinfectant tablets into the water jars, they fed water worms to animals in their scientific laboratories, and dying of laughter he told them through an interpreter don't be such horses' asses, misters, the only plague here is you people, but they insisted there was, that they had superior orders that there was, they prepared a syrup with preventive powers, thick and green, with which they varnished visitors' bodies all over without distinction of credentials from the most ordinary to the most illustrious, they obliged them to keep their distance in audiences, they standing in the doorway and he sitting at the end of the room where their voices but not their breath could reach him, parleying in shouts with highborn naked people who gesticulated with one hand, your excellency, and with the other covered their bedaubed little dove, and all that to guard from contagion the one who had conceived in the enervation of wakefulness the most banal details of the false calamity, who had invented earth-born lies and spread apocalyptic predictions in accordance with his belief that the less the people understand the more afraid they'll be, and who scarcely blinked when one of his aides, pale with fright, came to attention before him with the news general sir that the plague is causing tremendous casualties among the civilian population, so that through the foggy windows of the presidential carriage he had seen time stopped by his orders on the abandoned streets, he saw the awe-struck look of the yellow flags, he saw the closed doors even on houses where the red circle had been omitted, he saw the gorged buzzards on the balconies, and he saw the dead, the dead, the dead, there were so many everywhere that it was impossible to count them in the clay pits, piled up in the sun on terraces, stretched out over the vegetables in the market, flesh and blood dead people general sir, who knows how many, because there were many more than he would have wanted to see among the hosts of his enemies thrown out like dead dogs in garbage bins, and above the rotting of the bodies and the familiar fetid smell of the streets he recognized the mangy smell of the plague, but he didn't react, he gave in to no entreaties until he felt himself absolute master of all his power again, and only when there didn't seem to be any means human or divine to put an end to the dying did we see appear on the streets a carriage without insignias in which no one perceived at first the icy wind of the majesty of power, but in the interior of funereal plush we saw the lethal eyes, the quivering lips, the nuptial glove which went along throwing handfuls of salt into the doorways, we saw the train painted with the colors of the flag clawing its way up through the gardenias and terrified leopards to the heights of mist of the most precipitous provinces, we saw the hazy eyes through the windows of the solitary railroad car, the afflicted face, the haughty maiden's hand that went along leaving a trail of salt across the mournful barrens of his childhood, we saw the steamboat with its wooden paddle wheel and rolls of mazurkas in chimerical pianolas that bumped its way along among reefs and sandbars and the ruins of the catastrophes caused in the jungle by the dragon's springtime strolls, we saw the sunset eyes in the window of the presidential stateroom, we saw the pale lips, the hand without origin which threw handfuls of salt into villages deadened by the heat, and those who ate that salt and licked the ground where it had been recovered their health immediately and were immunized for a long time against evil omens and the rash of illusions, so that he was not to be surprised in the twilight of his autumn when they proposed to him a new disembarkation regime sustained by the same lie of a political epidemic of yellow fever but he stood up to the arguments of the sterile ministers who shouted bring back the marines, general, bring them back with their machines for fumigating plague-ridden people in exchange for whatever they want, let them come back with their white hospitals, their blue lawns, their spinning sprinklers, those people who ended their leap years with two centuries of good health, but he pounded on the table and decided no, under his supreme responsibility until the blunt Ambassador MacQueen answered him that conditions don't warrant any more discussion, your excellency, the regime wasn't being sustained by hope or conformity or even by terror, but by the pure inertia of an ancient and irreparable disillusion, go out into the street and look truth in the face, your excellency, we're on the final curve, either the marines land or we take the sea, there's no other way, your excellency, there was no other way, mother, so they took away the Caribbean in April, Ambassador Ewing's nautical engineers carried it off in numbered pieces to plant it far from the hurricanes in the blood-red dawns of Arizona, they took it away with everything it had inside general sir, with the reflection of our cities, our timid drowned people, our demented dragons, in spite of the fact that he had appealed to the most

audacious registers of his age-old cunning trying to pro-
mote a national convulsion of protest against the despoil-
ment, but nobody paid any attention general sir, they
refused to take to the streets either by persuasion or by
force because we thought it was a new maneuver on his part
like so many others to satiate even beyond all limits his
irrepressible passion to endure, we thought just so long as
something happens even if they carry off the sea, God damn
it, even though they carry off the whole nation along with
its dragon, we thought, unmoved by the seductive arts of
the military men who appeared in our houses disguised as
civilians and begged us in the name of the nation to rush
into the streets shouting out with the gringos to stop the
implementation of the theft, they incited us to sack and
burn the stores and mansions of foreigners, they offered us
ready cash to go out and protest under the protection of the
troops who were solidly behind the people in opposition to
the act of aggression, but no one went out general sir,
because nobody had forgotten that one other time they had
told us the same thing on their word of honor as soldiers
and still they shot them down in a massacre under the
pretext that agitators had infiltrated and opened fire
against the troops, so this time we can't even count on the
people general sir, and I had to bear the weight of this
punishment alone, I had to sign alone thinking mother of
mine Bendición Alvarado no one knows better than you
that it's better to be left without the sea than to allow a
landing of marines, remember that they were the ones who
thought up the orders they made me sign, they turned our
artists into fairies, they brought the Bible and syphilis, they
made people believe that life was easy, mother, that everything is gotten with money, that blacks carry a contagion,
they tried to convince our soldiers that the nation is a
business and that the sense of honor is a bother invented
by the government so that soldiers would fight for free, and
it was to avoid the repetition of all those ills that I granted
them the right to make use of our territorial waters in the
way they considered best for the interests of humanity and
peace among peoples, with the understanding that said

cession not only included the physical waters visible from the window of his bedroom to the horizon but everything that is understood by sea in the broadest sense, or, the flora and fauna belonging to said waters, its system of winds, the inconstancy of its millibars, everything, but I could never have imagined that they would be capable of doing what they did to carry off the numbered locks of my old checkerboard sea with gigantic suction dredges and in its torn crater we saw appear the instantaneous sparkle of the submerged remains of the very ancient city of Santa María de Darién laid low by the whirlwind, we saw the flagship of the first admiral of the ocean sea just as I had seen it from my window, mother, it was identical, trapped by a clump of goose barnacles that the teeth of the dredges had pulled out by the roots before he had time to order an homage worthy of the historic importance of that wreck, they carried off everything that had been the reasons for my wars and the motive of his power and left behind only the deserted plain of harsh lunar dust that he saw as he passed by the windows with a heavy heart crying out mother of mine Bendición Alvarado illuminate me with your wisest lights, because on those twilight nights he would be awakened by the fright that the dead of the nation were standing up in their tombs asking him for an accounting of the sea, he felt their scratching on the walls, he heard their unburied voices, the horror of the posthumous looks that spied through keyholes on the trail of his great feet of a dying saurian in the steaming bog of the last fens of salvation in the shadowy house, he would walk ceaselessly through the cross currents of the tardy trade winds and the false mistrals from the wind machine that Ambassador Eberhart had given him so that he would not think so much about that bad piece of business with the sea, on the top of the reefs he saw the solitary light from the rest home for refugee dictators who sleep like sitting oxen while I suffer, evil-born bastards, he remembered the farewell snoring of his mother Bendición Alvarado in the suburban mansion, her good birdwoman's sleep in the room lighted by the vigil of the oregano, if he were only her, he sighed, happy sleeping mother who never let herself be frightened by the plague, or let herself be intimidated by love or let herself be scared by death, and on the contrary he was so wrought up that even the flashes of the lighthouse without a sea coming at intervals through the windows seemed to him to have been befouled by the dead, he fled in terror from the fantastic starlike firefly that fumigated in its orbit of a spinning nightmare the fearsome outpouring of the luminous dust of the marrow of the dead, put it out, he shouted, they put it out, he ordered the building caulked inside and out so that even the slightest wisp of death's nocturnal mangy air would not creep in through cracks in doors and windows, not even concealed in other fragrances, he remained in the dark feeling his way, breathing with difficulty in the airless heat, feeling himself pass by dark mirrors, walking from fear, until he heard a troop of hoofs in the crater of the sea and it was the moon rising with its decrepit snows, frightening, take it away, he shouted, put out the stars, damn it, by order of God, but nobody ran to him in the former offices, the blind men on the stairs, the lepers pearled with dew who rose up as he passed the stubble of the first rosebushes to implore the salt of health from his hands, and that was when it happened, disbelievers all over the world, shitty idolaters, it came to pass that he touched our heads as he went by, one by one, he touched each one of us on the place of our defects with a smooth and wise hand that was the hand of truth, and the instant he touched us we recovered the health of our bodies and the repose of our souls and we recovered the strength and will to live, and we saw the blind men dazzled by the glow of the roses, we saw the cripples jumping on the stairways and we saw this my own skin of a newborn child which I go about exhibiting in carnivals all over the world so that everyone will know about the miracle and this fragrance of premature lilies from the scars of my sores which I go spreading over the face of the earth for the derision of the unfaithful and as a lesson for libertines, they shouted it in cities and on byways, at dances and parades, trying to infuse in the crowds the terror of the miracle, but nobody thought it was true, we thought it was just one more of the many aulic messages they sent to villages with an entourage of old quacks to try to convince us of the last thing we needed to believe that he had given skin back to lepers, sight to the blind, agility to cripples, we thought that it was the last resort of the regime to call attention to an improbable president whose personal guard was reduced to a patrol of recruits against the unanimous advice of the cabinet who had insisted no general sir, tighter protection was necessary, at least a unit of riflemen general sir, but he had insisted that no one had any need or desire to kill me, you people are the only ones, my useless ministers, my lazy commanders, except that you don't dare and never will dare kill me because you know that afterward you'll have to kill each other, so that all that was left was the guard of rookies for an extinguished house where the cows wandered with no law or order from the first vestibule to the hearing room, they had eaten the flowered lawns on the tapestries general sir, they had eaten the files, but he didn't hear them, he had seen the first cow come up one October afternoon when it was impossible to stay outside because of the fury of the cloudburst, he had tried to chase it away with his hands, cow, cow, remembering suddenly that cow was written with a c, he had seen it another time eating the lampshades at a moment in life when he was beginning to understand that it wasn't worthwhile moving toward the stairs to chase a cow away, he had found two of them in the ballroom exasperated by the hens who were flying up to peck at the ticks on their backs, so that on recent nights when we saw lights that looked like navigational signals and we heard a disaster of large-animal hoofs behind the fortified walls it was because he was going about with a candle fighting with the cows over a place to sleep while outside his public life went on without him, every day in the newspapers of the regime we saw his fictionalized photographs at civil and military audiences in which they showed him to us with a different uniform according to the character of the occasion, every year for so many years on the major holidays of the nation's anniversaries we would hear the repeated harangues on the radio, he was present in our lives as we left home, as we went to church, as we ate and as we slept, when it was public knowledge that he could barely make his way along with his rustic hiker's boots in the decrepit building whose service had been reduced at that time to three or four orderlies who fed him and kept the honey hiding places well supplied and chased away the cows who had made a shambles of the general staff of porcelain marshals in the forbidden office where he was to die according to the prognostications of oracles that he himself had forgotten, they stood hanging on his whimsical orders until he hung the lamp on the door and they heard the noise of the three locks, the three bolts, the three bars of the bedroom rarefied by the lack of sea, and then they would withdraw to their quarters on the ground floor convinced that he was at the mercy of his dreams of a solitary drowned man until dawn, but he would awaken with unforeseen starts, he would browse through his insomnia, dragging his great feet of an apparition through the immense building in darkness disturbed only by the patient digestion of the cows and the obtuse breathing of the hens roosting on the viceroys' coatracks, he heard moon winds in the darkness, he felt the steps of time in the darkness, he saw his mother Bendición Alvarado sweeping in the darkness with the broom of green branches with which she had swept away the leaf storm of the illustrious singed heroes of Cornelius Nepos in the original, the immemorial rhetoric of Livius Andronicus and Cecilius Stratus who were reduced to office trash on the night of blood when he entered the ownerless house of power for the first time while outside the last suicide barricades of the distinguished Latinist General Lautaro Muñoz whom God keep in his holy kingdom were resisting, they had crossed the courtyard under the glow of the city in flames, leaping over the dead hulks of the personal bodyguard of the illustrious president, he shaking from the heat of tertian fever and his mother Bendición Alvarado with no other arm but the broom of green branches, they went up the stairs stumbling in the darkness over the horses of the splendid presidential squiry who were still bleeding from the first vestibule to the hearing room, it was difficult to breathe inside the closed building because of the sour gunpowder smell of the dead horses, along the corridors we saw prints of bare feet stained with horse blood, we saw the marks of palms stained with horse blood on the walls, and in the pool of blood in the hearing room we saw the drained body of a beautiful Florentine woman in an evening gown with a saber thrust through her heart, and she was the wife of the president, and beside her we saw the corpse of a little girl who looked like a toy windup ballerina with a pistol shot in her forehead, and she was his nine-year-old daughter, and they saw the corpse of the Garibaldian Caesar who was President Lautaro Muñoz, the ablest and most capable of the fourteen federalist generals who had succeeded to power through successive coups during eleven years of bloody rivalries but also the only one who dared say no in his own tongue to the English consul, and there he was stretched out like a mullet, barefoot, suffering the punishment for his daring with his skull pierced by a pistol shot he had given himself in the palate after having killed his wife and daughter and his forty-two Andalusian horses so that they wouldn't fall into the hands of the punitive expedition of the British fleet, and that was when Commander Kitchener told me pointing to the body you see, general, that's what happens to those who raise their hands against their fathers, don't forget it when you're in your own kingdom, he told him, although he already was after so many nights of insomnia from waiting, so many postponed rages, so many digested humiliations, there he was, mother, proclaimed supreme commander of the three branches of the armed forces and president of the republic for such a time as was necessary for the reestablishment of order and the economic balance of the nation, it had been unanimously resolved by the last field commanders of the federation in agreement with the senate and chamber of deputies in joint session and the backing of the British fleet from my so many and so difficult nights of domino with Consul Macdonall, except that neither I nor anybody else believed it at the beginning, naturally, who could have believed it in the tumult of that frightening night since Bendición Alvarado herself still didn't believe on her bed of putrefaction when she evoked the memory of the son who couldn't find where to begin to govern in that disorder, they couldn't find a piece of grass to cook or to use to warm up that immense unfurnished house in which nothing of value was left except the moth-eaten oil paintings of viceroys and archbishops from the dead grandeur of Spain, everything else had been carried off little by little by previous presidents for their private domains, they didn't even leave a trace of the wallpaper with heroic episodes on the walls, the bedrooms were full of barracks trash, everywhere there were forgotten traces of historic massacres and slogans written with a bloody finger by illusory presidents who lasted one night, but there wasn't even a mat to lie down on to sweat out a fever, so his mother Bendición Alvarado pulled down a curtain to wrap me in and left him lying in a corner of the main stairway while with the broom of green branches she swept out the presidential quarters that the English were finishing sacking, she swept the whole floor defending herself with broom blows from this pack of filibusters who were trying to rape her from behind doors, and a short while before dawn she sat down to rest beside her son who was done in by chills, wrapped in the velvet curtain, the sweat pouring off him on the last step of the devastated main stairway while she tried to bring his fever down with her easy calculations of don't let this disorder get you down, son, it's only a matter of buying a few leather stools the cheapest you can find and they'll be painted with flowers and animals, I'll paint them myself, she said, it's only a matter of buying some hammocks for when visitors come, those especially, hammocks, because in a house like this there must be a lot of unannounced visitors at all hours, she said, we'll buy a church table to eat on, we'll buy iron utensils and pewter plates so they can suffer the bad life of soldiers, we'll buy a decent jug for drinking water and a charcoal stove and that's it, after all it's the government's money, she said to console him, but he wasn't listening to her, depressed by the first mallow light of dawn which was lighting up the hidden side of truth in living flesh, conscious of being nothing but a pitiful old man who was shaking with fever sitting on the stairs thinking without love mother of mine Bendición Alvarado so that was the whole mess, damn it, so power was that house of castaways, that human smell of burned horses, that desolate dawn of another twelfth of August just like all the others was the date of power, mother, what kind of a mess have we got ourselves into, suffering the original upset, the atavistic fear of the new century of darkness that was rising up in the world without his permission, the cocks were crowing at sea, the English were singing in English gathering up the dead from the courtyard when his mother Bendición Alvarado ended her merry accounting with the remnant of relief of I'm not frightened by the things we have to buy and the chores we have to do, what frightens me is the number of sheets to be washed in this house, and then it was he who leaned on the strength of his disillusionment to try to console her with sleep easy, mother, in this country no president lasts long, he told her, and not only did he believe it then but he kept on believing it for every instant of his very long life of a sedentary despot, all the more as life convinced him more and more that the long years of power don't bring any two days that are just alike, that there would always be a hidden intention in the proposals of a prime minister when he released the dazzling display of truth in the routine Wednesday report, and he would only smile, don't tell me the truth, counselor, because we'll run the risk that it will be believed, thwarting with that single phrase a whole laborious strategy of the cabinet to try to get him to sign without asking questions, for he had never seemed more lucid to me than during the time of the rumors that he urinated in his pants during official visits without noticing it, he seemed more severe as he sank into the backwaters of decrepitude with the slippers of a terminal case and the eyeglasses with only one temple which was tied on with a piece of thread and his manner had become more intense and his instinct more certain in putting aside what was inopportune and signing what was needed without reading it, God damn it, because when all's said and done nobody pays any attention to me, he smiled, see how I ordered them to put up a barrier in the vestibule so the cows wouldn't climb up the stairs, and there it was again, so boss, so boss, it had stuck its head through the office window and was eating the paper flowers on the altar of the nation, but he limited himself to smiling you see what I'm talking about, counselor, what's got this country all fucked up is the fact that no one has ever paid any attention to me, he said, and he said it with a clearness of judgment that seemed impossible at his age, even so Ambassador Kippling said in his suppressed memoirs that around that time he had found him in a pitiful state of senile unawareness which did not even permit him to take care of himself in the most childish acts, he told how he found him soaked in an incessant and salty matter which flowed from his skin, that he had acquired the huge size of a drowned man and he had opened his shirt to show me the tight and lucid body of a dry-land drowned man in whose cracks and crannies parasites from the reefs at the bottom of the sea were proliferating, he had a ship remora on his back, polyps and microscopic crustaceans in his armpits, but he was convinced that those sproutings from reefs were only the first symptoms of the spontaneous return of the sea that you people carried off, my dear Johnson, because seas are like cats, he said, they always come home, convinced that the rows of goose barnacles in his crotch were the secret announcement of a happy dawn in which he was going to open his bedroom window and would see again the three caravels of the admiral of the ocean sea who had grown weary of searching the whole world over to see if what they had told him was true who had smooth hands like his and like those of so many other great men of history, he had ordered him brought before him, by force if necessary, when other navigators told him they had seen him mapping the innumerable islands of the neighboring seas changing their old names of military men to the names of kings and saints while he sought in native science the only thing that really interested him which was to discover some masterful hair-restorer for his incipient baldness, we had lost all hope of finding him again when he recognized him from the presidential limousine disguised in a brown habit with the cord of Saint Francis around his waist swinging a penitent's rattle among the Sunday crowds at the public market and sunken into such a state of moral penury that it was impossible to believe that he was the same one we had seen enter the audience room in his crimson uniform and gold spurs and with the solemn gait of a sea dog on dry land, but when they tried to get him into the limousine on his orders we couldn't find a trace general sir, the earth had swallowed him up, they said he had become a Moslem, that he had died of pellagra in Senegal, and had been buried in three different tombs in three different cities in the world although he really wasn't in any of them, condemned to wander from sepulcher to sepulcher until the end of time because of the twisted fate of his expeditions, because that man was a fraud general sir, he was a worse jinx than gold, but he never believed it, he kept on hoping that he would return during the last extremes of his old age when the minister of health used pincers to pull out the ox ticks he found on his body and he insisted that they weren't ticks, doctor, it's the sea coming back, he said, so sure of his judgment that the minister of health had thought many times that he wasn't as deaf as he made one believe in public or as unraveled as he seemed to be during uncomfortable audiences, although a thorough examination had revealed that his arteries had turned to glass, he had beach-sand sediment in his kidneys, and his heart was cracked from a lack of love, so the old physician took refuge behind the shield of old comradeship to tell him that it's time now to hand over the tools general sir, at least decide in whose hands you're going to leave us, he told him, save us from being orphaned, but he asked him with surprise who told him I'm thinking about dying, my dear doctor, let other people die, God damn it, and he finished in a joking vein that two nights ago I saw myself on television and I looked better than ever, like a fighting bull, he said, dying with laughter, because he had seen himself in a fog, nodding with sleep in front of the screen, and with his head wrapped in a wet towel in accordance with the habits of his more recent nights of solitude, he was really more resolute than a fighting bull before the charms of the wife of the ambassador of France, or maybe Turkey, or Sweden, what the hell, they were all so much alike that he couldn't tell them apart and so much time had passed that he couldn't remember himself among them with his dress uniform and a glass of champagne untouched in his hand during the festivities for the anniversary of August 12, or at the commemoration of the victory of January 14, or the rebirth of March 13, how should I know, because in the rigmarole of historic dates of the regime he had ended up not knowing which was when or what corresponded to what nor did he get any use from the little rolled pieces of paper that with so much good spirit and so much care he had hidden in the cracks in the walls because he had ended up forgetting what it was he was supposed to remember, he would find them by chance in the hiding places for the honey and he had read one time that April 17 was the birthday of Dr. Marcos de León, we have to send him a tiger as a gift, he had read, written in his own hand, without the slightest idea of who he was, feeling that there was no punishment more humiliating or less deserved for a man than betrayal by his own body, he had begun to glimpse it long before the immemorial times of José Ignacio Saenz de la Barra when he became aware that he only knew who was who in group audiences, a man like me who had been capable of calling the whole population of the most remote village in his realm of gloom by their first and last names, and yet he had reached the opposite extreme, from the carriage he saw among the crowd a boy he knew and he had been so surprised at not remembering where he had seen him before that he had him arrested by the escort while I tried to remember, a poor man from the country who spent twenty-two years in a jail cell repeating the truth established on the first day in the court transcript, that his name was Braulio Linares Moscote, that he was the illegitimate but recognized son of Marcos Linares, a fresh-water sailor, and Delfina Moscote, a breeder of jaguar hounds, both with an established domicile in Rosal del Virrey, that he was in the capital of this country for the first time because his mother had sent him to sell two dogs at the March poetry festival, that he had arrived on a rented donkey with no other clothes except those he was wearing at dawn on the same Thursday they had arrested him, that he was at a stand in the public market drinking a mug of black coffee as he asked the girls behind the counter if they knew of anyone who wanted to buy two cross-bred dogs for hunting jaguars, that they had answered no when the bustle of drums began, cornets, rockets, people shouting here comes the man, there he comes, that he had asked who was the man and they had answered him who else could it be, the one who gives the orders, that he put the dogs in a crate so that the counter girls could do him the favor of watching them for me until I get back, that he climbed up on a window ledge to be able to see over the crowd and he saw the escort of horses with gold caparisons and feathered crests, he saw the carriage with the dragon of the nation, the greeting by a hand with a cloth glove, the pale visage, the taciturn unsmiling lips of the man who gave the orders, the sad eyes that found him suddenly like a needle in a pile of needles, the finger that pointed him out, that one, the one up on the window sill, arrest him while I remember where I've seen him, he ordered, so they grabbed me and hit me, beat me with the flats of their sabers, roasted me on a grill so that I would confess where the man who gave the orders had seen me before, but they had been unable to drag any other truth out of him except the only one there was in the horror chamber of the harbor fort and he repeated it with such conviction and such personal courage that he ended up admitting he had been mistaken, but now there was no way out, he said, because they had treated him so badly that if he hadn't been an enemy he is now, poor man, so he rotted away alive in the dungeon while I wandered about this house of shadows thinking mother of mine Bendición Alvarado of my good times, be with me, look at what I am without the shelter of your mantle, shouting to himself that it wasn't worth the trouble having lived so many splendid days of glory if he couldn't evoke them to seek solace in them and feed himself on them and continue surviving because of them in the bog of old age because even the most intense grief and the happiest moments of his great times had slipped away irrevocably through the loopholes of memory in spite of his naïve attempts to impede it with little plugs of rolled-up paper, he was punished by never knowing who this Francisca Linero aged ninety-six was, the one he had ordered buried with the honors of a queen in accordance with another note written in his own hand, condemned to govern blindly with eleven pairs of useless spectacles hidden in the desk drawer to hide the fact that he was really conversing with specters whose voices he couldn't even decipher, whose identities he guessed by instinctive signs, sunken in a state of abandonment whose greatest risk had become evident to him in an audience with his minister of war in which he had the bad luck to have sneezed once and the minister of war said your health general sir and he had sneezed again and the minister of war again said your health general sir, but after nine consecutive sneezes I didn't say your health general sir again but I felt terrified by the threat of that face twisted in a stupor, I saw the eyes sunken in tears that spat on me without pity from the quicksand of his throes, I saw the tongue of a hanged man on the decrepit beast who was dying in my arms without any witness of my innocence, without anyone, and then the only thing that occurred to me was to get out of the office before it was too late, but he stopped me with an authoritative wave between two sneezes not to be a coward Brigadier General Rosendo Sacristán, stay where you are, God damn it, I'm not such a damned fool as to die in front of you, he shouted, and that's how it was, because he kept on sneezing up to the edge of death, floating in a space of unconsciousness peopled by fireflies at midday but clinging to the certainty that his mother Bendición Alvarado would not give him the shame of dying from a sneezing attack in the presence of an inferior, never in a million years, better dead than humiliated, better to live among the cows than among men capable of letting a person die without honor, God damn it, for he hadn't gone back to arguing about God with the apostolic nuncio so that he wouldn't notice that he was drinking his chocolate with a spoon, nor back to playing dominoes for fear that someone would dare lose to him out of pity, he didn't want to see anyone, mother, so that no one would discover that in spite of the close vigilance of his personal conduct, in spite of his impression of not dragging his flat feet which after all he had always dragged, in spite of the shame of his years he felt himself on the edge of the abyss of grief of the last dictators in disgrace whom he maintained more prisoners than protected in the house on the cliff so that they wouldn't contaminate the world with the plague of their indignity, he suffered it alone on that evil morning when he had fallen asleep in the pool in the private courtyard while he was taking his bath of medicinal waters, he was dreaming about you, mother, he was dreaming that it was you who made the cicadas who were bursting from so much buzzing over my head among the flowering almond boughs of real life, he dreamed it was you who painted with your brushes the colored voices of the orioles when he awoke startled by the unforeseen belch of his insides in the bottom of the water, mother, he awoke congested with rage in the perverted pool of my shame where the aromatic lotuses of oregano and mallow floated, where the fresh blossoms from the orange tree floated, where the hicatee turtles floated aroused by the novelty of the gold and tender flow of rabbit droppings from general sir in the fragrant waters, what a mess, but he survived that and so many other infamies of old age and had reduced his service personnel to the minimum in order to face them without witnesses, no one was to see him drifting through the no man's house for days and nights on end with his head wrapped in rags soaked in liniment moaning with despair against the walls, surfeited with pain, maddened by the unbearable headache of which he never spoke even to his personal physician because he knew that it was only just one more of the so many useless pains of decrepitude, he would feel it arrive like a thunderclap of stones long before the heavy storm clouds appeared in the sky and he ordered nobody to bother me as soon as he felt the tourniquet tighten on his temples, nobody come into this building no matter what happens, he ordered, when he felt the bones of his skull creak with the second turn of the tourniquet, not even God if he comes, he ordered, not even if I die, God damn it, blind with that pitiless pain which did not even give him an instant of respite to think until the end of the centuries of desperation when the blessing of the rains fell, and then he would call us and we would find him newborn with the little table ready for dinner opposite the mute television screen, we served him roast meat, beans with fatback, coconut rice, slices of fried plantains, a dinner inconceivable for his age which he let grow cold without even tasting it as he watched the same emergency film on television, aware that the government was trying to hide something from him since they had repeated the same closed-circuit program without noticing that the film was backward, God damn it, he said, trying to forget what they wanted to hide from him, if it were something worse he would have known it by now, he said, snorting over the dinner he had been served, until it struck eight on the cathedral clock and he arose with the untouched plate and threw the meal down the toilet as every night at that time for so many years to hide the humiliation that his stomach rejected everything, to while away with the legends of his times of glory the rancor that he felt toward himself every time he fell into some detestable act of the carelessness of an old man, to forget that he was only alive, that it was he and no one else who wrote on the walls of the toilets long live the general, long live the stud, and that he had sneaked out a healer's potion to do it as many times as he wanted and in one single night and even three times each time with three different women and he paid for that senile ingenuousness with tears more from rage than grief clinging to the chain of the toilet weeping mother of mine Bendición Alvarado of my heart, despise me, purify me with your waters of fire, fulfilling with pride the punishment of his naïveté because he knew only too well that what he lacked then and had always lacked in bed was not honor but love, he needed

223

women less arid than those who served my comrade the foreign minister so that he would not lose the good habit since they closed the school next door, fleshy boneless women for you alone general sir, sent by plane with official exemption from customs from the shopwindows of Amsterdam, the film festivals of Budapest, the sea of Italy general sir, look at what a marvel, the most beautiful in the whole world whom he would find sitting with singing-teacher decorum in the shadows of the office, they got undressed like artists, they lay down on the felt couch with the strips of their bathing suits printed like a photographic negative on their warm golden honey skin, lying beside the enormous concrete ox who refused to take off his military uniform while I tried to encourage him with my most loving means until he wearied of suffering the pressures of that hallucinating beauty of a dead fish, and he told her it was all right, child, go become a nun, so depressed by his own indolence that that night at the stroke of eight he surprised one of the women in charge of the soldiers' laundry and threw her down with his claws on top of the laundry tubs in spite of the fact that she tried to get away with the frightened excuse that I can't today general, believe me, it's vampire time, but he turned her face down on the laundry table and planted her from behind with a biblical drive that the poor woman felt in her soul with the crunch of death and she panted so big general, you must have studied to be a donkey, and he felt more relieved with that moan of pain than with the most frenetic dithyrambs of his official adulators and he assigned the washerwoman a lifetime pension for the education of her children, he sang again after so many years when he gave the cows their fodder in the milking stalls, bright January moon, he sang, without thinking about death, because not even on the last night of his life would he allow himself the weakness of thinking about anything that didn't make common sense, he counted the cows twice again while he sang you are the light of my darkened path, you are my northern star, and he discovered that four were missing, he went back into the building counting along the way the hens sleeping on the viceroys' coatracks, covering the cages with the sleeping birds which he counted as he put the cloth covers over them forty-eight, he set fire to the droppings scattered by the cows during the day from the vestibule to the audience room, he remembered a remote childhood which for the first time was his own image shivering on the icy barrens and the image of his mother Bendición Alvarado who stole the innards of a ram away from the garbage-heap buzzards for lunch, it had struck eleven when he covered the whole building again in the opposite direction lighting his way with the lamp as he put out the lights down to the vestibule, he saw himself one by one fourteen generals walking with a lamp repeated in the dark mirrors, he saw a cow collapsed on her back in the rear of the mirror in the music room, so boss, so boss, he said, she was dead, what a mess, he went through the sleeping quarters of the guard to tell them that there was a dead cow inside a mirror, he ordered them to take it out early tomorrow, without fail, before the building fills up with vultures, he ordered, inspecting with the light the former offices on the ground floor in search of the other lost cows, there were three of them, he looked for them in the toilets, under the tables, inside every mirror, he went up to the main floor searching the rooms room by room and all he found was a hen lying under the pink embroidered mosquito netting of a novice from other times whose name he had forgotten, he took his spoonful of honey before going to bed, he put the bottle back in the hiding place where there was one of his little pieces of paper with the date of some birthday of the famous poet Rubén Darío whom God keep on the highest seat in his kingdom, he rolled the piece of paper up again and left it in its place while he recited from memory the well-aimed prayer of our father and celestial lyrophorous master who keepeth afloat airplanes in the heavens and liners on the seas, dragging his great feet of a hopeless insomniac through the last fleeting dawns of green sunrises from the turns of the lighthouse, he heard the winds sorrowing for the sea that had gone away, he heard the lively music of a wedding party that was about to die struck from behind by some carelessness of God, he

found a strayed cow and he cut off its path without touching
it, so boss, so boss, he went back to his bedroom, seeing as
he passed by the windows the block of lights of the city
without a sea in every window, he smelled the hot vapor of
the mystery of its insides, the secret of its unanimous
breathing, he contemplated it twenty-three times without
stopping and he suffered forever as ever the uncertainty of
the vast and inscrutable ocean of people sleeping with their
hands on their hearts, he knew himself to be hated by those
who loved him most, he felt himself illuminated by the
candles of saints, he heard his name invoked to straighten
the fortunes of women in childbirth and to change the
destiny of those dying, he felt his memory exalted by the
same ones who cursed his mother when they saw the taciturn eyes, the sad lips, the hand of a pensive bride behind
the panes of transparent steel in the remote times of the
somnambulant limousine and we would kiss the mark of his
boot in the mud and we sent him fetishes for an evil death
on hot nights when from our courtyards we saw the wandering lights in the soulless windows of government house,
no one loves us, he sighed, looking into the old bedroom
of the lifeless birdwoman painter of orioles his mother
Bendición Alvarado her body strewn with sawdust, have a
good death mother, he said to her, a very good death son,
she answered him in the crypt, it was exactly twelve o'clock
when he hung the lamp on the doorway wounded inside by
the fatal twisting of the tenuous whistles of the hernia,
there was no space in the world except that of his pain, he
ran the three bolts of the bedroom for the last time, closed
the three locks, the three bars, he suffered the final holocaust of his scant micturition in the portable latrine, he
stretched out on the bare floor in the pants of rough burlap
which he wore at home ever since he had put an end to
audiences, the striped shirt without the artificial collar, and
the slippers of an invalid, he lay face down with his right
arm doubled under his head as a pillow and he fell asleep
immediately, but at ten minutes after two he awoke with his
mind aground and his clothes soaked in the pale and warm
sweat of the eye of a cyclone, who's there, he asked shaken

by the certainty that someone had called him in his sleep
by a name that was not his, Nicanor, and once again, Nicanor, someone who was able to get into his room without
taking down the bars because he came and went as he
wished going through the walls, and then he saw her, it was
death general sir, his, dressed in a penitent's tunic of pita
fiber cloth, with a long-poled hook in her hand and her
skull sown with the tufts of sepulchral algae and flowers of
the earth in the fissures of her bones and her eyes archaic
and startled in the fleshless sockets, and only when he saw
her full length did he understand that she had called him
Nicanor Nicanor which is the name by which death knows
all of us men at the moment of death, but he said no, death,
it still wasn't his time, it was to be during his sleep in the
shadows of the office as it had always been announced in
the premonitory waters of the basins, but she replied no,
general, it's been here, barefoot and with the beggar's
clothes you're wearing, although those who found the body
were to say that it was on the floor of the office with the
denim uniform without insignia and the gold spur on the
left heel so as not to go against the auguries of their Pythi-
ans, it had been when he least wanted it, when after so
many long years of sterile illusions he had begun to glimpse
that one doesn't live, God damn it, he lives through, he
survives, one learns too late that even the broadest and
most useful of lives only reach the point of learning how to
live, he had learned of his incapacity for love in the enigma
of the palm of his mute hands and in the invisible code of
the cards and he had tried to compensate for that infamous
fate with the burning cultivation of the solitary vice of
power, he had made himself victim of his own sect to be
immolated on the flames of that infinite holocaust, he had
fed on fallacy and crime, he had flourished in impiety and
dishonor and he had put himself above his feverish avarice
and his congenital fear only to keep until the end of time
the little glass ball in his hand without knowing that it was
an endless vice the satiety of which generated its own appetite until the end of all times general sir, he had known
since his beginnings that they deceived him in order to

please him, that they collected from him by fawning on him, that they recruited by force of arms the dense crowds along his route with shouts of jubilation and venal signs of eternal life to the magnificent one who is more ancient than his age, but he learned to live with those and all the miseries of glory as he discovered in the course of his uncountable years that a lie is more comfortable than doubt, more useful than love, more lasting than truth, he had arrived without surprise at the ignominious fiction of commanding without power, of being exalted without glory and of being obeyed without authority when he became convinced in the trail of yellow leaves of his autumn that he had never been master of all his power, that he was condemned not to know life except in reverse, condemned to decipher the seams and straighten the threads of the woof and the warp of the tapestry of illusions of reality without suspecting even too late that the only livable life was one of show, the one we saw from this side which wasn't his general sir, this poor people's side with the trail of yellow leaves of our uncountable years of misfortune and our ungraspable instants of happiness, where love was contaminated by the seeds of death but was all love general sir, where you yourself were only an uncertain vision of pitiful eyes through the dusty peepholes of the window of a train, only the tremor of some taciturn lips, the fugitive wave of a velvet glove on the no man's hand of an old man with no destiny with our never knowing who he was, or what he was like, or even if he was only a figment of the imagination, a comic tyrant who never knew where the reverse side was and where the right of this life which we loved with an insatiable passion that you never dared even to imagine out of the fear of knowing what we knew only too well that it was arduous and ephemeral but there wasn't any other, general, because we knew who we were while he was left never knowing it forever with the soft whistle of his rupture of a dead old man cut off at the roots by the slash of death, flying through the dark sound of the last frozen leaves of his autumn toward the homeland of shadows of the truth of oblivion, clinging to his fear of the rotting cloth of death's hooded cassock and alien to the clamor of the frantic crowds who took to the streets singing hymns of joy at the jubilant news of his death and alien forevermore to the music of liberation and the rockets of jubilation and the bells of glory that announced to the world the good news that the uncountable time of eternity had come to an end.

1968–1975

read more

GABRIEL GARCÍA MÁRQUEZ

LOVE IN THE TIME OF CHOLERA

'An amazing celebration of the many kinds of love between men and women'
The Times

'It was inevitable: the scent of bitter almonds always reminded him of the fate of unrequited love ...'

Fifty-one years, nine months and four days have passed since Fermina Daza rebuffed hopeless romantic Florentino Ariza's impassioned advances and married Dr. Juvenal Urbino instead. During that half century, Florentino has fallen into the arms of many delighted women, but has loved none but Fermina. Having sworn his eternal love to her, he lives for the day when he can court her again.

When Fermina's husband is killed trying to retrieve his pet parrot from a mango tree, Florentino seizes his chance to declare his enduring love. But can young love find new life in the twilight of their lives?

'A love story of astonishing power and delicious comedy' *Newsweek*

'A delight' Melvyn Bragg

GABRIEL GARCÍA MÁRQUEZ

ONE HUNDRED YEARS OF SOLITUDE

'The greatest novel in any language of the last 50 years. Marquez writes in this lyrical, magical language that no-one else can do' Salman Rushdie

'Many years later, as he faced the firing squad, Colonel Aureliano Buendía was to remember that distant afternoon when his father took him to discover ice ...'

Pipes and kettledrums herald the arrival of gypsies on their annual visit to Macondo, the newly founded village where José Arcadio Buendía and his strong-willed wife, Úrsula, have started their new life. As the mysterious Melquíades excites Aureliano Buendía's father with new inventions and tales of adventure, neither can know the significance of the indecipherable manuscript that the old gypsy passes into their hands.

Through plagues of insomnia, civil war, hauntings and vendettas, the many tribulations of the Buendía household push memories of the manuscript aside. Few remember its existence and only one will discover the hidden message that it holds...

'Should be required reading for the entire human race' *New York Times*

'No lover of fiction can fail to respond to the grace of Márquez's writing' *Sunday Telegraph*

'It's the most magical book I have ever read. I think Márquez has influenced the world' Carolina Herrera

GABRIEL GARCÍA MÁRQUEZ

INNOCENT ERÉNDIRA AND OTHER STORIES

'These stories abound with love affairs, ruined beauty, and magical women. It is the essence of Marquez' *Guardian*

'Eréndira was bathing her grandmother when the wind of misfortune began to blow …'

Whilst her grotesque and demanding grandmother retires to bed, Eréndira still has floors to wash, sheets to iron, and a peacock to feed. The never-ending chores leave the young girl so exhausted that she collapses into bed with the candle still glowing on a nearby table – and is fast asleep when it topples over …

Eight hundred and seventy-two thousand, three hundred and fifteen pesos, her grandmother calculates, is the amount that Eréndira must repay her for the loss of the house. As she is dragged by her grandmother from town to town and hawked to soldiers, smugglers and traders, Eréndira feels herself dying. Can the love of a virgin save the young whore from her hell?

'It becomes more and more fun to read. It shows what "fabulous" really means' *Time Out*

'Marquez writes in this lyrical, magical language that no-one else can do' Salman Rushdie

'One of this century's most evocative writers' Anne Tyler

GABRIEL GARCÍA MÁRQUEZ

CHRONICLE OF A DEATH FORETOLD

COLLECTED STORIES

IN EVIL HOUR

INNOCENT ERENDIRA AND OTHER STORIES

LEAF STORM

LIVING TO TELL THE TALE

LOVE IN THE TIME OF CHOLERA

MEMORIES OF MY MELANCHOLY WHORES

NEWS OF A KIDNAPPING

NO ONE WRITES TO THE COLONEL

OF LOVE AND OTHER DEMONS

ONE HUNDRED YEARS OF SOLITUDE

STRANGE PILGRIMS

THE AUTUMN OF THE PATRIARCH

THE GENERAL IN HIS LABYRINTH

THE STORY OF A SHIPWRECKED SAILOR

He just wanted a decent book to read ...

Not too much to ask, is it? It was in 1935 when Allen Lane, Managing
Director of Bodley Head Publishers, stood on a platform at Exeter railway
station looking for something good to read on his journey back to London.
His choice was limited to popular magazines and poor-quality paperbacks –
the same choice faced every day by the vast majority of readers, few of
whom could afford hardbacks. Lane's disappointment and subsequent anger
at the range of books generally available led him to found a company – and
change the world.

*'We believed in the existence in this country of a vast reading public for intelligent
books at a low price, and staked everything on it'*
Sir Allen Lane, 1902–1970, founder of Penguin Books

The quality paperback had arrived – and not just in bookshops. Lane was
adamant that his Penguins should appear in chain stores and tobacconists,
and should cost no more than a packet of cigarettes.

Reading habits (and cigarette prices) have changed since 1935, but
Penguin still believes in publishing the best books for everybody to
enjoy. We still believe that good design costs no more than bad design,
and we still believe that quality books published passionately and responsibly
make the world a better place.

So wherever you see the little bird – whether it's on a piece of
prize-winning literary fiction or a celebrity autobiography, political tour
de force or historical masterpiece, a serial-killer thriller, reference book,
world classic or a piece of pure escapism – you can bet that it represents
the very best that the genre has to offer.

Whatever you like to read – trust Penguin.